Forever Julia

FOREVER JULIA

JODI CARMICHAEL

GREAT PLAINS
TEEN FICTION

Great Plains Publications gratefully acknowledges the financial support provided
for its publishing program by the Government of Canada through the Canada
Book Fund; the Canada Council for the Arts; the Province of Manitoba through
the Book Publishing Tax Credit and the Book Publisher Marketing Assistance
Program; and the Manitoba Arts Council.

Design & Typography by Relish New Brand Experience
Printed in Canada by Friesens

LIBRARY AND ARCHIVES CANADA CATALOGUING IN PUBLICATION

Carmichael, Jodi, author
    Forever Julia / Jodi Carmichael.

Issued in print and electronic formats.
ISBN 978-1-927855-20-1 (pbk.)

    1. Title.

PS8605.A7559F67 2015   JC813'.6   C2014-907247-3
                                        C2014-907248-1

As always to my family;
your love and support fuels me.
Emma and Sarah you inspire me.
Drew your confidence keeps me writing.

To the struggling writers:
no one but you can free the stories
locked in your imagination. So get to it!

CHAPTER 1

That was then. This is now.

Yoga has warped my mom. For the good.

I think.

Namaste. Chakras. Divine spark.

Seriously?

She's all "open minded" and "willing to let me explore my own boundaries." That's what she said when I asked if I could go on a ski trip with Jeremy. My mother, who has never let me ride the city bus on my own, is letting us go away together for a night. Alone. Well, not completely alone. We'll be with all his friends in a chalet they're renting. And Annika will be there too, but there won't be any parents, so it still counts.

I reach to the back of my drawer, searching for my thickest, coziest socks. Something scratches along the back of my hand, catching on my watchband. I yank it free from a tangle of mismatched socks. Ugh. It's the package of condoms we received from health class in September. If it were up to Jeremy we'd be long through this starter pack and onto a lifetime supply. I shove it back to the nether regions of my bureau.

"Hey Mom!" I call, swinging my duffle bag over my shoulder. "I'm ready to go."

"Cheese," she says, clicking her phone as I step out of my bedroom into the living room.

We live in the miniscule apartment above our bookstore. It is a seriously hideous space. Whoever lived here before us must've found a sale on pastel paints—every room painted a different pale colour. Lilac, butter yellow, powder pink—we've got them all. It's like living in a giant daycare.

I cross our baby blue living room into the mint green dining room, which are separated only by our overstuffed beige sofa.

"When did you get up?" I ask. Flour's powdered across the front of Mom's faded crimson apron. An old navy blue bandana sweeps her greying hair off her face.

"Close to five. I want to get the cookies baked for tonight's book club." My stomach sinks. Baking is my job. She's covering for me so I can go away this weekend.

"Sorry I won't be here to help," I say, hoping she doesn't ask me to stay. We usually run book clubs together. I watch the store while she makes sure the groups get everything they need.

"Not to worry. I can handle it." She picks an envelope off the dining room table. "Here's a little spending money. It's only $40, but…" her face flushes. A guilt tsunami hits me as I think of her sitting at the dinner table last night, sorting cash into envelopes: groceries, gas, clothing, utilities, and our monthly "fun night." She's handing me our movie money.

"You don't have to," I say.

"No, just take it—in case of emergency."

"Jeremy's got everything covered. The rooms, skis, meals and we're driving his dad's brand new Hummer. That thing is a tank."

"You really like this boy, don't you?"

"Yeah. He's pretty amazing."

I wish Annika could see what I see in Jeremy. She's convinced he's an arrogant control freak, but she's totally wrong. It sucks that my best friend can't stand my boyfriend. Plus, she has no idea what he's going through with his dad. He hasn't told me much, beyond the fact that his dad is never happy with anything Jeremy does. Apparently, making the football team wasn't good enough. Jeremy's dad was captain when he was in twelfth grade and anything less than perfection doesn't count in his books. Jeremy made me swear I wouldn't say anything to anybody about his dad. My heart breaks for him, when I think about how amazing my own dad was.

"Jeremy opens car doors for me, carries my backpack, and meets me between classes," I tell Mom.

"He sounds like a real gentleman."

"Yeah, he is." He reminds me of Dad that way, but I don't say that to Mom. Every time I mention Dad, she gets weepy which starts me crying, too. I can't let her set me off, especially not today. I don't want to ruin my weekend with Jeremy. I mean who wants to date a complete downer, right? He's got enough to worry about, without adding my depression issues.

"Even so," she says, tucking the money into the side of my bag.

"Thanks."

She pulls me in for a hug, and whispers, "You have your meds, right? Both sets?"

"*Mother*, of course I do." Jeremy hates that I take them. No matter how I explain how anti-depressants and anti-anxiety meds work, he still doesn't seem to understand why I need them. I've decided not to talk about it with him anymore. It's easier that way. I'm hoping to get off them soon, but that would mean another visit to Dr. Shapiro and I'm done being psychoanalyzed.

"Hey, I'm your mom. I'm allowed to worry. And Jules—" she pauses, biting her lip as if considering what to say next. "You know my concern about not having a chaperone this weekend."

"Yes, you've made that perfectly clear." It's like she memorized some pamphlet on "How to Talk to Your Teen About Sex." It gives me the heebies every time she says intercourse. Gack. Such a revolting word.

"Listen, you need to know that if anything happens that you aren't comfortable with, if he pressures you at all to have intercourse— "

"Ick. Mom. Please don't start about sex again."

The doorbell warbles, three times in rapid succession.

"That's Jeremy," I say, leaping by her to the staircase.

"Let's go let Romeo in, shall we?" she says.

"Mom, please do not call him that, and don't embarrass me."

"Jules, give me a little credit, would you?"

We creak down the stairs from our apartment to the landing at the bottom and unlock the door that stops our bookshop customers from traipsing upstairs. To the left is the sunflower yellow door that leads to the store. Mom painted, in scrolling black letters arching above the door's piano windows, "Beyond this door dreams come true between the pages of a book."

She swings the front door open to find Jeremy leaning on the snow-covered handrail, in the near darkness, texting. He stuffs his phone in his pocket, smiles his killer smile, and extends his hand.

"Nice to see you again, Mrs. Collins," Jeremy peers over Mom's shoulder inside the doorway to the bookstore.

"Good to see you too, Jeremy. Would you like to come in and look around? You may find something you'd like to read this weekend."

"*Mother.*" Why can't she understand not every moment is an opportunity to make a sale? "We're not going to be reading."

"I wish we could, Mrs. Collins," says Jeremy. His smile softens as he looks at me and reaches for my hand. The moment his fingers touch mine, my heart beat races, pounding hard inside my chest. My breath catches. "But I want to get to Holiday Mountain by nine, so we get as much time on the slopes."

"You kids had better get going, then. Maybe another time." She gives me one last hug. "I love you."

"Love you too."

"Remember to call me before you get on the highway tomorrow, so I know when to expect you."

"I will Mom. Don't worry."

"Not possible." Her eyes narrow and her voice grows stern, as her smile slides pencil thin. "Jeremy, you take good care of my girl. She's all I've got."

"*Mother!*" Is she purposely trying to embarrass me? My hand flies from Jeremy's and covers my face. Heat rushes up my neck. Soon my face will resemble a red spotted Rorschach test, if my blushing doesn't cease and desist. Time to exit. Now.

"I will Mrs. Collins. I promise, she'll have a great time," says Jeremy.

She slips back inside. The lock clicks into place.

Jeremy glides the backpack from my shoulder, wrapping his free hand around mine once more. It makes me feel small and safe at the same time. This is a remarkable feat for a 5'8" giraffe like me.

"Sorry about my mom. She's overprotective." The wind whistles around us, freezing my ears and my face. I pull up my hood as we head down the front steps.

"Don't worry about it. I'm just happy she's letting you stay overnight."

"I was shocked she said yes."

My foot slips on the first stair and my arms circle wide in a feeble attempt not to fall.

"I've got you, Beautiful," he says, pulling me upright.

"I wish you'd stop calling me that. It's so not true." *He's* the beautiful one—all square-jawed manly, with short sand-coloured hair and intense light grey eyes.

He laughs, plants a kiss on my lips and scoops me up like a bride. My legs dangle over his arm as I wrap my arms around his neck. Jeremy carries me down the remaining stairs and across our snowy parking lot to the other side of the dented BFI bin to his dad's canary yellow Hummer.

"Don't want you to break a leg before you've even made it to the hill."

I clamber inside, hoisting my body onto the warm leather seat. My home-slash-bookstore looms in the near-dawn light. The ancient white paint is peeling off in jagged one-foot chunks and the rickety front porch is falling away from the rest of the building. Mom appears in the dining room window up in our apartment. She waves, a slim smile on her face. I don't care what she says, even Buddha would be depressed if he lived in that puny two-bedroom above the store like we do. Whenever I'm with Jeremy I feel like I'm fleeing my sad reality.

Jeremy climbs in, plunking my bag on the seat between us.

"I wish Annika was coming with us." Annika can't leave the city until after her Taekwondo class. Jeremy didn't want to wait that long to hit the hill, which is understandable since this weekend was his idea.

"We don't want to miss any prime hill time. Plus, she's late for everything," he says. His voice drips disapproval. Jeremy is *never* late. Ever.

"Not always," I say, feeling defensive. The problem is, he's right. The only thing Annika isn't late for is Taekwondo. She says Master Wong would kick her butt if she were even five minutes late.

"And anyway, you don't have to spend every minute with her. You spend most of your time helping your mom in the store, studying, and tutoring. What little free time you get I have to share with Annika."

"Some of that time I spend tutoring you." In fact, since my other student moved to Toronto, Jeremy's the only one I currently tutor.

"Good point. Have I ever told you how grateful I am for your brain?" he says, laughing as he backs up. "The whole basketball team is thankful. Coach would've benched me if you hadn't got me through exams."

"You've only told me a million times." I smile. He is so good for my ego. "I'm actually grateful that you were having trouble."

"What? That's sort of twisted."

"Maybe, but I don't think we would've ever started dating otherwise."

"True. Thank God for my academic challenges and your academic genius. We're a perfect match, like puzzle pieces. We belong together."

My heart soars when he says that. *We belong together.*

Jeremy shifts into gear and drives over the boulevard onto the street. I reach for the dashboard to brace myself.

"Um, Jeremy. That was a curb you just ploughed over," I say.

"A curb's nothing for this beast," he says, pounding the steering wheel as our back end thumps onto the street. "It might as well be a grain of sand. Nothing can stop us." He hoots like a semi truck horn.

I laugh, feeling invincible. The cars beside us look like toys in comparison. One of the biggest thrills of being with Jeremy is that he makes me feel like anything is possible. He looks like he should be in a Hummer ad. His eyes shine, his short hair is styled to perfection as we rocket down the highway. Again, I have to wonder, why did he pick me? He is way out of my league and he could date anyone at school—anyone—but he chose me. *Me.*

I sneeze.

"Tissue?" I ask, knowing better than to search the glove compartment or console.

"Back seat," Jeremy says. I grab a few tissues, leaving the box right back where I found it.

He hates people snooping through his things. A few days ago, he left his English binder in the lunchroom, so Annika and I chased him through the halls and tried to tuck it into his backpack while he was walking. Big mistake. He totally freaked out, telling me to respect his stuff and not to touch his belongings unless I asked first.

I think he's so private because of his parents. I know something happened between his mom and dad. I'm pretty sure his dad cheated, but he refuses to talk about them. All I know is his mom spends most of her time in their condo in L.A., and his dad is rarely at home, jetting from city to city on business.

Struggling out of my jacket, I pull down the visor, flipping open the mirror. My auburn curls are behaving today, no frizzy square-head this morning. It's not exactly the straight hair perfection that I know Jeremy admires. He points out all the movie stars he thinks are hot. Not one has my coiled mass of hair. Pulled over one shoulder, it dangles down almost to my elbow. I give my makeup a quick inspection. Jeremy is particular.

"You look great," he says, as if reading my mind. "Just a bit more lip gloss and you'll be a knock out. Use the pink stuff, though. The red one is something my mom would wear and you are nothing like her. *Nothing.*"

"I threw that one out."

"You have a wicked body and you're gorgeous," he reaches over and strokes my thigh. Heat rushes through me. My face burns. "I'll teach you the ropes." He scans me. "We need to go shopping—my treat."

"Why?"

"What you're wearing isn't horrible. Not like that faded black U of M sweatshirt you wore to the game last week. What you have on is way better, but it's just not current enough. I know exactly what would look amazing on you."

"Sounds great."

Tears sting my eyes. I blink them away before Jeremy can notice. That sweatshirt was my dad's. And I love the soft grey sweater and jeans that I'm wearing. It took Annika and I over two hours of searching rack after rack of used clothes at St. Bart's Clothing Closet last fall to find this outfit, and Annika found the coolest black leather jacket and rolls of fabric ends for herself. She reworks old pieces and scraps of material into original Annika designs, sort of a clothes mashup. She gets a rush out of knowing that no one else on the planet will have the exact same outfit as her. We both walked away super excited about our finds...but now?

I sigh. How am I ever going to fit into Jeremy's life if I can't even figure out the basics, like what clothes to buy?

We pass the city limits, the snow-lit farmers' fields fly by, and to the east pink clouds stretch up from the horizon, hinting at a breathtaking prairie sunrise. Reaching into my inside jacket pocket, I find the smooth button with the beveled edge that I take with me everywhere. Dad's button—off his favourite sweater. It's round and smaller than a quarter. I clench it in my fist. Resting my head on the cold window, I close my eyes. Jeremy turns up the radio and starts singing to the hip hop song.

Dad. I miss you.

CHAPTER 2

Beautiful.
Perfection.
(Watch out for frozen chicken heads.)

Jeremy parks as usual, diagonal across two spaces, at the far end of the parking lot. He parks like this so no one can ding his car when opening their doors. Annika calls it the "Over-Privileged Asshole Park." OPAP for short. I've explained about his car countless times, but she only rolls her eyes and mouths, "OPAP" over and over until I stop talking.

"Okay, let's check in," he says, jumping out of the car. I grab my bag and slide down the seat. Slamming the enormous truck door closed, I lose my balance and careen backwards.

"Ouch," I groan, landing in a high gravel-permeated snowbank. Jeremy rushes around the truck.

"Are you okay?" he asks, pulling me to my feet.

I dust icy chunks off my butt. "Yeah, I'm good."

"Don't want you bruised," he says, gently freeing a clump of snow from my hair. "Maybe I should carry you inside?" He grins.

"Hardee har har. Pretty sure I can master solid ground."

Jeremy holds my hand as we walk to the other side of the Hummer, just as his best friend Harley pulls up next to us.

The music is blaring from Harley's rusted SUV. The bass echoes deep in my chest as the front passenger window winds down to reveal Madison. Her bright blonde hair is smoothed neatly into a high pony that sits near the top of her head. Of course there isn't one stray hair out of place. And of course she's draped in designer skiwear. There is nothing thrift store about her. Yet, there is something needy about the way she lays claims to all the boys in her circle. Like they all are her potential boyfriends. Even Jeremy—and they broke up last summer. I know I shouldn't be jealous, but she seems to be everything I'm not. Everything Jeremy wants me to be. I hate that I feel jealous of her. Annika says Madison has zero redeeming qualities, but since I started dating Jeremy I've seen a side of her that isn't so bad. Not 100% nice, but she seems to be trying hard to be friendly. And she does have a wicked sense of humour. It's just funniest if it's not directed at you. I'm still trying to figure her out.

Jeremy opens her door and as she emerges a wall of her La Chance perfume makes my nose run. I sneeze.

"Oh, are you okay?" Madison asks, her voice full of concern, even sweet. "I wouldn't want to catch whatever *you've* got." She waves her hand at me, laughing. Okay, am I paranoid or is she inferring that *I* am what's catching? *Ouch*.

Jeremy laughs with her, making me feel like the butt of some inside joke. I'm sure he doesn't mean anything by it, but still my heart shrinks. Like the Grinch but worse—catastrophic shrinking—imagine a heart the size of a spec of dust. I zip up my jacket, hiding my "uncool" sweater, and step behind

Jeremy in a feeble attempt to hide myself. My hand finds the button in my pocket.

"Just joking, Julia," she says, throwing me an air kiss.

"Sure," I say, pasting on a smile. "Funny."

Hannah, Madison's sidekick and co-captain of the Prairie Trails cheerleading team (or as I like to call them, "The Pom-Poms"), tumbles out of the backseat with some boy I've never seen. He's pawing her.

"Later," she says, pushing him away. "I don't want to mess up my hair." Her hair is pinned into a sophisticated bun. Gorgeous long copper-red wavy tendrils frame her freck-led face. I can't imagine what time she woke up to get this glammed up—for skiing.

"Your hair is flawless. Don't waste it on him," Madison says.

"I know, right? It took Kimmie almost an hour to get it looking perfect." Hannah glares at me; her olive green eyes dare me to comment.

"Looks great," I say, careful to keep my voice neutral. Kimmie, I now know from hanging out with Jeremy's friends for the past four weeks, is Hannah's housekeeper. I made the mistake of referring to her as an indentured servant. Now I also know that Hannah has zero sense of humour. And she claws and hisses like a feral cat.

"The Third!" Harley says as he and Jeremy high five. The Third. It's short for Jeremy H. Thurston III. Everyone calls him that. Only his girlfriend, otherwise known as me, is allowed to call him Jeremy.

"They said we could have early check-in and it's on my dad's credit card, so we're good to go," Jeremy replies.

"Your dad's paying for this? Sweet."

"Yeah, well he owes me."

I'm renting skis, so I stand alone and watch everyone grab their snowboards from the trucks. They're talking about their favourite runs and snow. Who knew there were so many different kinds of snow: powder, freshies, death cookies, chowder. I have no clue what they're talking about. The last time I went skiing I was eight, and I came away with a broken wrist and little desire to reattempt it. Until today.

"Come on Beautiful," Jeremy says, giving my hand a squeeze before picking up my bag. He's so much like my dad that way. Dad never let Mom carry anything anywhere either. I know it's totally old fashioned, but I like it.

Jeremy walks with Harley towards the lodge, continuing their snow discussion. From what I can tell, I should avoid "frozen chicken heads." I'll have to get a tutorial from Jeremy later. Madison and Hannah are busy chatting to each other as they race ahead. The unknown letch boy trails after Hannah, carrying her bag and her board as well as his own gear.

I follow Jeremy and his pals into the chalet lobby. Although the lodge is massive, it has a warm cozy feeling with high-gloss knotty pine covering the ceiling and every wall. The floors are a dark wide wood plank—possibly elm or ash. They look old—probably original. My eyes are drawn to the enormous flagstone fireplace that sits at the centre of the room. Whoever designed this building new what they were doing. I wish I'd brought my sketchbook with me, I could—

My thoughts are interrupted by a tap on my shoulder.

"Hey, Julia. You dropped this in the parking lot." It's Tyler McAlister. His voice is quiet, kind and he's holding my mitt. "I kept calling you."

"Thanks, I didn't hear you at all. Which is obvious, isn't it? Or I would've replied. And got my mitt. Out there." I point to the parking lot. Why am I nattering like this?

He laughs. "Anyway, here you go." He passes it to me.

Tyler's in twelfth grade with Jeremy, and they've been buddies since they were kids. Jeremy still talks about how inseparable they used to be, up until seventh grade when Jeremy started to focus on sports. He became a huge jock, playing both basketball and football for the Prairie Trails Vikings and is a full-fledged member of the Jock Clique. Tyler stuck with music and is in a garage band. He's edgy with dangerous bad-boy good looks—always wearing band T-shirts, has a tattoo of a flaming guitar on his arm, and a killer smile. He's also an incredible dancer. He's never spoken more than a handful of words to me. Not exactly shy, more aloof, I guess.

"I didn't realize you were coming," I say.

"I wasn't going to, skiing's not really my thing, but I changed my mind at the last minute. Actually Chloe changed my mind. She needed a ride. She called Harley but his car was full and The Third never replied to her text. I'm not staying over though."

"Oh. Good." That didn't sound right. My face burns. "Wait, what I meant was, you coming to Holiday Mountain is good… and it was nice to give Chloe a ride."

"You think so?" Tyler asks. Over his shoulder I see Jeremy, Madison and Hannah at the front desk. Jeremy's face is beet red. He slams his wallet on the counter and spins around, searching the crowd.

"Sure," I respond, not really listening. Jeremy looks like he's going to lose it. "I gotta' go."

"Hey wait," he says, taking a deep breath and looks around the lobby. "Is Annika here?"

"She's coming out later—sometime after lunch."

"Cool," he replies, his face all smile.

"I really gotta' go."

"See you later."

I rush to Jeremy. "Sorry, I lost my mitt."

"You need to get those strings they put in kids' snowsuits. What do you call those?" Madison asks.

"Idiot strings," Hannah says. She and Madison laugh. "We need to get your little girlfriend idiot strings."

"What?" I say, bristling.

"We're just joking. You're super cute," Madison says, her blue eyes sparkling. She links arms with Hannah and they weave their way through a throng of snowboarders and plunk down on an overstuffed leather couch that faces a large stone fireplace. Jeremy stares at me.

"What were you and Tyler talking about?" His voice is gruff. He's spinning his car keys around his finger, over and over.

I hold up my black ski mitt. "Nothing. He was just returning this and he was asking about Annika." Jeremy examines me, like he's trying to find a lie in my answer. I know Jeremy doesn't like it when I talk with other guys, but this is Tyler. They've known each other since kindergarten. Heck, they taught each other how to play guitar in third grade.

"Annika? I didn't see that coming."

"Me neither, but it sort of makes sense when you think about it. They're both alternative and—"

"Yeah, but that's where the similarity ends," Jeremy says interrupting me. "I mean, Tyler's cool and—"

"Popular?" I finish his sentence. "Annika's popular enough and it's not like I'm Miss Popularity or anything."

"Yeah, but you're different. You're gorgeous and smart and funny and—"

"Okay, okay," I say. "My ego can't take any more of this."

He pulls me in and kisses me. Shivers race from my lips across my face.

"Let's just say I picked the best girl for me," he says, staring down at me.

My mind spins as I stare into his eyes.

"So, are we all checked-in?" I ask.

"Pfff. No. These morons," he says, his voice grows loud, his face flushes. "They messed up the reservation. Our room won't be ready until close to five. We'll have to store our bags in lockers in the change rooms for now."

"It's okay, Jeremy. It's no big deal."

"They never would've done this to my dad." Jeremy's eyes darken, his fists ball tight, his knuckles whiten.

"Really, it's okay."

"I wanted this weekend to be perfect, for us. For you," he says. His anger dissolves from his voice as quickly as it escalated.

"I'm not expecting perfection. I just want to spend time with you," I say as he pulls me close.

"See this is why I need you, why we belong together. You keep me calm. So beautiful…" he whispers and kisses me lightly on the lips.

He smells of soap and cologne. My head swirls. One moment he seems like I irritate him and the next he says he needs me. He confuses me.

"Let's store our stuff then we'll get your skis sized. Our first stop will be the bunny hill to see what I need to teach you."

"Okay coach."

Jeremy picks up my bag and leads me away from the great room to the back of the lodge and the staircase that leads to the lockers in the basement.

"Hey, Julia," he pulls me close and we pause in front of the women's locker room. I close my eyes, waiting for another kiss. "Don't keep me waiting." He drops my bag at my feet. I watch him disappear into the men's room.

So much for romance.

CHAPTER 3

Stupid, stupid butterflies

Whoever came up with the term "bunny hill" was delusional. I cannot see bunnies strapped to skis, hopping down this slope. I am neither a literal or figurative bunny. Every turn sends me tumbling. My hat, poles, and toque fly across the snow as I bounce after them. Maybe that's what is meant by bunny hill. Whatever. I still fail at skiing. Not a huge surprise. I, Julia Collins, am not a born skier. I'm just relieved I haven't broken anything.

I've spent all morning on this same hill with zero improvement. Jeremy, on the other hand, is a flawless snowboarder and hasn't fallen once.

"Why me?" I ask the puffy white clouds that hang motionless above me as I lie sprawled on my back. If I were skiing with Annika, she'd join me here on the ground, and we'd make snow angels. I keep texting her, but I haven't heard back. I thought she'd be here by now.

Jeremy is far too boarding-focused for snow angels and has already carved—which I now know means turning on the edge of your snowboard—like a pro to the bottom. Sitting up,

I see him standing down there with a bored expression pasted on his face. It's been like this all morning. He's acted all irritated with me and when he hasn't been sulking, he's been busy texting.

"Who does he need to message on a second-by-second basis?" I mutter, as I struggle to my feet. I slip across the snow in my heavy ski boots to retrieve my scattered gear. Deciding it would be safer to walk the hundred feet to the bottom, I push my skis down the hill and clomp down the slight decline after them.

"Look out!" I call to Jeremy, but he doesn't hear me. He's too busy texting. One of my skis races into the side of his foot.

"Crap, Julia!" He glares at me, his jaw tight. "Here." He picks up my lone ski and shoves it at me at the exact same time a woman with a bright red ski jacket approaches.

"Julia?" she asks.

Jeremy forces his sneer into a blinding white smile and lays the ski on the snow.

"Yes?" I reply.

"I'm Wanda, your ski instructor."

Jeremy convinced me to take a skiing lesson for the afternoon. At lunch he and Harley kept talking about the black diamond runs and all the fresh powder at the top of the hill. Jeremy looked so disappointed that he'd missed out on all the fun. I hated feeling like I was ruining his weekend, so of course I told him that I thought a lesson was a great idea. It's the least I can do, since this weekend is costing me nothing.

"Hi. You've got your work cut out for you. I'm a complete lost cause," I say.

"So, you're good here, right?" Jeremy interrupts Wanda's reply as he walks backwards, his snowboard over his shoulder.

"Yeah, I guess—" I begin.

"K. Later," he says and darts away without a second glance.

"I've decided not to take that personally," I say to Wanda, forcing a laugh. I glimpse my reflection in her sunglasses. Horrified, I stuff a mat of tangled curls back into my haphazard bun. No wonder Jeremy took off so fast.

"Sure, honey," she says, pointing to the towrope. "Let's see what you can do."

I attempt to skate-ski, but it feels like I'm sliding on butter. I wipe out mere inches from the lift.

"I hope you enjoy a challenge," I say, looking up at Wanda. She laughs and gathers my poles.

"If you already knew how to ski, I wouldn't have a job. So let's start by teaching you how to get up once you fall," she says.

Jeremy texted me about an hour ago, asking to meet at the bottom of The Barclay Bowl run. I stack my skis and poles in the stand outside the lodge. Quarter-size snowflakes drift through the air. I squint into the sun and follow the well-packed path towards Barclay. The slopes are still crowded—everyone's trying to squeeze in a few more runs before the sun slips behind the hill.

My heart quivers when I see Jeremy standing in the shade of a thirty-foot Jack pine, leaning on his snowboard. I wave, but he's too busy texting to notice me. Who is he texting?

"Hey Jeremy," I call.

He holds up one finger to me, like my mom does when she's on the phone. My heart sinks. A minute goes by before he smirks and stuffs the phone in his pocket. He faces me and his smile lifts my spirits.

"Hey Julia," he says. He sounds serious—or something. I jam my hands into my jacket pockets. I would've worn my mitts, but they are soaked from my spills on the hill.

"How were the black diamonds?" I ask.

"Awesome. I smoked everyone up there."

"Oh. Good. I graduated off the bunny hill. I even did a few greens and only fell twice. And look no broken bones." I hold out my arms for his inspection. His eyebrows rise as he gives me a cursory glance. "Remember? Last time I went skiing, when I was eight—I broke my wrist," I explain.

"Right," he says and clears his throat, resting his snow-board against the pine tree. "Listen, Julia, I wanted to talk to you about something."

The wind picks up and snowflakes swirl around us, blowing my long bangs across my face. I tuck my curls under the edge of my toque, so I can see Jeremy. I cup my frozen, angry red hands in front of my mouth, blowing hot air into them. It doesn't help, so I stuff them back into my pockets.

He tugs me into his chest. "Tonight's *the* night." His mouth crashes down on mine. I try to respond, but my lips are so cold they barely move. They ache under the weight of his lips. He pulls back, his smile tight.

"What's wrong?"

"Nothing. I'm just cold."

"You won't be for long. Once we're back at the chalet, I'll get you hot." His lips caress my neck. "I need you, Julia. So much."

Shivers rush down my shoulders, spreading over my body. I toss my head back, close my eyes, and sink into his embrace.

"Tonight, we're going to finally do it," he murmurs; his voice is low, husky. My eyes flash open. The tiny hairs at the back of my neck prickle as I untangle myself from his arms, pushing him away.

"Wait," I say, fighting to comprehend what he's saying. My hands rise in front of me in the international accepted sign for "stop right there, mister," preventing him from saying anything more.

Jeremy opens a tin of his signature extreme mints and pops a few in his mouth. He crushes and swallows the tiny candies in seconds.

"Jeremy," I manage to whisper over the voice of panic that's doing laps in my head, "do you think we're having sex—tonight?"

"Of course. We're out here, with no parents, it's perfect."

"But Jeremy, I thought you understood."

"I do, and you wanting to wait to have sex is one of the best things about you. It makes you special, but it's been a long time. Now we're all the way out here..." his voice trails off as he runs his hand through his dark blond hair. It stands on end, looking like he just tumbled off a magazine spread. "And you do love me, don't you?"

"Love you?" I say, pausing. We've never said that to each other before. "Of course I do."

"And I love you."

He loves me. My breath catches. *But I'm still not ready.* I blink fast to stop the tears that gather, preparing to spill. My throat aches. I spin around, not able to look at him. Jeremy coughs—quiet at first and then louder, continuing until I turn and face him. He looks impatient. *What am I supposed to do?* Hot tears slip down my face, stinging my windburnt cheeks.

I try to speak, but all that comes out is a strangled, "I just can't."

"Julia, please don't cry. Having sex is no big deal, really. Everyone does it. You need to get over your sex issues."

"I know, but I'm just not—"

"Ready? I know, you keep saying that, but we've been dating close to two months and people who love each other have sex. Julia, I've been really patient. And generous. Do you know how much this weekend cost?"

"I—I—"

"You know, Julia, people ask me what I see in you, and I always stick up for you, saying how great you are. How we are meant to be together. Maybe you don't feel the same way I do."

"Jeremy," I plead. "That's not true."

"Maybe we need to take a break."

"*What?*"

This can not *be happening!* I'm 165 kilometres from home, being dumped at the bottom of The Barclay Bowl run. *How can this be happening?*

"No, please Jeremy. You just said you love me."

He cringes and inhales. He holds it for one, two, three seconds. He exhales and his spearmint breath stings my eyes.

"I do love you, Julia. But I need to know for sure that you love me back. I'll give you some time to figure out what you're willing to put into our relationship."

"What does that mean?"

"It means that you're on your own tonight."

"But, I'm staying with you—in the chalet."

"I don't think that's a good idea." His grey eyes darken to near black.

"You can't be serious?" *Oh my God, where am I supposed to sleep?* I only have $40. This isn't happening.

He yanks me close. His face is an inch from mine. He huffs his anger onto me.

"I love you, Julia, but I need you to figure out how much you love me, or we're done. For good."

My stomach recoils and then collides with my sinking heart. Jeremy still looks like his usual Tommy Hilfiger self, but I don't feel those dancing butterflies in my stomach when I look at him. I still feel butterflies, but they aren't in the mood for dancing. I turn my head, but those butterflies are too fast. They race up my throat. Macaroni and cheese splashes Jeremy's brand new, first time worn, Novella snowboarding boots. Four hundred and thirty bucks gone in one KD barf.

Seriously bad day.

CHAPTER 4

"Can this day get any worse?"

I stumble back to the ski lodge, slipping in my ski boots. I thought this weekend would be all romantic—just me and Jeremy at the ski hill. And then I barfed on him.

I've got to get out of here. No way can I let anyone see me this messed up. I grab my skis from the stand and tuck them under one arm. The poles I jam under my other arm and I take two steps. My skis slide down my side—the poles slip and jab into the snow. Wrapping the pole straps around my wrists like the ski instructor taught me, I stuff the skis back under my arm. Three more steps and the skis slide again. *This is totally awkward.*

"Fine, let them drag," I mumble.

At the top of the steps, I try to hurdle over the ice to the dry patch under the eaves. I've done this a half dozen times since we arrived at Holiday Mountain this morning with no problem. But this time, as I leap over the ice, the skis knock me off balance. My right foot shoots out in front of me and almost touches the door before my left foot even has time to leave the top stair. My skis fly through the air. I hear the rip of jeans as my entire body crashes hard onto the deck. The boards dig deep into my hip. I've likely just done the best splits of my life.

"My jeans," I moan. All that searching at St. Bart's and now they're ruined.

I'm lying on the stairs, legs akimbo, head pointing downwards, when the lodge door twangs open.

"Julia? Are you okay?" I can't see him, but I recognize the voice from this morning. It's Tyler.

I close my eyes. Crud. Nothing like a witness for your moment of extreme humiliation. Shifting my legs, I try to sit up. Gravity, trampled snow, and my ski jacket work against me and I glide, unhurried, head first down the steps. My poles, which are still wrapped tightly around my wrists, snag in the railing. I pull my hands upwards, trying to stop my descent, but I only free myself and continue my downward slide. My head nudges into a snowbank, while my skis clatter down the stairs behind me.

On any other day, I probably would've made some crack about Newton and the laws of physics, but today I'm too busy drowning under waves of embarrassment.

First Jeremy and now this? At that thought of Jeremy, tears well in my eyes, clouding my vision. Determined not to let Tyler see me cry, I fling my arm over my face with more force than I intended and whack myself hard across the bridge of my nose with my ski pole.

"Ow," I cry, as I lurch up and cup my hands over my nose. Warm liquid drips onto my fingers and my stomach flips over. Butterflies flutter inside my belly.

"I think I broke my nose," I mumble. *OMG, this day is actually getting worse! Even nightmares end...don't they?!*

The crunch of boots on packed snow shakes me from my misery. I'm too afraid to look up, so I keep my head bowed down towards my knees. Blood trickles through my fingers onto my jeans.

"Can I help you inside?" Tyler asks.

I tilt my head up and through my blurred vision I see only a shadow of Tyler standing above me.

"You have no idea how bad this day has been," I say, my voice trembles.

"I think I have a good idea." Tyler points to his phone as I peer at him through my bloody fingers.

Does Jeremy have to text his every freakin' move??

Too embarrassed to respond, I keep my face hidden behind my hands and we're left with silence. I'm not great with silence. It makes me nervous and then I begin to chatter. Mom says that's because I'm not comfortable with being alone with myself and I need to join her more often for her Sunday-morning yoga and meditation class. According to Mom's yogi, it will help me get in touch with my "inner me." I love my mom, but do I need to prove it to her by spending two hours lying on the boot-scuffed, beer-stained, and freezing community club floor at 9 AM, on the only day of the week I can sleep in?

"You might as well text them and let them know my one-woman disaster show is closed for the season," I say and bite the inside of my cheek to stop myself from rattling on. I came up with that technique in 8th grade after I was sent to the office for the thousandth time for talking too much in class.

"Funny girl," Tyler says. "Let me see."

Tyler kneels down beside me and I move my hands away to let him inspect the damage. I must look like a total mess. Blood's dripped down my face, my pants are ripped, and I smell like barf. He brushes my hair away from my face. The touch of his cold fingers on my forehead sends a shiver down my face towards my neck and shoulders. Tyler's over six feet and has enormous hands, so I'm surprised by how tender his fingers are, but even with his light touch, it's still painful.

"Ouch." I wince.

"Sorry. It doesn't look broken, and it's already stopped bleeding. I've had my fair share of bloody noses. You need to put some ice on it to keep the swelling down." He pulls a wad of tissues from his pocket and wipes the blood from my face. Another tingle shivers towards my shoulders.

"Right. Ice," I say, taking a quick peek at him. "Thanks for your help."

Tyler stuffs the tissue into his jacket pocket and rocks back on his heels. I wipe the blood from my fingers in the snow and dry them on my torn jeans. *At this point what is a little blood going to hurt?*

"No problem. I'm heading back inside to watch the hockey game. Are you coming?" He nods towards the lodge.

"I'm not sure," I pause, my voice wobbles. I take a deep breath to gather my courage. "Can I ask you something?"

Tyler's eyes hold such a look of pity that I'm not sure I want the answer, but I have to know.

"Does everyone know that I barfed on his shoes?"

"Yeah, we thought that was kind of funny." He points to his phone.

"Yeah, LOL!" I fake laugh, which makes my nose throb. "Ow-ow-ow."

Tyler grimaces. A surge of nauseous embarrassment rolls up my throat. *Oh God, please no more barfing.* I take another deep breath, unzip my jacket, and will my stomach to settle down. Snow has started to melt beneath me and is soaking through my jeans.

"I must look like the bride of Frankenstein." My voice breaks mid-sentence.

"Well…" he begins and smiles. His face full of sympathy, "you've looked better."

I groan. "As pathetic as that sounds, that is the nicest thing anyone has said to me today." Having a boy tell me he loved me for the first time in my life was right up there, until he dumped me, and I barfed on his boots.

"Yeah, that is pathetic," he agrees.

I untwist the pole straps from my wrists as Tyler stands up. He gives me his hand and draws me to my feet. I flail backwards, my poles fly from my hands but Tyler steadies me, stopping me from landing back in the snowbank.

We're standing so close that I can smell mint on his breath and a hint of something else—coffee? It tweaks a memory of my dad. It's like one frame of a film that stops in my mind and I can see Dad sitting at the kitchen table in his grey striped robe, drinking his coffee. Starbucks freshly ground dark roast, no milk, but heaps of sugar. My breath catches. A blanket of sorrow hangs heavy on my shoulders. *Please. Please, don't start crying.*

I cover my hands with my face. *Oh my God. My breath smells like a dungeon.* At that realization, my tears vanish. I take a quick step back. Tyler gathers up my skis and lifts them to rest on his shoulders while I grab my poles.

"Thanks. Can you do me one more favour?" I ask. "Can you walk me through the lions' den in there so I can pack up my stuff and get out of here before something even worse happens to me?"

"What's left for you to do?"

"Spontaneously combust? I've heard it can ruin a ski holiday…" I trail off.

"How about we sneak in the back door?" he says.

"Good plan." My smile shakes, but I force it out anyway. I follow him through the snow. A grey wave of sadness washes over me. My legs drag. My breathing labours. I stuff my frozen hand into my pocket and find the tiny bit of Dad I take everywhere, wedged in a corner of my pocket.

I just want to get home.

Home: what a laugh.

CHAPTER 5

Why, yes. It can always get worse.

We sneak up the back steps and into the lodge without incident. Nothing combusts. Not even the slightest spark. A small smile slips onto my face. I'll have to tell Annika that one. She always appreciates my warped sense of humour. Mom would just run her hands through her hair, shake her head, and tell me to "dial down the drama and embrace my inner calm." I'm not sure even my mom, with her newfound spiritual awakening, could find inner calm right now.

"So far so good," I whisper, "I'm not a cinder...yet."

"Shhh!" Tyler whispers back.

A lopsided grin creeps onto his ski-tanned face and he winks. Normally I find winking cheesy, but the colour of his eyes is startling. They remind me of my grandma's huge sapphire ring; bright blue and crystal clear. They are so unusual—almost hypnotic—that I don't know why I didn't notice them before

My Tyler inspection is interrupted by the roaring cheers coming from the lodge's great room. The Jets must have scored. I feel like an intruder. All I want is to get my stuff and get out before anyone sees me. *What if I run into Jeremy?* A smidgen of hope trembles deep in my belly. *If we could just talk, maybe he'd change his mind. Maybe we could skip this whole break idea. But then would he expect sex—tonight?* A shiver runs from the nape of my neck out across my shoulders. A hard lump forms in my throat. *Please don't cry. Not here.*

Taking one step down the stairs to the lockers, I'm made aware of the gaping rip in the crotch of my jeans. I swear I can feel wind on my privates. My face burns fire hot. I shift my body so I'm not facing Tyler and hope he can't see the rip in my pants and…*Holy Crap! Wasn't Tyler following me this whole time? Doesn't that mean he would've seen…Oh My God! What panties am I wearing? Think Julia.* Smiling with relief, I picture today's undies: pink, full butt, no thong. Thank God for Granny panties.

I take a sideways step down another stair and my ski pole jabs my leg. A small "ouch" escapes from me, which I turn into a cough. *Is this day for real?*

"I still have to return my skis," I whisper, my voice shaking. "And my poles."

"Don't worry, I'll return them to the shop for you," he says and flashes me another crooked smile, "but you'll owe me one."

"Sure. Thanks," is all I can manage to say.

He points to my feet. "Your boots."

"Rightio. Boots. Check." Did I seriously just say that?

Heat rushes across my face and down my neck. I'm melting under these layers of fleece. I bend down, careful not to expose anything, and unbuckle the clasps, wrenching my feet free. I wobble on the stair and grab the rail to steady myself. He mouths "*Good luck,*" heaves my poles and skis over one shoulder and tucks my boots under his other arm. Sauntering down the hall, Tyler disappears into the great room. I wait a few seconds to make sure he's gone and dash down the stairs, making little noise. The sounds of the hockey announcers' play by play on the TV, whooping boys, and chattering girls fades as I rush into the women's changing room.

I pad straight to the washroom to clean myself up. My reflection makes me moan. My green eyes are barely visible through my puffy eyelids and what little you can see is bloodshot. My nose is red and my hair has blocks of ice encrusted into the ends. Pink blotches splatter down my neck. Reason 352 why Jeremy wants a break. I'm a total mess. My reflection says more boxer than beauty queen. Whatever.

Please Dad, just let me just get out of here before anyone sees me.

I splash ice cold water on my face, rinse the rotten taste from my mouth, and half run from the bathroom to the lockers. As I get closer to my locker, my nose twitches and I sneeze on Chloe's musky signature scent, *You Wanna'*. What is with these Pom-Poms? Do they bathe in perfume? Chloe's locker's right next to mine and this morning she offered to lend me her hoodie when I realized I didn't pack one. If only she'd lay off the *You Wanna'* I could imagine the two of us becoming friends. Maybe I should be more thankful for Chloe's perfume addiction. At least it masks some of the revolting blend of b.o. and wet socks that lingers in the air.

Leaning against the lockers, I scroll through my texts, finding one from Annika. She said she was running late, but that was two hours ago. My fingers fly over the keypad.

JULES: Where r u?

A few seconds pass.

JULES: R u ok??

Where is she? Annika's never far from her phone and she uses hands-free when driving. She says if those telephone geeks need a guinea pig to test out phone implants on humans she'll be the first in line, as long as she gets to pick the implant site. She doesn't want anything getting in the way of her multiple ear piercings.

I wait a few seconds and send another text.

JULES: Jeremy dumped me—R U THERE?!

10 more seconds crawl by and I'm about to send another message when my phone pings Annika's reply.

TKD4EVR: HE WHAT???????

JULES: He didn't exactly dump me. He says we're on a break

TKD4EVR: What does that mean?

JULES: I'll tell u when u get here. Where r u?

TKD4EVR: I just pulled in

JULES: & he kicked me out of the chalet

TKD4EVR: What a prick

JULES: & i barfed on his novella's 😟

TKD4EVR: U barfed?! OMG. R u ok?

JULES: I don't know

TKD4EVR: Come out to the parking lot

JULES: K

TKD4EVR: Note 2 self—he is so dead when I see him

JULES: Gotta go. Someone's coming—luv you! 🙂

TKD4EVR: Luv u 2! Be strong! 🙂 No more barfing! 😟

Stuffing my phone back into my pocket, I focus on the hissing whispers heading my way. *Did I hear my name pop out of the muffled voices? Or am I just getting paranoid?* Tiptoeing, I follow the row of silver lockers and peek around the corner, where I see Madison and Hannah enter the bathroom.

"OMG, did you see Julia's jeans?" asks Madison.

"Yeah, they're last year's Accents," says Hannah. "So what?"

"They are *my* last year's Accents! Did you see the back pocket? It's been stitched up. I ripped the pocket on The Third's car door when we were at the lake last summer. I donated them to St. Bart's and she bought them!"

Horrified, I whip my head around to peer at my back pocket. I trace the jagged stitching with my finger. How did I think the diamond shape was part of the design? It now resembles more of a worthless lump of coal. *How stupid.* What did I think would happen? That a pair of designer jeans would make me less of an outsider with Jeremy's wealthy clique?

I stagger backwards unable to listen further. The cold edge of a metal bench hits me mid-calf and both knees buckle. I slump onto the bench, stunned.

I have to get out of here!

A numbness envelops and cushions me. Somewhere, in a remote corner of my mind, I know I should feel devastated by their gossip. But I don't feel anything at all. Is this what Mom's yoga-loving pals would refer to as an out of body experience?

I tie my ski jacket around my waist to hide my jeans, tug on my faux sherpa S. Saville boots, and tug my bag out of my locker. Rushing to the staircase, I give one last look toward the washroom. *Are Madison and Hannah still dissecting my wardrobe?* My stomach recoils at the thought. I trip up the stairs, crashing through the back door outside.

Dad, if you can hear me, please help me keep it together until I'm out of here.

A gust of wind swirls snowflakes around me. I'll take that as a sign. But I feel so desperate right now I'd take a full face-plant in a snowbank as a sign, too.

I am trying to negotiate an ESP *deal with my deceased father.* This, I can never share with anyone, not even Annika. For sure they'll think I'm sliding back into depression-ville. I slip my button into my hand, wrapping my fingers tight.

Dad, it's just you and me.

CHAPTER 6

"Confucius say: 'When you buy fancy pants, you get knocked on fancy pants' ass."

As I trace my steps through the snow to the front of the lodge, my brain flashes moments of the past few hours. I can't shut out the fact that I may have lost Jeremy.

"Enough!" I say and shake my arms in an attempt to rid myself of the bone-deep humiliation.

Back on the main walkway I stop and let out a long sigh. It's getting late and soon the sun will dip behind the ski hill and leave me alone in the darkness. I shrug my bag onto my shoulder and hike to the parking lot. Only a few people remain on the hill, and the laughter and cheering from inside the lodge has died away. It's quiet except for the crisp crunch of the hard packed snow under my feet. I shiver and pull my hands into my sleeves in a feeble attempt to stay warm. I should've accepted Chloe's offer to keep her hoodie for the weekend instead of giving it back to her after lunch. The temperature's falling fast.

In the middle of the parking lot I see Annika waiting for me in her rusted once-navy-blue Mini Cooper, Aunt Mildred. It stands out, parked at a permanent left tilt among the newer, cleaner and fancier cars that surround it. I named Annika's car after my old Aunt Mildred who at eighty kept telling people she was sixty-five, her dyed blonde hair an attempt to make up for her walker, hearing aid and varicose veins that ran web-like tracks up her legs.

Swinging the passenger door open, I climb into the warm car, brushing my forehead across the fuzzy lime-green dingle-balls that line the interior of the car.

"Hey," Annika says.

The moment I close the door, tears pour down my face. My chest aches. I close my eyes, trying to slow my breathing and calm my thoughts, but it's useless.

Annika leans over the stick shift and pulls me into her arms. Her pink and blonde hair floats across my face and smells of Granny Smith apples, a perfect blend of tart and sweet. I cry in ragged spasms, like I did when Dad died six months ago. Not like the few tears that spilled out when Mom first told me he was sick, but at his funeral. Until that moment, I fooled myself into believing he was just away and still alive. That's when the reality of his death hit me full force. I would never see him again. Never have him help me with advanced calculus. Never go ice fishing, just the two of us, at the cottage. Never overhear him telling Mom that I was beyond ordinary smart, I was Einstein smart. I loved hearing the pride in his voice, loved how his voice almost sang when he'd brag to Mom. *Dad, I miss you so much.*

My breathing eases, the shudders cease and I draw away. I dry my face with some crumpled tissues I find wedged into the furthest corner of my jacket pocket.

Annika looks at me like only she can. She stares straight into my eyes, like she's trying to read my mind or search my soul for the big mystery of Julia. When she's done her inspection, I don't know what she'll say. I never do. Sometimes she comes up with these wise and self-reflective statements and other times her comments are blunt and even rude.

"What a little prick," she pronounces.

I smile. Who needs wisdom?

"Yup, but I showed him. Jeremy loved those boots."

"Crap, Julia, only you could barf on command!"

"Like Pavlov's dog, but instead of drooling on cue, I barf!"

"But, only on Novella's!"

We laugh until I have a stitch in my side and I'm gasping for air. Tears stream down our faces. Annika's dark black mascara is smudged under her eyes.

"You look like a Viking linebacker!" I say.

She makes a growling face at her reflection in the rear view mirror and says, "I gotta' kick me some Third butt! Booyah!"

I feel a pang of sister love. Under the blonde and pink hair, the piercings, and the retro clothing, she's still the same eight-year-old girl old who rain-danced with me in my back yard. We played for hours, slopping mud on each other until we were completely encrusted. Mom said we looked like sludge twins and the only way she could tell us apart was my three-inch height advantage. Annika stopped growing at five feet but I keep growing taller. Now if we were covered in mud, there would be no mistaking us.

I pass Annika a tissue and she wipes off the smeared mascara.

"So what exactly happened?" she asks.

"Uhm, it's sort of embarrassing. I—we said we loved each other and then he said he wanted to have sex tonight. When I said no, he said we needed to take a break."

"Oh my God. Are you serious? Do you really love him?"

"Yes." My heart spasms. *I love Jeremy. He needs me.*

"Okay," she says, pausing, looking like she's trying to solve some complicated algebraic formula. "So, how many times have you told him you want to wait? Like a zillion, and if he really loved you, he'd be okay with taking it slow. I have no idea what you see in him. He treats you like crap—"

"No, he can be really sweet—"

"Stop making excuses for him! He kicked you out of the chalet, knowing you had nowhere to go. How sweet is that?!" Annika is furious.

"I'm sorry." I say and begin to cry.

"Ugh, don't start crying and stop apologizing," she turns off the car and grabs my hand. "You are better than this guy. Way better."

"No, I'm not, Annika. I'm not. He's been through a lot of crap and he's got it all together, and look at me! I'm a wreck. Ever since Dad died, I've been a mess."

"Julia, it's only been six months. That's nothing. My dad left us when I was three. It's been fourteen years and I'm still not over that. And my dad didn't die. He just left us."

"I guess."

"It's true. You're too hard on yourself."

"And I want to get off these pills. I want to be normal," I confide.

"Don't rush it."

"Okay, Doctor."

"Shut up." She punches me, but it doesn't hurt. Her mom's a doctor and is pressing Annika to follow her footsteps. She hates any reference to medicine and her future. Her sights are set on a career in fashion design.

"Where am I going to stay tonight?" I ask.

"We're going home. No way I'm staying anywhere near The Third tonight. For sure I'd take him out if I saw him."

"But you just got here! You didn't even do one run!"

"It's not like I was looking forward to spending an entire night with The Turd. The Turd! Hah! Why didn't I think of that before? I love it."

She flips the ignition. It turns over twice and on the third attempt, as usual, it shudders to life.

"I feel horrible. I'm wrecking everyone's weekend," I say, and if we leave, I won't have a chance to talk with him. I won't have a chance to make up.

"Okay, enough with the pity party. The Turd got what he deserved—barf toes. You get a break from his Quest for Sex and I won't be tempted to beat up Prairie Trails biggest douche bag! They'd take away my black belt if I fought out of the ring."

"Jeremy is not a douche bag. He just wants us to be a real couple. I love him," I say, feeling both defensive of Jeremy and touched by Annika's fierce protection of me. "And he needs me. He said we belong together."

Annika rolls her eyes.

"I hate to tell you, but the entire civilized world can recognize a douche bag when they see one. Except you, of course."

"Annika, stop it. Jeremy's not—"

"Zip it." She lurches Aunt Mildred into reverse and forces the car through its gears as she speeds through the parking lot towards the exit. "Are you even allowed to call him Jeremy? You are on a "break" after all."

I decide that's a rhetorical question, but it does make me wonder. *How long will this break last?*

Digging around my duffle bag, my fingers wrap around my half empty Xanax prescription bottle. My emergency anxiety drugs, or what I like to call my Panic Pills. My back-up in case my daily anti-depressant isn't enough. Dread fills me. I can't let Mom see me this upset or she'll call Dr. Shapiro and tattle on me. They were dead serious about group therapy and I have no intention of sitting around in a circle all kumbaya-style and crying my grief out in a room full of strangers. No. Thank. You.

I push the pills to the bottom of my bag. I am determined not to take them anymore. They dull me and harden my emotions to marble. On Xanax, nothing bothers me, but then nothing excites me either. I'm a walking Michelangelo statue—I look alive, but I'm dead on the inside. I haven't needed one in close to a month because I've gotten much better at understanding my body's early warning system. Like those emergency horns that blare when there's a risk of tornado, my body screams out a warning that a full meltdown is headed my way. If I don't stop the onslaught of emotions, I'm in for days of depression—hiding in bed, unable to eat, refusing to talk to anyone.

Annika slides around the last row of snow-covered cars. I fly into my door.

"Annika, I want to get home faster than you, but I'd like to first make it out of the parking lot."

"Fraidy, have I ever got us into an accident?"

Fraidy is short for Fraidy Cat. It's been Annika's nickname for me ever since I refused her double dare to go down her basement stairs when we were in fifth grade: alone, in the dark, at midnight. Forget it.

"No, but I'm sure you've left a trail of destruction behind you."

Annika just cackles and pulls onto Highway 3. I swear she didn't even look to see if cars were coming, but I don't say anything. I've learnt better than to backseat drive with Annika. She's a combination of racecar driver and long-haul trucker when she's behind the wheel. She's focused, fast, and highly coordinated. Throw in a little profanity and that's Annika.

I stare out the window as the mini picks up speed. Sleek silhouettes of windmills fly by. They glow in the setting sun as the last rays of pink sunset bounce off their spinning blades. They look nothing like the windmill on an Old Dutch potato chip box. Science has come a long way since the days of Dutch engineering. Dad would've loved seeing them. We would've discussed their increased efficiency and he would have even made a chart to summarize the improvements. He loved visuals.

"So, after Jeremy told me we needed a break, I ran back to the lodge and wiped out on the stairs," I begin. My heart twitches as I say the words, "we needed a break" out loud.

"Yeah, I got the summary from Chloe."

"Did she tell you that the jeans you and I bought together at St. Bart's were actually Madison's castoffs?" Their snickers echo in my head. How could she be so mean?

"Yeah, that sucks, but that's karma for you."

"How is that karma?"

"Confucius say: When you buy fancy pants, you get knocked on fancy pants' ass."

"Very funny," I say and look out the front windshield. The wind picks up, howling against the window. Snowflakes blow sideways across the road. Annika taps on the brakes. Our back end swerves to the left, but she gains control. A long finger of snow appears through the haze, jutting out from the shoulder, nearly blocking our entire lane.

"Look out!" I yell.

Annika swerves, missing the drift and yells back, "Julia! Relax. Your nerves freak me out more than the fricking road."

Knowing better than to mess with her when she's channelled her darker trucker side, I stare out my side window and try not to think. Usually you can see for kilometres across the farmers' fields, but the blowing snow has made it impossible to see more than thirty or forty metres in any direction. We crawl along the highway, the visibility grows worse.

I'm relieved Annika's driving. A few months after I got my driver's licence I got rear-ended and now any distractions like snow, pedestrians, or other cars make me nervous.

"I can't see the shoulder," Annika says, turning down the music. "I don't even know if we're on our side of the road. I need you to look for the white line on the edge."

I squint into the white haze. I can't see sky or the highway, let alone a skinny white line under drifts of snow. A break in the wind reveals the gravel shoulder.

"There! You need to get over my way about two metres."

"This is crazy." Annika guides Aunt Mildred towards the edge of the road.

"Just go slow."

"Thanks for the tip, Captain Obvious."

"Should we stop?"

"Are you nuts? If we can't see two feet in front of us, then neither can anyone else coming up behind us. If we stop, anyone could cream into us."

"Crap, Annika. That means we could plow into anyone in front of us."

"Thanks for the update, Captain."

I stare at the side of the road, searching for patches of pavement. Moments turn into minutes. My back is tight. My heart races.

"Keep talking to me Fraidy. I'm scared to death we're going to end up in the ditch. And check your phone. Make sure we have a cell out here."

"Okay," I say, my hands tremble as I pull my phone from my backpack. "Only one bar and it keeps cutting out."

"Crap." Her fingers tighten on the wheel. Oh my God. I've never seen her this scared. Our back end slips towards where I imagine the shoulder should be. "Crap," she says again, slowing to turtle speed. "Come on, Fraidy. Talk to me—still freaking out here."

"Okay," I say. My mind is as blank as the scene out my window. All I can think about is a semi suddenly appearing out of the whiteout, crushing us like sardines in the Mini. "Uhm, I—I," I stammer.

"Okay, Cosmo moment," Annika buts in, her voice strained. "Give me your top five things you're looking forward to, now that you're single."

"I'm not really single. We're just on a break," I pause. *Are we?* What if I just made the biggest mistake of my life? "Jeremy said he wasn't going to wait around forever for me to get past my sex issues." I can't help the tremble in my voice. That really stung.

"He said that?"

"Yeah. I don't want to lose my virginity to my first real boyfriend, not that fast. I can't help but wonder: if I love him, aren't I supposed to want to have sex?" Maybe something is wrong with me. What if I actually have sex issues?

"I dunno about that. Guys say whatever they want to get into your pants and then once they've had enough, they're on to someone new."

I don't reply, because I know she's talking about her dad cheating on her mom. He took off to Toronto with some woman when Annika was little and the last time she saw him was in third grade, when he had a stopover on the way to Vancouver. He never calls; he only sends cheques at Christmas and her birthday and she's never cashed one of them. Instead she burns them in her fireplace.

Annika slows down as we approach Highway 75. In about an hour we'll be back in the city and I'll have to face Mom. She'll have endless questions. I cringe. No way can I tell her that she was right, that Jeremy wanted sex. I'll never hear the end of it. And for sure she'll say the dreaded word—intercourse. Ick.

I shift to face Annika.

"When my parents met, it was true love. They met in a university biology class and Dad said as soon as their eyes met over a slide of a squashed amoeba, he was hooked on Mom. Mom always joked that Dad just thought she was an interesting specimen. Dad would blush and say, she was too special to be toe-tagged and frozen for future study," I say.

"Really? That totally sounds like your parents. Geek love."

"I know, right?"

We cross over the southbound lane, turning north towards Winnipeg. The wind has died down and we can see more pavement. Open prairie banks us on both sides of the highway. The sun is low on the horizon, turning the sky shades of pinks and oranges. The knots of tension in my back ease and my thoughts drift like the snow across the pastures. Annika's death grip on the steering wheel releases and colour returns to her knuckles.

"True love. I think you're crazy to think it's out there," Annika says.

"I just want my first time to be the perfect romantic moment with the perfect guy. And I want to know for sure that Jeremy is the one. So many times we've been close to doing it, but after today, I am almost happy to remain one of Prairie Trails last remaining virgins." As soon as I say it, I know it's a lie. I'm not anti-sex. At all. Dread fills me. *What if I just ruined it with Jeremy?* What if he is the perfect guy? What if he decides I'm not worth the wait? My stomach flips.

"Maybe we could form a lunch hour club. We could call ourselves, 'The Happy Virgins Club.' It would be very exclusive," Annika says.

"Sure," I say, trying to sound enthusiastic. All I can think about is how I can win Jeremy back.

"We could print shirts!" says Annika. "And have a theme song."

We always get carried away like this, beating a joke to death, until no one but us would find it remotely funny. The difference is this time I don't find it remotely funny.

"Hey, that reminds me," Annika says, pointing to a brown grocery bag that's tucked between our seats. "Reach in there and find the new CD I made. I used all my iTunes cards for this one."

She's got this smug grin on her face that immediately makes me suspicious.

"What have you created this time?"

Annika has very diverse tastes in music and likes to mix everything together with seemingly no logical segue between songs. Sometimes it works and other times it's just a mess of musical styles. I push the disk into the player and press play.

"Oh just a little CD that I've decided to rename, 'The Happy Virgins Club'."

Pink's song, "So What" blares through the car.

"Julia's dumped her boyfriend!" Annika belts out over the first line, replacing Pink's words with her own version of the lyric. It isn't anywhere near an accurate rendering of today's catastrophe, but having Annika so firmly in my corner lifts my spirits.

Pumping my fists in the air I join in at the chorus. We rock the car down the highway as the sun sets over the prairie's never ending fields of snow. Perfect song after perfect song plays and my heart soars. Annika has outdone herself. What would I do without her?

And what about Jeremy? Will I have to do without him?

CHAPTER 7

White, mammoth lies.

We pull into the parking lot behind my so-called house and I'm filled with that same unease I always get when I arrive home. To call the bookshop "home" doesn't sound or feel right. Who has a parking lot for a driveway and a store for a house?

Before Dad died we had a normal life. We had a real home on a quiet cul-de-sac. The only cars that drove by were our neighbours. There was a wide fenced back yard with a garden and trees, not a pockmarked gravel parking pad with no vegetation (unless you count the thigh high weeds that cling to the building's flat board siding in summer.) The gravel pad rolls downhill, merging into a heavily trafficked back lane. There's nothing like waking up to the sound of tires screeching to a halt and blaring car horns to make you long for the silence of suburbia.

"I guess I have to go in," I say to Annika.

"Yup," she replies. "That's what you do when you arrive home. You enter the building."

"Ha-ha. Very funny. My mom is going to have a zillion questions. It was a big deal for her to let me stay overnight with Jeremy. She's going to be so pissed off at him and at me for not calling before we got on the highway."

"If it was up to my mom, she would have a tracking device surgically implanted in my ass. She hates not knowing where I am. Do you want me to sleep over? It might distract her from The Mom Inquisition."

"I have a feeling nothing is going to stop her once she finds out what happened."

"Good luck."

"Thanks," I reach into the back seat for my bag. "Hey! I just remembered something from this morning."

"Before or after the Turd incident?"

"Annika, please don't start again."

"Okay, sorry."

"As I was saying, something very curious happened. I ran into Tyler McAlister at the hill and he asked about you."

"He did? What did he say? Give me all the deets."

"He wanted to know if you were coming to Holiday Mountain."

"And what did you say?"

"Obviously, I said yes."

"And then what did he say."

"He said, 'Crap, then I'm leaving.'"

"What?!"

"Joking. He said cool and grinned like a puppy in love," I say, tilting my head and rapidly blinking my eyes. "I think he has a crush on you."

"Yeah?"

"Wait. Do you like him?" I stop teasing mid blink.

"Uhm, I dunno'. He is super cute."

My phone pings. I check the display.

"It's my mom. I gotta go. Thanks for saving me today Annika. I promise I'll make it up to you," I say as I climb out of the mini.

"No worries, Fraidy. Ciao." She reverses Aunt Mildred and jerks around a snowbank into the back lane. She almost hits a car that has to veer to clear a path. Horns blare. Annika gives the other driver the finger.

Looking at the old wooden staircase that winds its way up to the second floor of our home-slash-bookstore, I think back to when Mom announced she had to sell the house. She said she had no choice; she just couldn't afford it. It was only two months after Dad died.

Dad had just turned forty-six when he got his cancer diagnosis. Stage four. The oncologist said it started in his lungs and spread to his bones and his brain. By the time Dad found out his prognosis was dismal. He was given three to four months to live. We felt lucky when that turned into five. He was a fighter.

The part that sucks the most is that they might have caught it earlier if he hadn't been in such great shape. Dad never smoked, ran five miles every day, and only drank on special occasions. Mom's pet name for him was "Golden Boy" after the bronze statue on the top of our Legislative Building, because he was so fit. One Christmas she gave him a mini Golden Boy Statue with his name engraved on the base and a bundle of plastic wheat. Dad thought it was hilarious so he hung a picture of himself holding his statue and his wheat above his framed degrees in his office at the university. His students got a kick out of it and began to call him Professor Golden. Dad loved that.

Now we live in the cramped two-bedroom apartment above Mom's bookstore. Most of our furniture is stacked in the attic, with a little area cleared for my drafting table and paint easel. His statue is up there somewhere. Packed away.

Dad, you would hate it here. Where would you set up your home lab?

I sigh, feeling like I've been holding my breath since we left Holiday Mountain. I could be sitting by a fire right now, snuggled up next to Jeremy. Or next to him in bed, having sex, possibly even enjoying it. I. Am. An. Idiot.

Trudging through a snowdrift, I tug open the shop's back door and stomp inside the landing. The bell jingles my entry.

"Mom, I'm home!"

No response. *Sweet.* Maybe I can sneak up the outside stairs and postpone any guilt trips. I push the door back open, prepared to dash when I hear Mom's voice. *Crud.*

"Why are you home?" she calls. Her voice is high, fuelled with worry. I know that tone too well. It's her Hospital Voice. The floorboards creak as she runs through the store. "Jules, what happened?" Mom rushes down the narrow hallway to me.

A long sigh billows out. All I want is a few minutes alone in my bedroom to work on my dream house plans or listen to music, or just stare at the ceiling. I kick off my boots and drop my bag.

"I—I…" My lip trembles and Amazon-sized tears crash down my face. "It was…" I can't continue through my heaving cries. Mom wraps me in her arms. I cry so hard my chest bone aches. She holds me, never shrinking away. My cries begin to subside.

"Come, upstairs," she whispers in my ear. Leading me by the hand across the store, she flips the "Come in, we're open" sign over, turns the plastic hands of the little clock to read

"Back at 6:00." The old pine stairs groan as we slowly make our way upstairs, my hand still safe in hers.

My eyes feel puffy and swollen as I shuffle after her across the small dining room into our even tinier living room. She guides me to the sofa and I sink into the cushions. Mom spreads the green and yellow afghan over me, tucking it under my arms and folding the end under my feet. She lays a light kiss on my forehead.

"Time for hot chocolate," she says.

I just nod.

Hot chocolate is Mom's answer to any ailment, physical or emotional. Not being invited to Jenna Mooney's birthday party in second grade—hot chocolate. Twisted ankle only twelve minutes into last year's half marathon—hot chocolate. Dad getting cancer—daily mugs of hot chocolate.

I hate it.

Just the smell of it reminds me of Dad's final days in the hospital. But I can't tell her that. We don't talk about Dad. Ever. And I can't tell her that the thing she takes so much pride in makes me want to hurl.

I curl up on my side and slide my hands under my head. This day has been brutal. All I want to do is crawl into my PJs, cuddle up on the couch and watch an old movie. I close my eyes and will myself to think of anything but Jeremy.

"Here you go," Mom says. I sit up and she passes me a cup of frothy hot chocolate, piled high with mini marshmallows. It's the oversized latte mug Grandma gave me last Christmas. Enough cocoa for three. The sweet scent of melted mallow and milk chocolate is intense and sours my already queasy stomach. Gak.

"Do you want to talk about it?" she asks.

I take a deep breath and blow on my hot chocolate, making valleys in the melted marshmallow, taking a moment to decide how much to tell her. Since Dad died and I went through that rough patch, she's become a total self-improvement, new-age therapy freak. Plus, every time I seem slightly upset, she threatens to ship me back to counselling.

I feel detached as the words leave my lips. "Not really."

Mom strokes my hair, tucking it behind my ear.

"Jules," she says, "Did he try to force you—"

"No! Mom, please. I don't want to talk about that with you."

"I realize that, but you need to know you can talk to me about anything."

"Ugh, Mom I know," I say. "Jeremy said we need a break—that's all."

Of course that's not all. It's a mammoth lie, but there is no way I'm telling her the truth. She'd go berserk if she thought she'd been right. She'd start on her "Sex Talk" or send me back to counselling. Or both. No thanks.

"Oh Jules," she murmurs and rubs my back. "He has no idea what he's missing out on."

"Sure." I give her a weak smile.

"I'm serious. You're one special girl and any boy that is too dumb to miss that," she pauses and looks me straight in the eye, "is a jackass."

"Mom!" I gasp, setting the mug on the coffee table. Foam splashes over the sides, pooling in a ring around the cup.

She absolutely never swears. Never. Mom's not swearing is sort of like one of the Fundamental Laws of Physics, but instead it's a Fundamental Law of Mom. It is absolute and unbinding that when speaking my mom will use correct grammar; she'll never use lingo, or abbreviations, and never under any circumstances use profanity. Ever since I can remember, she's said, "Julia, if you truly want to express yourself, do it with flair. There are too many classy words in the dictionary that never get used, so there's no need to use common curse words. Be better and smarter than that." She's said it so many times that I can hear her voice in my head, like a recording.

Mom looks away and blushes. She presses the creases out of her sweater around her middle and does this tiny shake of her head. She looks at me out of the corner of her eye and her face crinkles. She makes this small sound. *What the…?* My mom, my English teacher turned new age, meditation-loving Mom is giggling. I mean, it's not like she dropped the F-bomb, but jackass is huge for my mom. This is a big deal for her and I know I should be concerned, maybe she is cracking up, losing it, needing to see that counsellor herself, but her giggle is infectious.

She puts her arm around me and I cuddle into her, we laugh until tears run down our cheeks. It feels so good. Our laughter runs its course and we pull away from each other, grabbing tissues to wipe our faces.

Mom tucks the curls that have popped loose from my ponytail behind my ear. "I am serious about one thing," she says. "If anyone messes with my girl…Pow, right in the kisser!"

That was Dad's favourite saying from an old Tweety Bird cartoon. I'm completely stunned. She's so careful about never saying his name or referring to him at all. I give her a long hug.

"Love you, Julia." She whispers and gives me a light kiss on the top of my head.

"Love you too."

"Are you going to be okay?"

I wish I could tell her the truth. That I don't know what I'm doing and that I want to have sex with Jeremy, but at the same time I can't, or I don't want to—or something. I want to share with her that I'm completely messed up and confused, but if I start confessing my innermost fears, I'll probably start crying again. And for sure, that'll push Mom over the edge and I'll be shoved back into therapy. Instead I'll tell her what won't make her worry.

"Yeah, I'll be fine."

She tucks the afghan back around me.

"I'll be downstairs, going over the accounts, if you need me. There's leftover chicken in the fridge and cookies in the jar."

"I almost forgot. I have your $40."

"You keep it, sweetie. Everyone should have some emergency money."

"Thanks Mom." I'll pass on the chicken, but guaranteed, I'll polish off every last cookie crumb.

I change into my PJs, snag the remaining five snickerdoodle cookies, and snuggle under the afghan with the remote. I search the list of movies saved to our PVR and look for a movie to match my mood. I narrow down my choices to *An Affair to Remember* and *Sleepless in Seattle*. Old or older? The original, Cary Grant and Deborah Kerr "let's meet on top of the Empire State Building and declare our love" movie or the Tom Hanks and Meg Ryan newer version that is inspired by the first? I pick *Sleepless in Seattle*, because it always makes me cry harder. And I need a good cry—when Mom can't see me. Plus, it's more current and somehow I just know Jeremy would think me watching Cary Grant would be lame. Sort of like my old clothes—tired and out of date. Placing the tissue box on my lap next to my stack of cookies, I settle in for an hour and a half of rom-com dreamland.

As the movie intro music plays, I sink further into the sofa and further away from the reality of my day.

Hello movie magic, goodbye harsh world.

CHAPTER 8

Traitor.

Come on Annika, hurry up! I'm freezing out here.

Before the wind hits me, I see the tall elm trees bend under the force of the arctic air that then rushes down the lane towards me. My hood blows off, freezing my ears in seconds. With one hand, I struggle to pull it back up, while I grip my mug with the other, trying not to spill my tea. I turn against another gust of wind, but it pummels my back and cold seeps through the seams of my jacket, making it feel way colder than -20 degrees.

Hunkering into my coat, I take another sip of my Earl Grey, inhaling its homey aroma and hide my face under my soft, knobbly turquoise blue scarf. Mom and I start each morning sharing a pot, and she always makes enough for both of us to fill a thermos cup. It's my morning ritual, and if I ever skip it I feel out of sorts, all fuzzy headed and muddled, and my day goes a bit sideways.

I hear Annika approaching before I see her car leap down the back lane towards me. Her horn blares out two extended honks followed by two staccato notes and ends with an ear piercing three-second warble. It sounds like a squashed goose that's letting out its last desperate gasp. Annika has a bizarre fondness for her dead-bird horn that I don't appreciate, and neither do our neighbours. When she first inherited her car from her brother, she blared it every morning when she picked me up for school. She calls it "Annika's Serenade." I call it "Annika's Invasion." Mr. Hanson, our back lane neighbour, threatened to call the cops. He's a retired lawyer and at 90-something I'm not sure how much law he remembers, but he is still intimidating enough. I told Annika to save her strangled honk for emergencies and world-shattering news only.

Annika slides into our parking pad, missing the few remaining rotten boards of our peeling salmon-coloured picket fence by inches. I believe that salmon is a colour that should never be used to describe anything but salmon. You'd never find salmon-coloured nail polish. Can you imagine it competing against polishes like "Pink-Me-a-Go-Go" or "Princess-Pinkilicious?" What funky name would they give salmon nail polish? "Once-Upon-a-Glamour-Pink?"

I swing open the door and a wall of music smashes into me. The thump is so loud, I'm surprised her ears aren't bleeding. Mr. Hanson's back-door light flashes on.

"TURN IT DOWN!" I shout into the car as I climb in, my feet squishing into a large black garbage bag that is stuffed under the dashboard. My knees almost touch my chin as I huddle on the seat.

The bag will be full of clothes for the Salvation Army drop box. Every few months Annika cleans out her closet and gets rid of piles of clothes that she's found at various thrift stores. The clothes that don't work themselves into one of her designs she recycles back to various charities, like St. Bart's. Jeremy hates the way she dresses. He says she's embarrassing to be around because her clothes are so different. But that's exactly what Annika wants—to be unique.

Mr. Hanson is standing on his back step in his slippers and robe, waving his phone over his head. What remains of his hair drifts above his ears like wispy snow-white clouds. His mouth is moving, but I can't hear him because Annika is deafening me with her so-called good music. I can only guess he's screaming that he's "only one number away from dialling 911." It's his monthly threat, but he never dials the last 1.

"Oops," Annika mouths to me and grins as she turns down the music.

She cranks down her window and yells out, "Good morning Mr. Hanson! You're looking hot in that bathrobe!"

"Annika! Shut up. He's going to think we're a bunch of pervs."

"Are you kidding me? We're sixteen, sitting innocently in my car while he's an ancient geezer in his bathrobe," she says and races down the back lane past a possessed-looking Mr. Hanson. "Fraidy, you've got to chill."

Annika careens down the back lane bouncing over the snow ruts and throwing me around the front seat as I try to get my seat belt fastened. Every time I get the buckle lined up to snap it in, she swerves and my hands go flying.

"Would you please slow down," I say, my head slamming back against the headrest. Dingle balls sway frantically across my field of vision.

She slams on the brakes and I'm thrown up against the dash as we slide on an angle to a stop just before the intersection at the end of the lane. My side of the car is snug to the snowbank that lines the alley. Luckily, there's no traffic.

"Better?" she asks, shifting the car into park.

"Ow!" I rub my chest. "That really hurt."

She sounds way too happy for 8 AM. Is she deranged? Is she high? That can't be it. After her brother OD'd two years ago, she's like a walking anti-drugs ad. I still give her the once over and notice that *she* has her seat belt on. Now I'm pissed off.

"What the F is up with you? You could've got me killed!"

I crank the music off.

"First of all, no one dies bombing down a back lane in Prairie Trails. Secondly, only you and Anglican nuns say 'what the F', and thirdly, don't you want to know about my news?"

It's too hard for me to stay mad at Annika for long, especially when she's looking all wide-eyed enthusiastic like she is right now. She resembles one of those anime girls that she doodles all over her binders.

"What news?" I ask.

"Did you not hear 'Annika's Serenade?' I played it special because I have news!"

Annika claps her hands. Her news must be huge if she's all bright and shiny this early in the morning.

"Okay..." I say.

"Master Wong thinks I'm ready for the Junior National Team! He said that if I step up my training I'll have a good shot at the National Championships."

"Annika, that is awesome."

"Yeah, but my mom isn't quite as happy." Her smile melts and she stares at her steering wheel.

"Why? You've been dreaming about this since you got your black belt."

"All that extra training has to happen on Sunday mornings. Mom wasn't too thrilled when Master Wong showed her my new schedule." Sundays are off limits with Annika. Her mom works crazy hours with her medical practice, so Sundays are their "girl's day" and Annika doesn't let anything derail that.

"She'll change her mind when she sees you standing on the podium with a gold medal around your neck at Nationals."

"I sure hope so."

Annika shoves Aunt Mildred back in drive and the tires spin in place. She shifts the gear into reverse and we move three inches backwards. The tires keep spinning. She cranks the car into drive and the wheels continue to spin. We sink a few more inches into the snow.

"Fraidy, we're stuck."

"No kidding," I say. "We're going to be late and I have a math quiz first period."

"What are you worried about, Mr. Jacobs loves you. You just have to ream off equations, bat your eyelashes, and he'll be panting all over your higher intelligence," she says and grins. "He'll let you take the quiz if you miss it."

"Annika, math is more than 'reaming off equations' and Mr. Jacobs doesn't pant over anything."

"Aw, so cute," she says. "You're blushing."

"Cut it out Annika," I say, trying not to smile. "What have you got first period? Gym?"

"How'd you guess? And since we're taking dance right now, I'm in no big rush," she says, jumping out of the car. She runs to the back of the vehicle. I open my door and it smacks into the snow. I squeeze out and climb over the snowbank to join her. We stare at the Mini.

"We're going to be late," I say. "We're never going to get out of this snowbank."

"'Dial down the drama," Annika says mimicking my mom.

"Don't bring her into this," I say. "She'd ground *you* if she saw how you drive!"

"No way. I've got your mom wrapped around my little finger." She waggles her fuzzy-black-gloved pinkie at me.

Annika can do no wrong according to my mom. Annika was only eleven the first time she dyed her hair. She used a bottle of peroxide. When she rinsed it out, hunks of hair fell out leaving sporadic bald spots. What was left of her blonde hair turned grandma-hair white. Annika braided her hair every day for two months until her hair grew back. She wove in beads, ribbons and silk flowers to make herself look more exotic. I thought she looked like a circus freak with ringworm, but Mom said she was "precocious with a unique sense of style." Please. If I had bleached my hair, I would have been grounded for the rest of my life.

"What are we going to do?" I ask her, stomping my feet to get some warmth to spread to my toes.

A burst of wind carrying large fluffy snowflakes blows Annika's pink hair round her head. She looks like a rocked-out pixie having a bad hair day. I'm just about to tell her this, when I look over her shoulder and see a silver car approaching. The car stops a few feet away, but I can't see the driver because of the sun glaring off the windshield. Cupping my hand over my eyes I take a few steps towards the car.

"Hey, it's our knight in shining BMW armour," remarks Annika. She slides over Aunt Mildred's trunk and lands behind me. Annika's like a tiny cat. She's fierce and uber coordinated. She masters every sport she tries. My total opposite. Mom says we're like ying and yang. If I tried sliding over a car, I would've dented the metal or broken a bone.

The BMW's passenger side window slides down.

"Look at her beater. It's totally stuck," says Hannah. Her nasal whine pierces the air. She snickers and I hear a muffled response coming from within the car. Hannah laughs harder as her window rolls back up.

Annika looks at me and puts her finger in her mouth, making retching sounds. She stops mid gag when the driver's side door swings open and Madison steps out of the car.

"Do you need a ride?" she asks.

Annika yanks out her phone and turns her back to us.

"I'm not sure. We're stuck pretty badly."

"It's okay," Annika says, turning to face me. She takes a step to my side, hands on her hips. Her eyes are scrunched up and her chest is puffed out. Her hair is still whipping around her head and she looks ready for a fight. "I texted my brother. He'll come and get us."

Madison tilts her head and examines Annika like it's the first time she's ever seen her, which is crazy because we used to be friends. Best friends. But that was years ago and a lot has changed since middle school. Madison's eyes narrow. A slow smile spreads across her face. She's scrutinizing Annika, sort of like the way Annika does to me. It's unnerving to see Annika put under the microscope like that and I can see by the way she's holding her ground, maintaining her fighter's pose, that she's doesn't like being studied.

"Yeah, thanks for the offer Madison, but we're good," I say in an attempt to get both of them to back down. "No reason for us all to be late."

"Okay," she says, shrugging. "No biggie."

She climbs back into her car as the passenger window rolls down. Hannah's face appears.

"Are you sure you don't want a ride?" she asks.

"No, we're good," Annika says.

"I actually wasn't talking to you, Small Freak. I was talking to Julia."

"Uhm, can you give me a moment?" I ask.

"Sure," Hannah says and she leans back into the car. The window slides closed.

I pull Annika away from their car.

"You aren't really going to get a ride with them are you?" Annika asks.

"I have a test. I can't be late." And maybe it'll give me a chance to find Jeremy before the first class.

"So you're fine ditching me here?"

"Annika. I'm not ditching you. Joel is coming to help you, and all you have is gym. I have a test and I need to keep up my grades. What choice do I have?"

"Fine."

"Please don't be mad," I pull at her arm, trying to get her to face me.

"Don't be mad? She called me a freak! She's a total skank and she's drawing you in," Annika's words shoot out rapid fire.

"What do you mean she's drawing me in? She only offered me a ride."

"Whatever." Annika glares at Madison's car.

"What is going on with you?" I lower my voice, hoping that they can't hear us in the car.

"What is going on with *me*? That's a laugh." She rolls her eyes, scoffing.

"I have no idea what you're talking about."

"Oh my God, Julia you are so naïve. Do you really think Madison has changed and is now this sweet person who wants to be your new BFF?" Annika growls her words at me.

"She's not perfect, but she's been really nice to me since Jeremy and I started dating."

"You are insane? Almost everyone in that group is messed up and they're dragging you into their clutches."

"They aren't dragging me anywhere. *And* you don't have to act like my mother. I'm capable of taking care of myself without you butting in like that."

"Really?" Annika's voice is getting louder and each word sharper. "If you're so good at taking care of yourself, then how do you explain dating that misogynistic asshole for the past two months?"

She yells the last few words at me, and they bounce off the houses that bank the intersection. Her face has turned beet red and clashes with her bubble gum pink hair, which is now covered with a light layer of fluffy snow. Her breath puffs out in tiny white clouds. Annika and I seldom fight and we've never had an actual blowout like this.

"The last thing I need right now is you screaming at me," I yell back. "You're supposed to be my best friend."

"Your best friend?" She sneers. "Only when it's convenient for you."

"Oh my God, Annika, you're totally acting crazy. Just because I'm friends with Madison, doesn't mean I can't still be friends with you.

"Whatever. Just go."

"Annika—"

"Go hang with your new BFF. I hope you have a super time comparing nail polish. Traitor."

"Traitor?" I say, my voice low and threatening. "Fine. I am out of here." I shove by her and stomp to her car. I yank the door open, grab my backpack and mug and slam the door with all the fury in my body.

"Julia," Annika calls. "I'm sorry...I didn't mean to... you're not..."

"Forget it," I say without looking at Annika. "I need to cool off. See you at school." I don't trust myself to say anything else.

I give her a backwards wave and run to the far side of Madison's car. As soon as I sit down inside, I feel like I've entered a different reality. New car smell fills my lungs and I melt into the warm leather. Heated seats. No holes in the cushions. The exact opposite of Aunt Mildred.

"Nice car," I say.

"Thanks," Madison replies. "It was my sweet sixteen gift from Daddy."

"Hey, what was that all about? You and Annika looked like you were ready to start punching each other," Hannah asks. She sounds almost disappointed that it didn't come to blows.

Madison rolls down the window, biting wind rushes into the car as she extends her slender wrist out the window. Her chunky silver bracelet chimes as she gives Annika a queen wave.

"*Ta-ta dahling*," she drawls, raising her voice so Annika can't help but hear.

She pulls away and I turn in my seat and watch Annika out the back window. She runs into the snow-packed street, chasing the car like a wild dog, both middle fingers raised high. She scoops up a handful of snow, packs it into a loose ball and chucks it after us. The snowball flies apart in the air, never coming close to the car.

"Nice friend, you've got there," Hannah snorts.

"She's not normally like that," I say, quietly. I close my eyes, trying to block the burn of tears.

"Sure," Madison says, but she doesn't sound convinced.

"It's—I shouldn't have left her. I, uh, had to get to class," I say. It sounds so lame now. So very lame.

I am a terrible friend.

What have I done?

CHAPTER 9

To swoon or not to swoon. That is the question.

I have seriously pissed off everyone I care about.

I want to clear the air with Annika but I can't find her anywhere. She normally hangs out in the sewing room between classes. She's working on her own line of skirts and her designs are going to be featured in the school's spring fashion show. She never skips class so she has to be around the school somewhere.

And Jeremy hasn't replied to even one text.

As I reach up to put my binders on the top shelf, a large shadow darkens my locker. *Jeremy?*

"I'm really sorry about—" I say, spinning around. I'm surprised to see Tyler. "Oh, you're not Jeremy."

Smooth move, Julia.

"Not the last time I checked." He smiles. "I heard you're a math genius."

"I don't know about genius, but I like math. Why?"

"I'm actually, I—I," he stops and looks down at his hands, his face grows pink. "It's sort of embarrassing. I'm having trouble in calculus and I need a tutor."

"And you want me to tutor you?"

"Yes. I can pay you."

"That is how it works," I say, wondering what Jeremy will think of me taking on another student. Now that we're "on a break" will he even care?

"Of course."

"I'm not sure if I have time."

"If you could just think about it, that would be great," he says, turning towards the music room. "I've gotta' go to a Battle of the Bands practice. I'll see you later."

"See you."

He turns and runs down the hall, weaving between other students and nearly running into the back of the custodian but dodging out of the way at the last second. He's as light on his feet as Annika. Annika. Where is she?

I grab my lunch and see Jeremy across the hall, staring at me. How long has he been standing there?

"Jeremy," I call. His face is pale and he looks sad. He throws his arm around Harley's shoulder and they careen down the hallway. Jeremy glances back at me before disappearing into the cafeteria. This time, I can't read the expression on his face.

Oh my God. I messed up big time. Should I go after him? What do I do?

I need Annika! I scan the corridor and spot Madison at the far end. Hannah as usual, is right behind her whispering something in her ear. Madison smiles at me and waves. I wave back.

"Want to join us for lunch?" she calls to me.

"Uhm, okay," I say, searching the hall, hoping to see Annika. I feel weird, sort of like I'm dumping Annika for Madison. Madison and I haven't been friends since the summer of seventh grade, when she went to the lake for the summer and came back with boobs, a boyfriend, and according to Annika, a bitch complex. Before that summer though, Annika, Madison and I were inseparable.

"So, what happened with you and Jeremy at the hill?" Hannah asks as we walk towards the cafeteria. The click-clack of her high heels echoes down the hall.

"Oh, I—uh—" I stumble over my words, not sure what to say. Hannah only ever snarks at me, so I'm suspicious that she's actually speaking to me like a normal human being.

"Hannah, don't be rude," Madison says and then faces me. "You don't have to answer that."

"Thanks," I say, relieved. And really, how could I answer her? I have no clue what's going on with me and Jeremy. I texted him this morning before school and he never replied. And just now when he walked away with Harley...what was that all about?

"Sorry to hear about your break up," Madison says.

"We're just taking a break. It's not forever."

"Oh, okay. I just thought," she pauses, looking apologetic. "That you knew."

"Knew what?" My heart begins to race, my head pounds in rhythm.

"We were on a break last summer and then..." she shrugs her shoulders and her blonde eyebrows arch high. "We weren't a couple anymore."

"That's—that's not what is going to happen to us."

"Oh, okay. I just thought—" she shrugs her shoulders again and pulls me by the elbow down the hall.

"We're going to be fine. Really," I say, drawing away from her. "I, uh, just remembered, I have to go to the library and get some books for my science project."

"Ugh, I hate science. Isn't Mr. Benoit a dweeb? How about I call you later? Maybe we can go to a movie or something?"

"Sure."

"Toodles," she says, linking arms with Hannah. Their heads, like magnets, bend to each other. I watch them whisper their way down the hall towards the cafeteria.

"Julia?" says Annika, from behind me.

"Yishe!" I scream, lurching to the side and bash into the wall. "You scared me to death. Where have you been?"

"Around," she says, her eyes squint tight as she watches Hannah and Madison. "I still can't understand what you see in that demented Barbie doll and her evil sidekick."

"Hannah's still Hannah, but Madison isn't as bad as we thought. She's—changed."

"Do you have selective amnesia, or something? Have you forgotten all the names she used to call you? In grade eight it was Amazon because you were taller than all the boys. In grade nine she called you Curb Stomp, because you were in that car accident with your grandma and your face hit the airbag. And after your dad—"

"I know, I know, but she seems different now," I say not needing her to remind of Madison calling me Little Orphan Annie after my dad died. That one was too fresh. Too painful. Too close to how I felt. "I think she's trying hard to be nice. To make amends. She used to be our best friend."

"Best friend? That was sixth grade. You're crazy if you think she wants to be best buds again."

"Annika, I really don't want to talk about Madison."

"At least that's something we can agree on."

"About this morning," I begin, and stall out. What do I want to say?

We just stare at each other, then speak at the same time, and stutter to silence. Annika runs her fingers over her dangling blue feather earring.

"I don't know what happened," I say.

"Me neither. I kind of lost my mind."

"And I shouldn't have gotten so defensive. Some of what you said was true, but your delivery was harsh. I'm not a traitor."

"I know and I'm sorry, Fraidy." She lays a hand over her heart. "*Really* sorry. You are not and never will be a traitor."

"Apology accepted, and I'm sorry I stormed off and left you by yourself to wait for your brother."

"Truce?" She gives me a quick hug.

"Let's hit the library," I say.

"BFF?" she asks, like always.

"For-effferrr!" We sing, fist bumping into an explosion.

"Julia?"

I spin, nearly knocking Annika over. Jeremy's walking toward us. A huge smile engulfs my face.

"Can I talk to you?" His words are soft, meek.

"Of course," I say, my words catch in my throat. Butterflies, good ones this time, dance madly in my belly.

"So, we're not going to the library?" Annika asks. Her voice is tight, sarcastic.

"Sorry, Annika. I just—" I look from her to Jeremy, silently pleading with her not to make me choose between my boyfriend and my best friend.

"Whatever. I'll talk to you later," Annika says, pausing. "Or not."

"Annika, wait," I reach out to her, but she twists away and storms down the hall.

"Julia. Julia," Jeremy says, his hand grasping mine. "I need to talk to you."

"I am so sorry about the ski hill," I say. "I didn't mean to wreck the weekend."

"I know, and I'm sorry I got so angry. It won't happen again." He wraps his arm around my waist. "I just can't stay away from you." He kisses my neck, tiny shivers arch across my back, tingle down my shoulder, and race across my face. I look into his eyes and my legs tremble.

"Jeremy, let's not fight anymore."

"Oh God, I love you so much." His voice is three octaves deeper and trembles as much as my legs.

He bends into me and his lips lay a perfect kiss on mine. He tastes like spearmint. My body moulds into his, and his kiss becomes crushing. The shiver gathers strength and warmth and lights my body on fire. Part of me wants to push him away; we're in public, it's too intense. But another part of me wants to prove that we're solid, to show him I love him, to thank him for loving me.

Jeremy steps back, his arms a lazy loop around my waist.

"Come on Beautiful," he says, "let me buy you lunch."

"That's okay. I have leftovers," I say, patting the plastic grocery bag that's tucked under my arm. Jeremy grabs my lunch and tosses it like a basketball into a trashcan.

"No way is my girlfriend eating second-hand food," he says.

"Second-hand food? It's not like I'm eating a hand-me-down lunch," I say and dive after the bag. "That was my mom's lasagna. And her Tupperware!"

"Julia, leave it," he says. "We don't dig through garbage cans."

"Hah-hah-hah," I say. "*We* also don't throw away my mom's best plastic containers."

"Julia. Leave it." His voice is serious as he pulls me to him.

"But it's right there." I point to the can that's less than a foot from us.

"You don't need to worry about plastic containers, okay? I'll buy your mom a lifetime supply. Now, I will treat you to lunch." With one finger, he strokes my cheek, down to my jawline, along to my chin. He pauses and I swear my heartbeat pauses in response. *Oh my God, he is so hot.* And not ordinary hot. He's smokin'-caliente-fire hot. His finger runs to my lower lip, which he traces. Slowly. My knees jellify and I lean into him for support. I think I may be swooning.

"You're mine," he whispers.

Without thought a reply sighs out of me as I melt into his arms, "Yes, I am."

I adore swooning.

CHAPTER 10

Not fair.

Annika won't return any of my texts. Despair creeps after me as I trudge the last block home. I bite back tears and my head begins to pound. I searched the entire school for her and her car wasn't in the parking lot at the end of the day. We've never fought like this before. Not ever. Jeremy said a real friend would understand that I'd want to be with my boyfriend, which I suppose is true, but having her mad at me still hurts. A lot.

I feel a pang of disappointment when I see our little bookshop at the end of the street. If only I could have more time before my shift started, I'd escape to the attic and work on the draft of my dream house plans.

Jeremy's going to call me later, so at least that's something to look forward to.

Stomping in the back door, I slip my wet boots off and hang up my coat. There's a long black coat hanging on the spare hook next to Mom's grey one. Strange.

"Hey Mom," I yell down the hall as I walk towards the storefront.

"We have a surprise guest," she replies. She sounds excited. I haven't heard her sound this happy since before Dad died.

"Who is it?"

I run smack into our "guest."

"Grandma!" I tuck a long wayward strand of curly hair behind my ear and give her a hug. She feels tinier than usual. "Shouldn't you be in Arizona?"

"Julia!" says Mom.

"Oh Ruth, a little honesty isn't going to shock this old bird," says Grandma.

"I *am* happy you're here. I'm just surprised." Grandma winters down south and spends the summer at the cottage. The thought of Grandma being referred to as old is laughable. Even though she's sixty-three, she's way trendier than Mom. You'd never see Mom in the tight dark jeans, striped grey designer T-shirt, and diamond-studded ballet flats that Grandma's wearing. The olive green silk scarf wrapped around her head is a bit over the top, but it *is* the exact hue of her eyes. Tufts of curly auburn hair peek out from the edge of her scarf above her ears. Our eyes and hair are the same colour and Grandma says that makes us forever connected.

Mom says Grandma's had more "procedures" than all of Hollywood put together. Dad used to say, "When the world comes to an end, Grandma will be there to turn out the lights."

"Julia, we're closing up early to celebrate Grandma's visit," says Mom.

"Pardon me?" I'm stunned. "We're closing the store?" This goes against Mom's OCD need to sell books, so this is not just surprising—it's world stopping.

"Yes, your Grandma is worth losing two hours of revenue."

Grandma links her arm through Mom's and leads the way up to our apartment. Their heads bend into each other and I can hear snippets of Grandma's "never asked for but always offered" advice.

"Ruthie, about your hair. You'd look years younger if it was a rich chocolate brown. Grey is truly a color only for tweed and the ninety-year-old crowd…"

I follow behind them.

When I get to the top of the stairs, the first thing I see is a suitcase tucked just inside my bedroom doorway. That's odd. I glance towards Mom's bedroom and stop when my eyes travel across the vinyl folding door of the den. Inside the tiny room, sitting on the worn-out sofa bed is my comforter and my stuffed bear, Sampson. All the muscles in my back tighten. Something is up.

"Jules, we need to talk to you," Mom says as she runs her hands through her hair, then reaches for Grandma. Grandma gives Mom's hand a squeeze and she continues.

"Grandma's going to stay with us for a little while, until…" she stops to look at Grandma. Mom's eyebrows rise, almost touching her hairline, and her shoulders shrug as if silently asking Grandma for a timeframe.

"Until?" I ask, looking from Mom to Grandma. They both look uncomfortable.

"It's only temporary," says Grandma, sounding like she's apologizing, but for what?

"Which means Grandma will be in your room until we get things straightened out. You'll be in the den, but it should only be for a few months."

"Oh," I say, stunned. *Only a few months jammed into the den?* The den. Such a polite way of describing our home office/

library/dump-all room for all our odds and ends. It's eight feet by eight feet of clutter—the same size as a prison cell. *Where will I put all my stuff?*

"I know this must be a shock. I, I mean we want—" Mom begins, but I cut her off.

"That's okay," I lie. There's a bite in my voice as the lump in my throat grows, making it hard to swallow. I turn my back, determined not to let them see me cry. I'm losing my room? It's not much, but it's mine. It's the only cubbyhole of privacy I have. I can't cry or express any "scary" emotion around Mom or she'll threaten to ship me back to Dr. Shapiro. At least I could cry behind that closed door. The den doesn't even have a real door. *This is totally not fair!*

"Oh, sweetie," Mom says, her hand rests on my shoulder. "It's just until we get things straightened out," she says, repeating herself.

I spin around, forcing a smile. Tears are gathering in Mom's eyes and something else that seems familiar but I can't place it. Whatever it is, I don't care. Her crying isn't fair. I mean "she who cries first gets all the pity" right? So what gives her the right to start crying? It's my room we're talking about. A surge of hot anger rumbles in my chest. I can't contain it. I don't want to contain it.

"What's she going to straighten out? Your life? My life? This dumpy apartment? Not even Grandma can straighten this place out. This place is embarrassing Mom! What would Dad say?"

"Julia!" Mom says. She bursts into tears. Her hands fly to cover her face.

"Oh right, I forgot about our unspoken pact," I say, my words bitter. They sour my mouth. "We shall never speak of Dad again!"

"Julia! That's enough," says Grandma.

I step back. Grandma never gets mad. She claims that anger causes wrinkles that no amount of Botox can erase.

"Fine. Let me just grab my stuff," I say, shoving past them into my room. I slam the door so hard that I hear the mirror on the living room wall rattle.

Locking my bedroom door, I scan the room. Already there are bits of Grandma everywhere. Her plush white robe's on the back of my door, a large stack of unopened mail sits on my bed, and her leather jewellery box perches on the top of my dresser. Even the scent of her lilac perfume is here, filling my room.

A few months. *Only* a few months.

Nothing's been the same since we moved here. Mom says it doesn't matter where we live as long as we're together. I know that's true, but when we moved it was like we left Dad's aura behind. That might sound crazy, but that's how I feel, like we left a part of Dad at the old house.

We have photos and my old birthday cards with his hand-writing that I read over and over. I can hear his voice in my head when I read what he wrote to me. I even dressed Sampson in Dad's slate grey cardigan—the one I took the button from. I like to fall asleep on Sampson's belly, because the sweater still smells like Dad's aftershave, so that's something. But it's not the same.

I can hear Mom and Grandma speaking in hushed voic-es outside my door. *Oh great, Mom's still crying.* Nudging Grandma's suitcase out of the way, I flop on my bed and close my eyes. Why does she get to cry and no one threatens to send her to a shrink? It's my room we're talking about.

There's a tap at my door.

"Jules...please open the door." Mom's voice sounds ragged

"Why can't you just leave me alone for a minute?"

"Jules, please."

Sitting up on the edge of my bed I reach over, unlock the door, and swing it open. Mom stands in the threshold.

"Can I come in?" she asks.

"Might as well. Not like it's going to be my room much longer."

She eases the door closed and sits down next to me and lays one hand on top of mine. After a moment she clears her throat.

"Jules, I know this has been a tough time for you. First your dad and then moving here and now you're losing your room. I get that."

"*Really?* Then why isn't Grandma in your room?"

"That's what I want to talk to you—"

I yank my hand away.

"Are you trying to make my life suck even more than it does?"

"Of course not!" Her voice cracks mid-sentence. She closes her eyes and takes one of her yoga breathes and begins again. "Please let me talk—without interruptions."

"Fine."

Mom's face contorts and flushes. She takes another deep breath. "The reason your Grandma left Arizona and came home is because she's sick," she pauses. My breath catches.

"No," I whisper. I don't want her to finish.

"Grandma has breast cancer."

Please God, not cancer again. Thoughts of Dad fly through my head.

"No, it's not fair. Grandma *can't* have cancer; she doesn't *do* sick."

A head scarf?

Scorching waves of guilt wash over me. Nausea burns my stomach. We aren't having Grandma straighten *us* out; *we* are straightening Grandma out.

I slump into Mom's embrace and we cry together, wrapped in each other's arms. I draw away before Mom does and grab a few tissues from the top of my nightstand to wipe my face. My legs are limp as I walk to my closet. I pull my purple paisley jewellery box down from the top shelf, finding what I'm looking for safely stored in its original gold silk bag. Tears stream down my cheeks again.

Mom's hand flies to rest above her heart; her eyes crinkle. "*Oh Julia.*"

"Grandma," I call as we leave my room. She's standing in the den staring out the window, looking down the back lane. "I have something for you." In my hand is the necklace she gave me when I was in a spelling bee in fourth grade.

She swivels around.

"It's a bit scratched, but it still has a lot of luck left in it," I say. The pink horseshoe charm hangs from the tarnished silver chain as I hold it out to Grandma.

"Now that's my girl," Grandma says.

Grandma blinks away tears as I rush into her arms and sob against her. She comforts me even though I know I should be comforting her. Mom's strong arms then cocoon both of us.

"Alright, alright," Grandma gently pushes us away, "you're mussing up my bodacious scarf."

We try not to laugh, but then Grandma lets out a hoot that's contagious. I feel my whole body loosen as we huddle together on that beat-up couch, all three talking at once.

Looking at Grandma, my heart aches for her. Guilt floods through me, and my vision blurs with tears.

A bedroom. How could I have been so shallow?

CHAPTER 11

When all else fails, run from the truth.

Their laughter wakes me, but I don't get up right away. I love lying here, listening to their hushed whispers. Closing my eyes, I can almost imagine myself back in my old bedroom at the house, with Mom and Grandma at the dining room table playing canasta for hours into the night. Everything would be the way it was supposed to be. Dad would be alive and I would be safe in my bed. I want this feeling to last. I close my eyes tight, shutting out the reality of the cramped den.

I roll onto my side, hoping that I'll fall back asleep, but the musty sofa bed is narrower than I remember. My lips almost kiss the couch's brown tweed arm and the half peanut that is stuck to its fabric. *Gross.* When was the last time we vacuumed this piece of junk?

Shoving my feet into my bunny slippers, I hug my fuzzy purple robe around me. I still can't believe Grandma's been back from Arizona for two months and she never called. She didn't even let us know she had started chemo, she never asked for an ounce of help. We would've completely fallen apart without her when Dad was sick. She cooked meals, washed clothes, coordinated hospital relief, and manned the bookstore; all without being asked. She instinctively knew when and how we needed her, yet she's was too stubborn to ask us for help. Until now.

I stretch, take in a big breath, and the homiest smell from my childhood hits me—cinnamon! My eyes fly wide, fully awake. Grandma must have made her world-famous buns. I pull at the bi-fold door. It clicks, but doesn't open. I shake it and pull again. It rattles, but the magnet won't un-stick. The door is made of cheap brown plastic and is ripped in several places. This would never happen in Jeremy's pristine mini mansion. His bedroom is larger than our living and dining room combined.

"Come on," I mutter, shaking the door harder and pushing it at the same time. "Whoa!"

My hand goes through the vinyl next to the magnet closure. I pull my hand out, careful not to scratch it on the jagged opening, and crouch down to peer through the hole. I can see all the way across the apartment into the kitchen. Mom and Grandma are staring back at me. Mom has her hand over her mouth and looks like she's trying not to laugh. Grandma's busting a gut. The smell of fresh bread mingled with brown sugar and cinnamon makes my mouth water. My stomach rumbles in response.

"Can one of you get me out of here before I do an Incredible Hulk and bust the door down?"

Grandma hands her oven mitts to Mom and marches to me. She's got a different scarf wrapped around her head this morning, pale yellow swirled with a hint of orange. It's like a bright flag, waving to the world that she's sick. My stomach churns at the thought.

"How in the world did you get yourself locked in there?" Grandma asks as she pulls at the door, which remains shut. I hear a quiet click and she ratchets the door open. "Ta-da! Grandma to the rescue!"

"How'd you open it?" I squeeze by her, trying not to look too long at her scarf-wrapped head, pretending like I'm fascinated by the faulty lock.

"Well, the door must have been put on wrong. The lock was on the outside of the door rather than the inside and when you went to bed, somehow it must have automatically locked."

"Or you two locked me in!" I tease and force on a grin. *Don't look at her scarf. Keep your eyes on her face.*

"Aw, you discovered our evil plan," Mom says. "We were going to keep you caged in there until we polished off all of Grandma's famous cinnamon buns."

"Did you say cinnamon buns?" I say and sprint to the kitchen, breathing deep on the cinnamon sweetness.

The table's already set and Mom's served us each a bun, poured orange juice in all three glasses.

"Who's ready to eat?" says Grandma, as she sits down at the table.

"I'm starving," I say, sitting down across from her, careful not to let my gaze wander from her face. My heart races.

Grandma takes a big bite of her bun, and her lip curls up like she's just tasted poison. She gags and spits her cinnamon bun into her hand. Dumping the chewed mess onto her plate she grabs her glass, slopping orange juice across her hand in her haste. She gulps at the juice, her eyes shut tight.

"What's wrong?" I ask, knocking my chair over as I jump up. "Are you nauseous?" I run around the table.

"What do you need us to do Grandma? Are you okay? Should we call your doctor?" My heart beat gallops. I can't catch my breath.

"Julia, calm down," says Mom, her voice remains even, no trace of worry. How can she be so calm? "You need to give Grandma a chance to answer."

With a corner of her napkin, Grandma wipes the orange juice from her hand and around her upper lip.

"Good Lord, child. You need to relax. The buns taste like a salt lick. Somehow I put in far too much salt." Grandma tips her head back and hoots like she does, sounding like a strange mix of owl and wolf.

"What?" I say, barely above a whisper. I thought she was going to throw up and the only problem was she ate a salty pastry? My heartbeat won't slow down and my hands start to shake. Feeling woozy, I lean against the wall for support.

Mom gets up from the table, removes the cinnamon buns, and dumps them in the garbage can. They both start giggling. I watch them for a minute or so, growing more agitated. I have to grit my teeth to stop my stomach from lurching up my throat.

"So you're not feeling sick from the chemo? I was really freaked out and you two think its some big joke!" I say, my voice getting louder. "I thought Grandma was going to be sick." Beads of perspiration form across the bridge of my nose.

Grandma stops laughing and adjusts her scarf, tucking a few short curls under the edge behind her ears.

"Julia, I don't think this is a joke," Grandma says and swoops across the room. "We need to talk."

"No! I can't handle this right now."

I stumble into the living room, my vision narrows. I fall onto the couch and sit with my head between my knees, trying not to hyperventilate.

"Sweetie," says Grandma. She plunks down next to me and rubs my back. "Sometimes I forget how much you worry about everyone. I should've thought this through."

Mom sits down on the other side of me.

"Just breathe, Jules," Mom says, her voice soft. A few moments pass and I sit up, breathing easier.

"Grandma, not even you can predict when my emotions are going to go berserk," I say.

"I'm going to get us some bagels," Mom says, running her hands through her hair.

Grandma watches Mom in the kitchen for a moment before pulling the afghan from the back of the sofa. She drapes the blanket over my shoulders. I turn to face Grandma and the smell of her Dove soap mixed with a light whiff of lilac helps calm me. I lean into her.

"I'm not sure I can handle the details," I say.

"We can't hide from—"

"Don't push her. You need to let her decide when she's ready," Mom says from the kitchen, interrupting Grandma.

"Hmm. I'm not sure I agree. I know it has been terribly difficult for both of you since Richard passed, but that doesn't mean you shrivel into a ball and cry in the corner every time bad news comes your way."

I stiffen at the mention of Dad's name and glance at Mom. She freezes. She stares down at the counter for a second and then closes her eyes. Her whole body stiffens statue still. Is she even breathing? A moment goes by and her nostrils flare. She must be centering herself. It's a yoga technique. It's supposed to calm your chi or something. A few more deep breaths pass and her eyes open. She returns to prepping our breakfast, as if Dad's name was never mentioned, sticking to our unspoken pact.

Grandma examines Mom, her eyebrows attempting to crease. Of course they no longer move on demand. They just quiver for a few seconds but never rise. She nods her head, looking resigned.

"Alright," she says, focusing her inquisitor eyes on me. "We'll give it some time."

Grandma reaches over and cups my chin, like she's done since forever.

"But I have my eyes on you," she says.

There's something about her face looks different, beyond just looking thinner. I can't quite figure out what it is. *Is she tired?* My breath catches.

Grandma doesn't look tired; she looks old.

CHAPTER 12

Why can't everyone just get along?

Running late, I shove my lunch and books into my backpack and gulp down my daily pill. I'm going to have to sprint to school to make the bell. I check my phone for texts from Annika. Still nothing. I'll just have to track her down and make her talk to me. Somehow.

I cut though the pitch-black store and trip over the life size cardboard cutout of Laura Ingalls Wilder. She goes flying into the cash desk, knocking over the wheat bouquet Mom spent over an hour arranging. We're running a month long "Books of the Prairies for the Prairies" campaign. Book themes liven up the store and entice our customers to check out titles and authors they've overlooked. I gather the shafts that are strewn across the counter as best I can in the dark and shove them back into the plastic vase. Thank goodness Mom didn't use her usual container or I would be sweeping up broken pottery too.

"Is everything okay down there?" Mom calls down the stairs.

"Yup, don't worry," I reply. "See you after school."

"Jules," she calls again. "I—" she stops mid-sentence.

"Yes?"

No reply.

"Mom?" I call. Louder.

"Have a good day," she finally says.

"You too." That was weird. It totally sounded like she wanted to say something more. Whatever.

Deciding it safer for both me and the store, I fast walk through the rest of the shop to the back door. I pat my jeans pocket, checking for Dad's button before slipping on my coat and boots.

A quiet duck honk greets me as I take my first step into the crisp morning air. *Annika!* She's parked Aunt Mildred at the bottom of the staircase. Music pumps through the closed windows. As usual. A tentative smile quivers to life on her face as she waves. She mouths the words, "Sorry."

"Me too," I say out loud, flying down the stairs.

I tug open the door and practically fall inside.

"I'm sorry," we say at the same time. And then I burst into tears. As usual.

"Annika," I say, between sobs. "I am so sorry. I never meant to hurt you."

"I know, I know. It's just—" she pauses, a blush rushes up her neck, engulfing her face. "I felt like you were dumping me for that whole crowd."

"I'm not. Nothing will stop you from being my best friend. Having Jeremy as my boyfriend doesn't change anything."

"I guess." Annika says, sounding uncertain.

"Hey, why don't you come over after school tonight and we can have dinner and watch *Rock Star*?" Tonight's her only Taekwondo-free evening.

"Sure, that would be great," Annika says. Her smile is huge. "Buckle up, Fraidy. We gotta' boot it if we're going to make school on time."

As promised, Annika flies out of the parking lot, and races down the lane. Houses zip by so fast that they're only a blur of snow-shrouded stucco.

"Annika…" I begin.

"Trust me," she says and cackles.

I close my eyes, hoping that what I can't see won't kill me. We turn a corner and I crash against my door.

"Youch," I say. My eyes pop open. "I've decided I don't mind being late."

"Ach, Fraidy, we're almost there."

We speed around the last corner. Prairie Trials is only five hundred meters down the road.

"Thank God. We're going to arrive alive," I say, fighting a rising urge to cover my eyes with my hands and scream like a lunatic.

"You seriously need to chill."

We pull into one of the last remaining spots at the back of the parking lot. My hands shake as I climb from Aunt Mildred. If I were Catholic, this would be the perfect time to cross myself. Twice.

Weaving through the cars, we pass Jeremy's glistening black BMW. Of course it sits on an angle, covering two spots.

"Over Pretentious Asshole Park!" Annika calls from behind me.

"Annika!" I moan, but a giggle escapes. It *is* sort of pretentious.

She catches up to me as we enter the school and just as the morning bell blares.

"Okay, truce," she says. "I will try to keep my opinions to myself, but you must swear not to turn into Madison's second evil sidekick."

"Annika, she is really not that bad."

"See, she already has her talons in you." She holds her hands up like claws and caws like a jackal. I push her hands down.

"She does not. She is different. Nicer. Her jackal side has been tamed."

"You can't tame a wild beast and there is no way that even six months ago you would've said that. No way."

"Listen, I will prove it to you"

"Good luck with that," she replies and laughs. I can tell she has no faith in my appraisal of Madison. We thread our way through throngs of students to the far end of the school.

"Jeremy," I call. He's standing by my locker with a black gift bag in his hands. Hot pink and lime green tissue pokes out the top. I race to him.

"Beautiful," he says, kissing me on my cheek. "I have a present for you."

"That is so nice. Can I open it?"

"Of course," he says. He folds his arms and leans against the lockers watching me with a satisfied grin.

"Hey Jeremy," Annika says. I stop mid tissue pull, and stare at her. She looks at me, her eyes grow wide and her eyebrows arch so high they disappear under her angled bangs. "*What?* I can't say hi to my best friend's boyfriend?"

"No, that's good," I say, thrilled that she's already making an effort with him.

"Hey Annika," Jeremy says. He doesn't exactly sound pleased to see her, but it's a start.

I pull the rest of the tissue from the bag.

"Oh Jeremy, it's gorgeous." With care, I pull out a black leather jacket. I hold it up against me and stare down at myself. It comes just to my waist and is form fitting. The tag flips over revealing the $450 price.

"That is a De la Vega, Julia. A Rosa De la Vega. I didn't even know you could get her line in Winnipeg," Annika says. Wanting to be a designer herself she knows all the hottest designers' works. She razzes Madison for wearing designer threads only because she thinks Madison is too much of a trend follower, not a trendsetter.

"You can't," Jeremy says, looking at me. "I ordered it in for you."

"That is so sweet, but I can't accept this. It's too much."

"I told you—I like to buy you things. And anyway, we can't return it so you have to wear it."

I slip off my bulky winter coat and pull the jacket on over my T-shirt. The leather is soft and fits like a glove. It even smells expensive.

"Fraidy, you look amazing," Annika says, her eyes wide in appreciation.

"For once I agree with you," Jeremy says. He takes a picture of me with his phone. "You look hot."

"It is the nicest piece of clothing I have ever worn, but—" I say, pausing. I'm torn. I love the jacket and I want to keep it, but something about the price of the coat feels wrong. "You shouldn't be spending so much money on me. Really."

Madison walks up behind Annika.

"Julia, you look like a model," she says. Her eyes narrow as she gives Annika a head to toe inspection. Annika ignores Madison. Annika is wearing one of her older "creations"— a one of a kind jacket over her artfully torn black jeans. She took bits and pieces of two khaki army jackets and melded them together. It has a sort of Igor look to it, which she says is supposed to be both intriguing and harsh. Madison smirks at me, points at Annika and rolls her eyes. Thank God, Annika's too engrossed in the stitching of my coat to notice, her hands busily tracing each seam of the smooth leather.

"Thanks. It's a present from Jeremy."

"Wow, that's some sort of gift," she says, her voice is tight. She sounds miffed. "You never bought me anything so posh when we were dating."

Jeremy shrugs.

"Can I try it on?" Annika asks.

"Ah—" Jeremy begins.

"Of course," I say, slipping out of the luxurious jacket. Annika drops her bag to the floor and yanks off her Igor threads, laying her jacket on top. She extends her hands to me. They're trembling. She holds the coat like I would if handed the original plans for the Eiffel Tower or The Taj Mahal or anything from Frank Lloyd Wright: gently and with great care.

"Oh. My. God. It feels better than I ever imagined," she says, zipping it up. Her voice is soft. Her smile full of wonder and awe.

"Like you would have any clue," scoffs Madison.

"What?" Annika says.

"You look ridiculous," says Madison.

Annika's smile vanishes. She rips the coat off like it's burning her skin and shoves it at me.

"Nice," she says, brushing by me.

"Annika, wait," I say, following her as she grabs her coat, slinging her bag over her shoulder.

"She is a total bitch," Annika says.

"No, no she's not. Really," I say. "The jacket is just a little too big for you."

"Oh my God, Julia. You're taking her side."

"Annika," I say. My gut churns. "Of course not, what I meant was—"

"Come on, Julia," Jeremy calls.

"One second," I say, pulling at Annika's arm. "Please listen—"

"It's fine," she interrupts. "I couldn't give a crap what princess thinks. She's a complete fake. But you?"

This is not going as planned, and I'm pretty sure Madison can hear every word we say. I need to change the subject.

"Are we still on for tonight?"

"I thought you would've forgotten," she says. "With your new friends taking up all your time."

"I want to hang out with you. I don't want to fight anymore."

Annika stares down the hallway and then sighs, facing me. She looks wary, her lips purse.

"Okay."

"And I need to tell you about my grandma." My voice catches. Emotion swells. My chest tightens.

"Is everything alright?"

"No, not really." My voice hushes to a whisper. "She has breast cancer."

"Oh my gosh, Fraidy. Why didn't you say anything in the car?"

"I was just so relieved to see you. I guess it slipped my mind." I bury my head in my hands. Please don't start crying. *Dad, help me.* Annika's arms are around me.

"Fraidy, are you okay?" she whispers.

"Yeah. No, I dunno. It's just a lot. You know?"

"Yeah."

The second bell rings. We're going to be late for class.

"Julia, is everything alright?" Jeremy asks.

I pull away from Annika.

"Are you *okay*, okay?" she asks.

"Yeah. Thanks." I say.

"Hey, no tears," Jeremy says, drying the one tear that escaped. He shoots Annika an accusing look, like she made me upset. "We've got to get to class."

I slip on his gift, warmed by the soft leather. If my blues could be so easily lifted by high fashion, I'd go shopping with Jeremy every day.

"I'll take care of this," he says, picking up my coat that I dropped by my locker. "See you at lunch."

"Sure," I reply.

"And don't be late." He nods at Annika, then sprints down the hall, tossing my old jacket in a garbage can before racing up the stairs towards the third floor.

"He just threw out a perfectly good—never mind," Annika says, adjusting her bag on her shoulder. "Text me if you need me. Seriously, Fraidy," she says, her voice insistent.

"I will."

"If I find you in a puddle in some corner of the school, and you didn't—"

"I get it. Please don't worry."

"See you at lunch," she says, giving me another quick hug.

"See you." I wave and we run to our first classes.

I squeeze through Mr. Foster's doorway right as he's closing the door. Once he closes the door, the only way in is with a late slip from the office.

"Almost got you that time Miss Julia," he says, his grey wiry eyebrows arched high up his forehead. He hisses his s's like a snake. It always makes me fixate on his mouth, half expecting a forked tongue to dart out between his lips. "Take your sssseat. Pronto."

I slip into my desk at the front of the class by the window and pull out my binder while Mr. Foster hands back our last test papers. He stops when he gets to my desk and waves my test above his head, drawing the class's attention.

"Students," he hisses, "this is what perfection looks like. 100% Miss Julia. Well done."

Thank God I aced it. Every test score counts if I want a shot at the University of Southern California. Its architectural program ranks top five in North America and there's no way I can afford to go without winning an academic scholarship. USC is my ticket out of here. Out of the apartment above the bookstore. Away from Mom's deep sighs and silence about Dad. In California, I can begin a new life with Jeremy. He's applying to USC too, so we can be together, but with his dad's money he doesn't have to worry about tuition.

Mr. Foster passes out the remainder of the tests, instructing the class to correct their errors for the rest of the period. Opening my textbook, I turn to the next chapter and scan the picture of a pig fetus's small intestine. My stomach burbles, so I take my pencil case, cover the photo, and just read about it. I'm about three quarters down the page when someone walks down the aisle and bangs my book with their leg. My textbook crashes to the floor.

"Oh sorry, I didn't mean to interrupt your precious study time," says Hannah. She crouches down beside me and places the textbook back on my desk. That was oddly decent of her. "Don't you ever do anything just for fun?"

"Of course I do."

"Like what?"

Nothing comes to mind. Most of my spare time is taken up by the bookstore. Working in the bookshop isn't water-boarding type torture, but no one would classify it as fun.

"OMG. So you never shop, party or even go to a movie? How lame. You should try socializing with other human beings."

"Annika and I do lots of those things."

"Yeah, I meant socializing—partying—with people *other* than the mini-freak."

"Annika is not a freak." Hannah's idea of partying is drinking until she passes out. With my meds, I'm too scared to drink even one beer.

"Hey, I'm just saying the girl's a bit of a style circus and you seem to have more potential than that." She stares at my face and hair as if considering my worthiness.

"She's unique," I say.

Hannah rolls her eyes at me. I flip over my page and pretend to find a pig's digestive secretions fascinating. Maybe she'll get the hint and leave me alone.

"She's uniquely freakish. You'd have a lot more friends if you'd ditch her. She's totally keeping you back. " She returns to the back row where she hides from Mr. Foster.

What a cow. Seriously, like I'd ever dump Annika. And who cares about what she wears. My heart sinks. Jeremy. He's all about being trendy. Annika and Jeremy are complete opposites. Maybe if I convince Annika to tone down her wardrobe, Jeremy would see how incredible she really is and then maybe everyone would get along.

It's good to have goals, right?

CHAPTER 13

Everyone has a complicated root system.

I grab a French fry from Annika's plate before she douses them with vinegar. She pops a few into her mouth, munching like she hasn't eaten all week. She has a monstrous appetite for someone so tiny.

"Is that new?" I ask, pointing to her top. It is—unique.

"Yeah, I put the finishing touches on it last night. The leather strips were a bit tricky, but I love the way it turned out." She runs her fingers over the light grey pieces that weave through each arm of her black long sleeve T-shirt.

"I've never seen anything like it." I suppose I can understand why people don't appreciate her sense of style.

"Thanks."

"You are not going to believe the run in I had with Hannah," I say.

"Well—" she begins, but stops as fry bits threaten to spill out of her mouth. She drops her fork and gingerly nudges the food back into her mouth with her pinkie.

"What?" I begin, but a flash of movement in my peripheral vision distracts me. Tyler is standing across the room, waving in our direction. My first impulse is to wave back, but I hesitate and look around the lunchroom, scouting for Jeremy. I glance back at Tyler who's still waving. I cautiously wave back.

Annika turns around and when she sees Tyler her entire body stiffens. She grabs a napkin and splashes water on it from her bottle. Like a bird she cleans any signs of French fry from her face. She pats down her hair and fiddles with the peace charm that she always wears around her neck. Tyler's eyes are locked on Annika.

"Hey," says Tyler.

"Hey," Annika and I say together.

"Can I join you?" He sits down opposite Annika before we reply and takes a long slurp from his straw. His eyes never leave Annika's face.

"Be our guest," Annika says. Maybe she's being sarcastically funny. She's playing with her earring, which usually means she's either nervous or annoyed.

"I've been looking for you all day," Tyler says to me.

"Why?" I ask.

"I wanted to talk to you about tut—"

"Hey, Beautiful," Jeremy interrupts, laying his hand on my shoulder. He leans over me and places a Caesar salad with grilled chicken in front of me. "Somehow, you didn't see me in the food line." There's an edge to his voice. He's glaring at Tyler and Annika.

"I'm so sorry Jeremy. As soon as I saw Annika I sat down, and Tyler just got here. Thanks for the salad."

I don't dare look at Tyler. I don't want to encourage him to keep talking about tutoring. I haven't had a chance to tell Jeremy yet. I'm pretty sure he may go mental. Jeremy moves my stack of textbooks so he can sit down beside me. My test paper slips from the pile and floats to the floor. He picks it up and hoots.

"Look at this. She's gorgeous and smart. And look at this," he says, pulling a crumpled test from his binder. "I got an 82! I have never gotten above a 70. All thanks to Julia." He kisses me on the cheek.

"Yes, Misssss. Julia," Tyler says, doing an impression of Mr. Foster. He's put two fries on his eyebrows mimicking Mr. Foster further. Oh my God. I totally forgot he was in my anatomy class. "Sssssо, if you're already a geniussss, why do you sssssstudy sssssso much?"

"Because she's not a dimwit, like some people," snaps Annika. Tyler scoots back in his chair and raises his hands in front of his face, as if fending off an attack. One fry slips down his cheek.

"Hey, I was just asking. It's not every day you meet a real live genius." He peels the fries off his face. He examines them thoroughly before stuffing them in his mouth. *Ick.* He bows to me and chants with his mouth full of face-fries, "I'm not worthy. I'm not worthy."

"What Annika meant to say, is that I need top grades to get into my dream university. Annika's just overly protective of me. She's actually very sweet, once you get to know her."

Annika crosses her eyes and sticks her tongue out at me.

"So she's complicated?" Tyler asks.

"I wouldn't say complicated. She's like an onion."

"She has layers?" he asks.

"She's bitter and makes your eyes water?" Jeremy asks.

"No," I laugh. "She's a certain type of onion—a Vidalia. Its taste surprises you: sweet, but still stings your eyes. When I was little my dad and I used to eat them like apples."

"Okay so she's a 'sweet on the inside and bitter on the outside' kind of onion," Tyler says.

"Hey, the onion in question is sitting right here and she has ears," Annika says.

"It's the hugest complement, Annika! Vidalias are like my BFFs of the vegetable world."

"Well, if I'm an onion, you've got to be a carrot."

"A carrot?" I ask.

"Yup. All fresh and shiny green on top, making everyone think that what they see is what they get, but in reality under the surface, there's a whole bunch more of you with a complicated root system."

She teeters back in her chair with her black ankle-high leather boots resting on the edge of the lunch table while a satisfied smile spreads across her face. Her ruby nose ring sparkles in the rays of light that stream through the window.

"I do like a good carrot," I say, glad she didn't say anything else about me. I really don't want to discuss any of my complexities. Pretty sure Jeremy's idea of perfection doesn't include complications like depression and anxiety.

"Okay, well if Annika is a special onion and you're a complex carrot, what am I?" Tyler asks. "Asparagus? Squash? How about a red pepper?"

Annika and I stare at each other and at the same time blurt out, "Broccoli!" We high five.

"I hate broccoli," he complains.

"But broccoli has two sides—the flowery top—like your super fine hair and the sturdy stems are—" I say, not finishing because Annika buts in.

"The sturdy stems are your legs and everyone knows you've got great dance moves. And if you smother broccoli with cheese you have a masterpiece that hits every taste bud, mmmm, mmmm," says Annika in this throaty sexy voice that I have never heard her use.

Tyler looks like he's died and gone to heaven and Annika, obviously flustered, jams a large fork full of fries into her mouth. Her face glows bright red.

"Hey," replies Tyler, oblivious to Annika's embarrassment. "I'll be your broccoli, any time…anywhere. I'll even bring the cheese." He high fives Jeremy and then turns to Annika, flashing an enormous smile. "We should hook up. I'll call you."

Annika gives him a slight head nod, her face somehow reaching a darker red. She looks like she fell asleep while suntanning—for two days straight.

Tyler rises and catches his leg under the table, which rocks all our drinks.

"See you later," he says. I avoid making eye contact, even though I can feel him looking at me. They leave the three of us in an uncomfortable silence. Annika breaks the tension.

"Okay," she stands up and grabs her tray. "I'm going to take my Vidalia self out of here."

"I'll see you at 3:30," I say.

"See ya'," Annika says, not meeting my eye. She turns and zigzags around the tables, dumping the leftovers from her tray into the trashcan before heading out of the cafeteria.

We sit for a moment and I tap my fork rhythmically on the table.

"That was…" I say.

"Strange?" Jeremy finishes for me.

"More than strange. I've never seen Annika like that."

"Maybe she's a rare 'complicated' hybrid Vidalia," Jeremy suggests. "With many, many layers of bitter before you get to the sweet." He makes a sourpuss face that gives me the giggles.

"Hey, that's my BFF you're talking about." I mock punch him.

"We've got time before our next class. Do you want to go for a walk?"

"Sure," a surge of joy courses through me, "I like to walk."

As we leave the cafeteria, Jeremy slips his hand over mine, sending electrical shocks up my arm, jellifying my knees in the process. If we were on a cover of a trashy romance novel, this is when I'd faint into his well-muscled bare arms. We walk down the corridor toward the gym and climb the stairs to the third floor.

"Where are we going?" I ask.

"It's a surprise."

He leads me to the end of the hallway to a little nook in the wall of frost-rimmed windows that run the back length of the school. We sit down on the cold ledge.

"So what's the—" I don't finish my sentence because although Jeremy is still looking directly at me, he's tracing tiny angel-wing light circles in the palm of my hand. It feels so…sexy. He leans over and kisses me. It's thrilling and exciting and…perfect.

"Wow," I say. "That was—wow."

He pulls me close and we kiss again. I lean into him, my hands run through his hair. Desire races through me. His hand glides from the small of my back, across my stomach and up to cup my breast. My eyes flash open and I push against his chest, breaking our kiss.

"Woah. That's way, way too much," I say.

"Julia," he moans. "You're driving me mental."

"Sorry, I just—I can't—that was—no, just no." Confusion clouds my mind. It was so amazing and then poof—I panic. "Why do you always do that?"

"Do what? Kiss you?"

"No, the other stuff. You keep rushing me, Jeremy."

"You're my girlfriend. I'm supposed to want you. You're supposed to want me." He crosses his arms. "You're not into someone else, are you?"

"Of course not. Why would you say that?"

"Why else would you push me away?"

The bell rings. I jump off the ledge, relieved to have an excuse to end this conversation.

"We have to get back to class," I say, taking a few steps down the corridor. Jeremy doesn't move.

"Jeremy," I reach for his hand, but he draws it away, glaring at me. He storms by me. "Jeremy, please."

He doesn't turn. Walking faster, his hands tighten to fists. I sprint to catch up. He spins to face me and I almost run into him.

"I don't get you, Julia. What do you want? Do you even want me?" His voice is deep and dangerous. He lunges at the lockers beside us and smashes his fist hard, denting the metal. His knuckles are bloodied.

"Oh my God, Jeremy!" I reach for his hand, but he yanks his arm back, seething in anger or pain. I'm not sure which.

"See, what you do to me?" He says. "I need you and you keep pushing me away."

"I didn't mean—" I begin.

"Never mind. I'll text you later."

"But, Jeremy,"

"Later," he growls. I watch him storm back down the hallway. He vanishes around the corner.

What just happened?

CHAPTER 14

Simple math.

I sprint to my locker. My throat aches and my tears finally let loose. At least I made it through the afternoon. Slamming the door closed, I run to the parking lot doors and to my escape. My bag, thrown over my arm, bashes against my side. My vision blurs.

The crisp air freezes my damp cheeks as I stagger outside and wind my way through the cars to the back row. Annika's sitting on Aunt Mildred's hood, earbuds in and swaying to her music. She glances up and her impish smile shifts into concern.

"Boys," I say and attempt a smile. I fail, by epic proportions. A sob escapes as I lurch towards the car.

"I'm going to call my brother and we're going to whip The Third's—" I grab her phone out of her hands.

"No, it was my fault."

"What?"

"Get in the car and I'll tell you the details. I don't want anyone seeing me like this."

Annika starts the car and we slide out of the snow-packed lot as I recap the entire scene with Jeremy.

"What an ass," Annika says.

"It was all my fault. I keep leading him on."

"You've told him billions of times to take it slow, but he keeps pushing you. Correct? Thus, he is pressuring you into sex when you are so not ready. Hence asslike behaviour; hence he acted like an ass; hence he is an ass. Simple math. If a = b, and b = c, then a = c."

"Your logic is wacked," I say.

Annika zooms toward the intersection, slamming on her brakes at the last moment. We fishtail across the ice to a stop.

Annika frowns and takes a sideways glance at me. She shifts into first gear.

"Don't you think you should talk to your mom about this? I mean, you're pretty upset."

"No way. She'll totally go nuts."

"I don't know Annika."

"When was the last time I had to call my mom?"

"When you had that anxiety attack at Starbucks and you locked yourself in the bathroom."

"Yeah, after I ordered my dad's favourite coffee, which was a huge trigger."

"It was a pretty severe meltdown, Fraidy."

"I know, but that was two months ago. You have to believe me. I can handle this."

"Okay, but if I see you crumbling—"

"Yeah, yeah. You can tattle to my mom."

"Hey," she says, punching me hard in my bicep. "It's not tattling when it's your best friend's, frickin' emotional well-being you're worried about."

"Okay, okay!" I laugh. "No need to go all martial arts crazy on me."

I pull out my compact and peer at my reflection. Jagged black mascara lines track down my cheeks. I am a total disaster.

"Any guy would be a fool to pass up this vision of beautiful." Beautiful.

What does Jeremy see in me?

CHAPTER 15

Best friend or boyfriend.

I pull the last tray of chocolate chunk cookies from the oven to help Mom get ready for tomorrow night's book club. Three nights a week and on Sunday afternoons, we rent out the back room for groups so they can discuss books. It helps bring in extra cash and right now we can use every penny.

When Mom first dreamed of owning a bookstore, I was totally hooked on the Little House on the Prairie books and I jokingly said she should call it, "The Little Bookshop on The Prairie." Mom loved it and the name stuck. She's always looking for ways to stand out from the big box chains. It was my idea to serve cookies and tea or coffee to our book club members to make their night more memorable. The book clubs love it and now I'm our official baker. I crank out three to four dozen cookies for every club night.

My dream is to add a small café-style restaurant and another meeting room, and I've already sketched out the plans. We would still have plenty of room for customer parking, but Mom keeps harping about our tight cash flow. She says it's good to keep dreaming but for now we need to focus on creating new varieties of our "Little Bookshop Cookies." Like another version of chocolate chip cookie is going to make a huge difference in our sales.

Taking a bite of a cooled cookie, I open my cookbook to my favourite cinnamon oatmeal raisin recipe to make sure I have all the ingredients. My head pops up at the high-pitched beep of the stair sensor. When we moved into the apartment the thought of strangers walking around downstairs freaked me out, and since we didn't always remember to lock the door at the bottom of the stairs I was scared that some book-crazy axe murderer would slink up when Mom was busy with customers. Mom had the sensor installed so I wouldn't get wigged out by every little sound.

I can hear Annika taking the stairs two at a time, getting to the top in a few seconds. We've been multi-tasking all night—first *Rock Star*, followed by a movie, all while baking cookies. We paused the movie while I finished the last batch and Annika went downstairs to scour the shelves for her next big read.

She grabs two cookies and scarfs back one before she drops the books she's holding.

"Piggish, much?" I tease.

"These...are...like heaven," she burbles, cookie crumbs tumbling from her mouth.

I pour us each a glass of milk and pile the cookies into tins. She gulps down her entire glass and holds it out for a refill. She grabs another cookie before I can smack her hand away.

"Hey, these are for our book clubs."

We return to the couch and start the movie. Under afghans we nibble on cookies and sip milk, just like we have since we were kids. My phone buzzes in my pocket. I check the display. *Jeremy*. I sneak to the washroom and lock the door.

THE3RD: Hey

JULES: Hey

THE3RD: Whaz up?

JULES: Movie w Annika

THE3RD: Oh

What do I say? Should I apologize? Annika says he's the one who was wrong, but I still feel guilty. A few seconds pass. My legs begin to shake so I sit on the edge of the bathtub. With my luck my legs would buckle and I'd collapse and smash my head on the sink, and to finish myself off, I'd knock my front teeth out.

THE3RD: I'm really sorry about today

JULES: Me too

THE3RD: U just do something to me

JULES: U too. To me. I mean. 😳

THE3RD: I need to see u

Annika will kill me or possibly Jeremy if he comes over right now, but I really want him to.

JULES: I don't think that's a good idea

THE3RD: Why?

JULES: Annika

THE3RD: How about later?

I glance at my watch. It's only 8:20, but the movie is almost over.

JULES: How about 10?

THE3RD: See u

I sneak back to the sofa and glance at Annika. Her eyes are glued to the screen. I don't think she even noticed I left the room. The credits roll.

"Awesome movie," she says, yawning and pulling Grandma's afghan to her chin.

"Yeah, totally," I agree. *Silver Lining Playbook* is our new most favourite chick flick and we've seen it at least seven times. She looks like she's getting ready to hunker down for the night. No last-minute sleepovers tonight.

"Hey, so what do you think about Tyler?" I ask." He's super cute—a total rock star in the making. I think he's totally into you."

"Cute? Really?" she thinks about that for a second, her face flushing. "Even after he French-fried his face in the lunchroom? It's nearly impossible to redeem yourself after doing something so moronic."

I truly think Tyler would be a good match for her, but the memory of him eating those face-fries gives me the willies. "That really was gross."

"But that butt…" she says, fanning her face with her hand. "Smokin' hot!"

"And you call me the Drama Queen?"

Laughing, we turn at the sound of footsteps bounding up the staircase, which can't be Mom or Grandma—neither one of them moves that fast.

"Jeremy!" I say. *Oh my God, he's really early, like an hour and a half early*. "I said 10:00." Did he call from the parking lot?

"Hey, I get here, when I get here," he replies, shrugging off his jacket.

"10:00—what? Why is he here?" Annika asks, her tone sharp.

"I, uh, invited him," I say, walking around the couch to the dining room. Annika is close on my heels.

"Why?"

"He wanted to apologize in person."

"Oh my God, and you're going to fall for that?" Her voice is angry and urgent.

"Fall for what?" Jeremy asks.

"Nothing," I reply.

"No, it's not *nothing*," Annika says to me, then directs her Annika fury onto Jeremy. "You are an asshole. You are a deep dark stinky butt. If Julia doesn't want to have sex with you, you need to respect that and stop pressuring her."

"Oh my God. Annika!"

"What? Like you didn't want me to say that?"

"No, I didn't."

"*Seriously?!*" Annika grabs my shoulders and stares into my eyes, searching like she does. She throws her arms off me and backs away. "Oh, okay, then fine. I am out of here." She shoves Jeremy out of her way as she heads to the staircase.

"Annika!" I call after her.

"Don't bother," Jeremy says, holding me back.

"But Jeremy, she's my best friend."

"You've got me."

He wraps his arms around me, encasing me. I cry. Hard. I'm unstoppable.

"Beautiful. I've got you."

Is that enough?

CHAPTER 16

1,000 volts of Jeremy.

"I can't believe that just happened," I mumble between sobs. My wet face is buried in Jeremy's shoulder.

"Annika is a total head case," Jeremy says. He sounds disgusted. Which I guess is fair. Who wants to be called a deep dark stinky butt?

"No, she's—" I stop. How do I defend her? She was totally out of control. My chest feels tight. I struggle to take a full breath.

He kisses me softly on my forehead. It makes me feel safe.

"You need to stop worrying about her. Let's head down to The Creek. Everyone's going to be there."

"Oh, I'm not sure…"

My body feels heavy. My arms are deadweight and my legs feel like logs. The last place I want to be right now is freezing in the bush, huddled around a fire in the snow, surrounded by people. I just want to snuggle here with Jeremy and block all thoughts of my fight with Annika.

"Come on, Julia. You can't say no forever. You've never been and I know you'll love it. It would mean a lot to me."

"I guess."

Annika and I have never been into drinking, but since her brother Joel got home from rehab, it's like she's the poster child for MADD. Plus, she's so anti-Madison that she'd never go to a party at the creek and I'd never go by myself.

"Great. Now," he pauses and holds me at arm's length. "You need to clean yourself up and try to flatten this." He picks up a lock of my snarled curls, pulling my hair across my face.

"Oh, okay," I reach up and push my hair behind my ear.

He pulls out his phone and begins texting. He glances up, looking annoyed. "What are you waiting for? Hurry up, slowpoke. I don't want to miss all the action."

My throat burns. I hurry to my room, stuffing down the near hysteria that is growing inside me. He doesn't understand. Annika's my best friend. We've been through everything together. I slide the bi-fold door as closed as it will go. I hope Jeremy doesn't notice the silver duct tape that we used to cover the hole I made the other day. I search my purse for my Panic Pills. Only four left. I've been so careful only to take one if it's my only choice. I have to visit Dr. Shapiro if I want a refill, and she'll ask me a million irritating questions like: How many times in the past week have you felt anxious? And have you considered harming yourself and have you had any thoughts of death? Most likely, I'll have to fill out another dozen questionnaires to convince everyone I'm sane enough to "function within the rest of society."

I am too familiar with this out of control feeling. I swallow one tiny pill, knowing the panic will soon lessen. I close my eyes and concentrate on slowing my breathing, willing my body to relax.

Spraying leave-in conditioner on my hair, I grab my paddle brush and carefully work the tangles from my curls. Jeremy is going to hate how long this is taking, but you can't rush your way through frizz and expect perfectly straight doll hair. I gather my hair into a low pony and inspect myself in the mirror. At least my bangs are somewhat smooth. I hairspray them into place, hoping they will behave themselves tonight.

"I'm ready," I call as I push on my plastic door handle. It doesn't budge. *Please don't jam. Please.* I lift up on the handle and wiggle the door. Nothing. I push harder. It jerks open a few inches and makes a loud cracking sound as the top of the door falls out of the track that runs along the doorframe.

"No, no, no," I whisper, trying to hold the door up as I squeeze out of my room. I have one leg free when the entire door collapses into the living room.

"Heh heh. I'm ready," I say, trying not to look as embarrassed as I feel. Heat engulfs me. *Is it possible for your entire body to blush?*

I step around the crumpled vinyl disaster, pretending I don't see it, and grab Jeremy's hand.

"*What the?*" he asks. "Are you okay?"

"Yup, let's go, before I change my mind." I pull him to the stairs.

"We just need to make a beer run on our way," he says.

I pause, peering down the stairs, expecting Mom to come flying through the doorway from the bookstore. It must have sounded like I destroyed the entire apartment. "Just don't say anything to my mom or grandma about the beer. They'll flip out."

"No worries. I am a pro with mothers," he says, but his smile slips just a bit. "It's just dads I have a problem with." My heart aches for him. He deserves to have a dad like mine. But if he knew how wrong he was about my mom, his grin would completely disappear. She doesn't even know we're back together, and she's livid with him.

What will Grandma think of Jeremy?

Mom appears at the base of the stairs.

"Hey," I call.

"I heard a crash? Are you okay?" she asks. She frowns when she sees Jeremy coming down the stairs behind me. Her jaw sets. She runs her hand through her hair, finding her glasses perched on top. Slipping them on, she squeezes her lips into a long thin line. She's in full-on pissed-off teacher mode. Grandma joins her. Crap. This is not going to be pretty. All four of us squeeze into the small landing that leads outside or into the bookshop.

"Why is he here?" Mom asks.

"I invited him."

"Do you think that's smart, after what he did to you?"

"Mom, we had a fight. We were both wrong," I explain. "And you and Dad always said it takes two to make or break a relationship."

Mom steps back, her face pales.

"Don't you throw my words back at me," her voice hushes to a whisper.

"But you—"

"Listen to your mother," Grandma interrupts. Her voice sombre.

"We're just going to go…" I hesitate. No way can I tell her where we're going, "…for a drive."

"Oh really," she says, glaring at Jeremy from above the rim of her glasses. "Can I expect you to return my daughter yourself this time?"

"Mrs. Collins, I am so sorry about the ski trip. I promise it won't happen again."

Grandma's hands are on her hips, the tails of her turquoise and grey headscarf billow down her shoulders.

"So this is the young man who left my granddaughter stranded, with no place to stay?"

"Grandma!"

"I really am sorry," Jeremy says again. I squeeze his hand, hoping he can tell that I am dying of embarrassment along with him.

Neither Mom nor Grandma says anything to him. Neither accepts his apology. They just scowl. At this point, it's a dead heat as to who is more angry: Mom or Grandma.

Mom ignores him and faces me.

"Jules," says Mom. She closes her eyes for a moment and pauses. "Do you have your cell?"

"Yes, but it's going to be okay."

"And you," Mom points up at Jeremy her finger an inch from his face. Her entire body is shaking. Jeremy blanches, takes a step backwards and bumps into the wall. "Don't you ever, ever, do something so stupid like that to my daughter again. Do you understand me?"

"Mom! Stop it!"

Grandma wraps her arm around Mom's shoulder and draws her away from Jeremy.

"It's okay, Julia. She's got a right to be mad," Jeremy says.

Silence fills the landing, smothering us. Mom is still shaking.

"You can go," Mom says, her voice thick. "But be home no later than midnight."

"Midnight? We have an in-service tomorrow; we don't even have school," I say.

"I need you in the store first thing tomorrow. It's twelve or you can stay home. Your choice."

"I'll have her home by twelve," Jeremy promises.

"You had better," says Grandma. "Because if you think Julia's mom is frightening when she's angry, you don't ever want to see me riled."

Red blotches creep over Jeremy's face, in stark contrast to the deathly pale colour that Mom scared into him.

Is this truly happening? My family sounds like a bunch of mafia dames.

I can't even look at Jeremy as he opens the door for me. He must think we're a bunch of lowlife scum. We walk across the lot to his car in silence. He's left the Hummer at home. This one is a brand new black Jag. I've never seen this car before.

He opens the car door for me, but he doesn't look at me or say a word.

"Thanks," I say. No response. He must be fuming.

Jeremy climbs in. The car starts without a sound. Only the crunch of the tires on the snow-packed gravel parking pad interrupts the silence. Even I, miraculously, am silent.

"You're lucky you have your mom and grandma." His voice is lower than usual and barely above a whisper.

"I guess. I'm really sorry they gave you the third degree."

"It's because they love you." He pauses, and clears his throat. "But Julia, I've gotta' know. What did you say to your mom about me?"

"I just said we were taking a break. But, I never told Mom about the details. I would never—" I begin.

"Julia you've got to stop talking about what happens between us. That's private. It's only between you and me. I meant it when I said we belong together. What we have is special, and I don't want the whole world knowing everything."

"I don't tell anyone intimate details," I say, flushing at the words. "But I always tell my mom stuff. She's pretty intense about not keeping secrets. It's one of her big rules. Especially after I had that trouble after Dad died."

"Julia, you have me now. You don't need to go telling anyone else anything. I am here for you. If you have problems, you can talk to me. No one else. Promise?"

"What about Annika?"

"No one. Julia, you have to trust me, or this is not going to work. I love you. I am willing to keep our personal life private." Every time he says loves me I get this rush.

"I love you, too."

"Good. Now let's get something to drink. My dad keeps the bar fridge loaded."

"Something to drink? Won't he notice that you've taken some?"

"He doesn't care what I do. He always says: 'If you're going to run with the dogs, you better rise with the roosters.'"

"What does that even mean?"

"That I can party all I want, but I'm not allowed to miss any school. Most importantly, I can't embarrass him."

"Oh. He doesn't care what you do?" My dad was so involved in my life, I can't imagine if he had been like Jeremy's dad.

"He's only in town a few days a month. He has no clue."

"What about your mom? I know she spends a lot of time in California, but still."

His face clouds over.

"Change of subjects. What did you think about the last basketball game? I totally dominated," Jeremy says.

"Yes you d—"

My words dry up as he places his hand on my knee, sending a jolt of electricity up and down my leg. I look down, half expecting to see tiny white lightning bolts shooting out his fingertips.

"Uhm, okay," I mumble. All moisture in my mouth evaporates as my sandpaper tongue scratches the roof of my Sahara desert-dry mouth. I've just been zapped by 1,000 volts of Jeremy.

As we drive down the winding streets, I am acutely aware that Jeremy has not removed his hand from my leg. This is good and bad. Good because it feels incredible. Bad because I can't concentrate on what he's saying. He's talking about basketball and playoffs. I think. I can't be sure because all I can think of is his hand. It started on my knee but slipped up my leg to rest on my thigh after the first turn, and there his hand, his very hot hand, has remained. This would be fine, except that I can't get my mind to stop imagining what would happen if that very hot hand slipped further north. *Would I stop him? Would I want to stop him? Would Jeremy think I was a skank? But that's what he wants, so he can't think I am a skank? Right?*

My head is reeling and now my pits have begun to sweat. Seriously, I now have drippy pits. *If just thinking about sex causes my body to go into overdrive, what's next? Will a massive boil suddenly erupt from the middle of my forehead if he kisses me again?*

Jeremy's voice breaks through the insane skank-babble that is cluttering my brain.

"Julia...hello Julia???"

"Oh sorry, I just..." I am completely flustered.

We turn into Jeremy's long driveway. Lights twinkle from the windows of his enormous Tyndall stone house. Nothing seems welcoming about the large black double door entrance-way. Jeremy's two older brothers are away at university in the States, so it's just him, his parents, and their live-in housekeeper, Angelina, in the six bedroom, six bathroom monstrosity. There are more bedrooms and bathrooms than people—a complete pointless wasted space. The exact opposite of my ideal home plan. To top off their over-built design, they even have two kitchens, and Angelina rarely cooks for more than herself and Jeremy. His mom spends most of her time at their condo in Los Angeles, and his dad is rarely home for dinner, even when he is in town. Oh, yeah, and their mock castle has a turret. I made a joke once about his princess tower. Jeremy didn't find it funny. I decided to keep my moat comment to myself.

"Do you want beer or vodka?" Jeremy asks.

"Neither."

"One drink isn't going to kill you."

"I guess." He has no idea I took a Xanax. What am I going to do? Dr. Shapiro drilled it into me—never mix booze and anxiety pills. Ever.

"Hey, didn't I say you have to trust me?"

"Yeah."

"Then trust me. I'll make you a drink and you won't taste anything."

"I don't know…"

"I'll be right back." He hops out and runs to the side door.

My hand instinctively finds Dad's button. I close my eyes and take a deep breath, releasing the tension in my shoulders. My meds should kick in any minute. My eyes blink open.

Oh, crap.

CHAPTER 17

"Best night. Ever."

My phone pings. *Annika?* I yank it out of my pocket and stare at the display. It's not her. Who is LEDZEP? I read the text.

LEDZEP: Hey teach! Have u made a decision?

JULES: Who is this?

LEDZEP: Tyler

Teach. Right.

JULES: Hey

LEDZEP: Sorry 2 bug u. Will u tutor me?

Will I tutor him? Good question.

JULES: Haven't decided

LEDZEP: What if I beg? Lol. I'm desperate

JULES: Lemme think

LEDZEP: K. I heard you're going to the creek. Is Annika coming?

JULES: I am. Not Annika

LEDZEP: 2 bad

JULES: Yeah. R u going?

I glance up. What is taking Jeremy so long? Maybe Angelina caught him sneaking his dad's alcohol. *What if she calls my mom?*

LEDZEP: Maybe later

The front door light goes out, snuffing the light in the car. Jeremy's jogging this way, a cooler bag slung over his shoulder.

JULES: Gotta go.

LEDZEP: Bye

He stuffs the bag into the trunk and jumps in the car.

"Ready to go party?" he asks, pulling onto the street.

"Sure," I say, staring out the window, watching the houses fly by.

"Trust me, you're going to have fun."

We park down the street from the bush party, behind Harley's SUV. Black shadows trudge across the snow-covered soccer field and disappear into the trees that line the winding creek. The Creek runs behind the soccer field and banks most of our neighbourhood. It's one of Prairie Trails' favourite party spots. Annika and I checked it out back in ninth grade—just to see what all the hype was about. We didn't go to a party, instead we went to The Creek during the day, when there was zero chance of running into older kids, and the only trace of the party crowd were beer cans and roach clips.

"Thanks for coming," Jeremy says.

"It's going to be fun," I say, trying to sound like I mean it. At least I'm not freaking out anymore. The Xanax' mellowing effect is in full gear. Now I just need to avoid drinking without Jeremy knowing. Should be a cinch. Hah.

He grabs my hand and slings the cooler bag over his shoulder. We follow the trail of footprints. As we get closer to the edge of the field, I can hear voices. And music.

"Follow me," Jeremy says, leading the way through a narrow opening in the bush, down a steep monkey trail. He holds the branches back, so they don't slap me in the face. Totally something my dad would do.

"Thanks," I say.

Peering through the bush, I can see flashes of orange. The acrid smell of smoke immediately makes my nose itch.

"We're here!" Jeremy shouts. "Let the party begin!"

About fifteen or twenty kids are standing around a crackling bonfire. It's stacked high with driftwood logs, an old picnic table, and discarded Christmas trees. Flames leap high.

"Third! Third! Third!" They chant.

This is going to be insane.

"Woohoo!" Jeremy shouts.

"Hey, Julia!" Madison calls. "I never expected to see you here."

"Yeah, me neither."

Jeremy wraps his arm around my waist, tucking his hand into my back pocket. A tingle fires across my butt, heading directly to my nether regions. Whoa.

"I never doubted it," he whispers in my ear. His voice is husky, sexy, and his fingers, the ones that are hanging out in my back pocket, are now caressing my ass.

"Jeremy," I whisper. "People are watching."

"Never mind them," he says, yanking me to his chest. He kisses me. It's intense. He jerks away and howls. Shadows dance across his face, making his features look hard, more defined. I have never seen him like this. He's like himself times a billion.

He flings open his cooler and grabs a beer.

"Who's going to count?" he asks.

"Me," says Harley.

Jeremy holds the can on its side and then grabs a pen from the cooler and jabs it into the can, near the bottom.

"Let me know when to start," he says. His legs are shoulder-width apart and he has one hand on the tab as he holds the hole close to this mouth.

"3, 2, 1, go!" Harley shouts.

"Chug, chug, chug," the crowd chants.

What the...? Is this for real?

"Eight seconds!" Harley announces as Jeremy crushes the now empty can in his fist.

"Impressed?" he asks me. Is he serious?

"Sure." I reply.

"No one can chug like The Third. He's a legend," Madison says, smiling. "Have you ever tried?"

"Uh, no," I say. *Please no one ask me to chug a beer.*

"No beer for Julia. She's too much of a lady," Jeremy says. The smile on Madison's face quivers for a second before stretching even wider.

"I am going to make Julia my specialty." He crouches over his cooler, blocking me from seeing what he's doing.

"Oooh, you're in for a real treat," says Madison. Hannah and Chloe join us. Madison turns to them. "The Third's making Julia his world famous Thurston Temptation."

"Yup, because once you have one, you'll be tempted to have another." Jeremy says, handing me a large red plastic cup.

I smell it.

They all laugh.

"It's not going to bite you," Madison says.

"If you only have one," Chloe adds. I notice she's the only one not laughing.

"What's in it?" I ask, stalling.

"A good chef never shares his recipes and a good bartender never shares his secret ingredients," says Jeremy. "Trust me, Julia. You're going to love it."

Everyone is staring at me, like I'm a lab rat stuck in a cage.

I look from face to face. They all look thrilled except for Hannah and Chloe. Hannah rolls her eyes, looking bored, and scrolls through her texts. Chloe's eyebrows knit. She looks worried.

"You know, you don't have to drink," she says.

"Aw, lighten up Chloe. Julia is a big girl," Madison says.

If it were summer I could throw my drink in the fire and run screaming through the bush, pretending I'd been bitten by a bee. But every last stupid insect is frozen under four feet of snow. I have zero options.

"Okay," I say, my breath rushes out. I'll take one tiny sip, just enough to get them off my back. I lift the cup to my lips and the first thing I taste is orange juice and something effervescent, maybe ginger ale. I don't taste any alcohol.

"Woohoo!" Madison says. "Finally. Initiation is over. You're one of us."

I laugh. That was easy.

"It tastes really good," I say to Jeremy, taking another sip, searching for the bitter taste of booze. I swallow another mouthful. It still only tastes crisp and refreshing. What could a few sips hurt? I'll just have to be careful how much I have. "Sorry I doubted you."

"It's okay, Beautiful," he leans down and kisses me gently on my lips. "You'll soon learn."

"Hey! Lovebirds," Harley calls. "We're playing 31."

"You're going to love this game," Jeremy says. "Take a couple more gulps, so I can top you up."

"Uhm, okay." I pause for a moment. What are my options? If he would just stop staring at me, I could just chuck some out.

"What's wrong?"

"Nothing." I'll dump some later. I take a few large swigs. As the cool liquid slides down my throat, a warm fuzziness slips into my arms and legs. They feel heavier.

I hand him my half empty cup and watch the campfire. The flames leap high, nearly touching the black gnarled oak branches that canopy the creek bed. Shadows bend and dance across the snow, reminding me of the monsters from that kids' book, *Where the Wild Things Are*. I giggle.

"Let the wild rumpus start!" I say, giggling harder.

"What?" Jeremy asks as he passes me my drink. I take a sip. It tastes even better—tangier.

"Didn't your parents ever read you *Where the Wild Things Are* when you were a kid?"

"Ah, no. My parents didn't read me much of anything," he scoffs, and grows quiet. "But my grandpa did. Before he died."

"Oh, I'm sorry."

"Don't worry about it. It was a long time ago," he says, leaning against the enormous tree trunk that is twice as wide as he is. "He was pretty cool, though. My grandpa loved baseball. He used to take me to see the Goldeyes play and always bought the cheap seats. He said it made us remember our roots. He'd make this big show of having to use his binoculars to watch the plays and he'd always buy me whatever treats I wanted. Popcorn, candyfloss, hotdogs—whatever. Then we'd take the bus home, because he never learned to drive. The bus ride was my favourite part because he would tell me all the stories of when he was a kid and when his family emigrated from England. They were dirt poor, you know."

"Really?" I'm stunned. I just assumed his family had always been rich.

"Yup. My grandpa built our company from scratch and then my dad took over and brought in partners and expanded it nationwide."

"He must have been proud of your dad."

"Yeah, I guess," he stares into his cup. "Nobody's ever asked about my family before. None of my other girlfriends bothered to ask." There's a softness to his words that I've never heard before.

"Oh."

"Hey, aren't you guys coming?" Harley calls. He beckons us over as he takes a puff of something. A cigarette or joint?

I take a large gulp of Jeremy's secret concoction so my drink doesn't spill over the edge as we walk. I feel funny, lighter and sort of wobbly.

"Let's go," Jeremy says, leading me by the hand. I trip on my first step and careen forward, spilling most of my drink. Jeremy keeps me from crashing into a willow tree.

"Are you okay?" he asks. Chloe runs over. I can hear Hannah's cackle. Of course, she'd find my near wipe out hilarious.

"How much have you had to drink?" Chloe asks.

"Not a lot," I say, which is true. It must be the Xanax. Crap. "And I spilled most of this cup. Sorry Jeremy."

"No worries, I'll just add a bit more," he says.

"Are you sure that's a good idea? I mean, she nearly—" Chloe begins, but Jeremy cuts her off.

"Mind you own business, Chloe. I'll take care of Julia." His voice bites at her.

"Okay," she says, her eyes wide. She backs away with her palms facing him. "No need to go all caveman."

Chloe gives me a quick smile and returns to the fire. I guess she's not playing the game with everyone else. My vision blurs for a moment and then clears.

Jeremy quickly mixes another drink.

"I'll carry this one, just in case you have another klutz moment."

"Sure," I say and giggle. "Did I just slur my s's? Shure, shure, shure." I say, testing it out. "Yup, they're slurly, slrry." I pause and concentrate. "They are slu-rry."

Jeremy laughs.

"You are a lightweight aren't you?"

"I've only ever had a few sips of wine with my parents at Christmas and Easter."

"I'll show you the ropes. Just remember, fun drunk is cool. Falling down drunk is cheap. So, no more tripping."

"Sure," I say, as the giggles surge through me.

He takes my hand and walks me carefully over the snow and around some bushes to the gang of kids who have already started playing. I'm feeling lightheaded, but in a good floating-on-air sort of way.

"Hey, rookie," says Harley. "Come sit by me. I'll show you how it's done." He passes what I can now see and smell is a joint to Hannah.

"Back off, buddy. I'll be the only one showing Julia how it's done." Jeremy says, slapping my butt.

"Ow, Jeremy, don't!"

"Ow, Jeremy, don't!" Harley mimics. Everyone laughs.

"Hey, I'm just teasing," he says. He nibbles my ear and whispers, "I love you, Beautiful." My anger thaws. I sit down on a frozen tree stump next to Madison. Her white jacket glows in the firelight.

"Okay, my peeps," I say, conscious that my words are getting muddled. "Wazz' up?"

"Woohoo! I had no idea you could be this much fun," says Madison, wrapping her arm around my shoulder. Her perfume tickles my nose.

"Yes, that's me—party central."

"Whatever," snarks Hannah. The fire throws shadows across her face, but I can still see her eyes roll.

"Oh Hannah, you are such a cow," I say.

Harley spits his beer over the rotting picnic table, laughing and coughing.

"Ewww, Harley," says Hannah, swaying as she stands up. "Grow up." She thrusts the reefer back at Harley and stomps off to join Chloe and a few others at the campfire.

Madison yanks Harley's hat off his head and mops up his drink.

"Third, you know how to pick 'em," Harley says. "Cheers, Julia. Welcome to The Creek!"

"Cheers," I say, and clink my plastic cup to Madison's beer bottle. "This is soooo musch, must, musched—whatever. It's tons of fun. And Harley, you're hot! Not Jeremy hot, but still."

"Julia that's—" Jeremy begins.

"No, don't stop her," Madison interrupts him. "You go girl! You're hilarious."

"K. Madiss, Madson. I'm gonna' call you Mads," I say. "Mads, you're beautiful. I'm so glad you stopped being a be-atch."

"Gee. Thanks," she says.

"Yup. I told Annika you shed your bitch-like outer skin—like a snake—but she doesn't believe me."

"Oh. Really."

"Yup, yup, yup. She says you're a she-devil."

Harley spits his drink out again and hoots.

"You do have some fire in you, don't you?" Jeremy whispers in my ear. "I'd like to see more of that."

"Okay, sexy boy."

Harley takes a long drag of his joint and passes it to me. I shake my head as he blows it out in smoke rings above my head.

"The girl is on a roll!" Harley slams his beer can into Jeremy's. Beer sloshes onto the trampled, muddy snow.

I pull my phone out of my pocket. I gotta get Annika down here. She'll never believe how fun it is. My fingers feel fat as I type.

JULES: U gotta come to the creek. Soooo fun

I sway on my stump, to the beat of the music. I had it so wrong. The Creek is awesome. My phone pings.

TKD4EVR: I'll pass

JULES: Pls come. liiss gr8

TKD4EVR: R u ok?

JULES: Yesss Jeremy made me his secrt drnk

TKD4EVR: What? U shouldn't be drinking.

Whatever. I turn my phone to mute.

This is going to be the best night. Ever.

CHAPTER 18

"Everyone should totally looooosen up!"

"How much have you had to drink?" Annika whispers in my ear.

"Hey!!!" I say, swaying on my stump stool. "You're here! Bestiesssss!" I hold out my hand so we can do our fourth grade secret handshake. Annika bats my hand away.

"Fraidy, you're wasted," she says, her voice low.

"No, no," I whisper to her. "I spilt most of it. On porpoise. I mean purpose. But don't tell Jeremy. And anyway, I'm just having fun. You should try it sometime. You need to loosen up. Everyone should totally looooosen up! WOOHOO!"

"Oh my God, Fraidy. You need to sober up before you go home."

"No thanks," I say. I stand and drape my arm around her neck. "You know who's here? Fry Face, Tyler. You two should hook up."

"Julia,'"

"Hey, TYYYYYLERRR!" I call. "Someone's got a crush on you!"

Annika shrugs herself out from under me, and I stumble into a tree.

"Hey!" I say. "That hurt."

"Stop it, Julia. You're being an idiot."

"No I'm not. You like him." I crank my head around her and shout, "Tyler, she like-likes you!"

"Shut. Up."

"Hey, what are you doing here?" Jeremy asks, pulling me to his side.

Annika backs away, shaking her head. "I have no idea," she says.

"She needs to loosen up," I say.

"Your mom is going to kill you," she says.

"Pffft. My mom won't even notice. She's too into her own crap." Slinging my arm around her shoulder, I sway into her. "PARTAY!"

She staggers for a moment, but regains her balance.

"Julia, we need to go," Annika says.

"No way," I say.

"Mind your own business, Annika," Jeremy says. He wrenches me from Annika and I wrap my arms around his waist, feeling woozy. "I'll take her home."

"Julia is my business."

"She can take care of herself," Jeremy snaps.

"That's obviously not true. Look at her. She can't even stand up." Her index finger jabs upwards at Jeremy.

"Jeremy's got me, Annika. He loves me, like for real."

"If he loved you he wouldn't give you booze."

"Just back off. She doesn't need you. I'll take care of her," Jeremy says, his arms tighten around me, protecting me from the world and Annika.

"Yup, yup yup. I'm all good," I say.

Annika glares at me. "So that's it? You don't need me anymore, so I can go?"

"You don't have to leave," I say, pointing over to the fire pit. "Why don't you hook up with Tyler?"

"Holy Crap. I'm outta' here," Annika says, brushing past Jeremy and me. Chloe runs to her, but she only shakes her head and keeps walking. I watch her as she climbs up the path to the soccer pitch. She pauses for a moment at the top of the ridge before disappearing into the night.

"Why can't she just have fun with me?"

"She's a total buzz kill," Jeremy says, leading me to his cooler. "Are you ready for a second?"

Why not?

CHAPTER 19

Party Girl. Out.

Voices. I can hear voices. Must be dreaming. They get louder and more insistent. A cool hand taps me on my cheek. I try to move my head. Pain shoots up the back up my neck, branching out over my skull.

"Ow!" My eyes fly open. Blurry faces stare back at me. I'm on the ground. "What—what happened?"

"Julia, are you okay?" someone asks. I turn to find the voice and wince as another lightning bolt of pain shoots across my head. My teeth start to chatter. I'm freezing. My vision clouds. Blinking my eyes, I slowly sit up.

"Everything's spinning," I mumble. "And my head kills." I cradle my head in my hands, holding it still.

Jeremy squats down next to me.

"You totally passed out," he says, sounding horrified. "You hit your head when you fell."

"Yeah," agrees Madison. "One minute you were sitting there, laughing and having a great time and then bam you went down. Hard."

"Maybe we should take her to the hospital," Chloe suggests.

"Over-react much?" replies Jeremy.

"What time is it?" I ask him.

"11:00."

"What? How long was I out?"

"Only a few seconds."

"But, we've been here almost two hours. The last thing I remember was…" *What?* I can't remember anything. "I feel like I'm going to be sick." A nauseous wave cramps low in my belly. My arms are shaking.

"Crap," Jeremy says. Tears sting my eyes as he lifts me under my arms. He wraps his arm around my waist and helps me walk further down a path that snakes deep into the bush.

"I'm sorry, Jeremy. I'm ruining your whole night." Branches slash across my face, stinging my cheeks.

"Forget about it," he says, his words clipped. He props me up against a tree. I close my eyes and take a shallow breath, trying to stop the world from spinning.

"Thanks," I say, my voice is small. Away from the smoke of the fire, I can breathe easier. My stomach stops cramping. "I think I just needed some air."

"You scared me." His fists clench, his nose is almost touching mine. His beer breath makes my stomach roll. He kisses me, but his lips taste like bitter Muddy Waters 49, his beer of choice. I push away from him. The bush whirls as I turn my head. All I can think about is not puking on his shoes.

"Maybe we should walk a bit. It might help," he suggests.

"Okay." I step a few paces. Everything around me, including Jeremy, spins. I moan. "My head."

"What did I tell you about being a cheap drunk? Not okay, Julia."

"You made me the drinks." I don't dare tell him about the anxiety pill. He'll freak.

"Just forget it. It was your first time. You'll get better at it, but right now we have to get you sobered up. Your grandma is never going to let me see you again if she sees you like this."

"You really don't need to be scared of her." I'm still embarrassed by how they treated him.

"Oh, yes I do."

Jeremy leads me by the hand through the woods. I stumble after him, off balance. My feet slide into the deeper snow that lines the trampled path until we finally emerge from the trees. We're at the furthest end of the field where the bleachers run along the edge of the snow-covered soccer pitch. I feel drained. Jeremy sits me down on the bottom plank of the wooden stand.

"Are you okay?" he asks.

I nod my head. "Just cold." I clench my jaw to stop my teeth from chattering. He shrugs off his jacket and drapes it around me.

"Wait here. I'll go get my car."

I can only nod, because I'm too frozen to talk. Jeremy's car is about five hundred meters down the street. My whole body is shaking now. At least the constant pounding in my head has eased to clenching pain every ten seconds or so.

Jeremy sprints to his car. I wrap my arms around myself, rocking back and forth to try and keep warm. I look to where we first went through the bush to The Creek. *Is everyone talking about me?*

As I stare at the trees, a black figure emerges from the riverbank and waves at me. I wave back, squinting hard. I can't make out who it is. A smaller shape joins the first one. They both wave at me.

Jeremy honks and I jump, nearly tumbling off the bench.

"Who's that?" he calls, nodding his head at the waving shadows. He treads across the snow and picks me up. My arms encircle his neck as I command my stomach to stay put.

"I have no idea," I say. I can no longer stop my teeth from chattering. My vision grows blurry as I stare at the two figures.

"Huh," he says, there's an edge to his voice, like he doesn't believe me.

"Maybe it's Harley."

"No, it's not Harley," Jeremy says, his voice grim.

He sits me in his car and slams the door. I watch him face the shadowed people, staring, not moving. My shakes cease as the heat from the seats thaw me out.

Finally, Jeremy gets in the car.

"Who was it?"

"I don't know," he says. He presses down hard on the gas, we fishtail around the first corner, but he doesn't slow down. We accelerate faster, houses sail by, blurring in the dark. Looking out the window turns my stomach, so I close my eyes and take shallow breaths. I take a quick peek out the front window. We blow through a stop sign.

"Jeremy!"

No response.

We soar through another intersection. He didn't even look to see if anyone else was coming.

"Jeremy! Slow down! You're scaring me!"

He taps on the brake. We slow.

"I couldn't handle it if you cheated on me," he says, his voice strained.

"What are you talking about?"

He brakes harder and veers onto the shoulder.

"Julia," he says. His knuckles whiten as he grips the steering wheel. He stares out the front windshield. "You know I love you, right?"

"Yes and I love you."

"Which means you're mine," he says.

"Uhm, That's sort of archaic, Jeremy. You sound like a Neanderthal."

He releases his seat belt and leans across the car. "I wanted to do this all night." He caresses my face, his fingers feather light as they trace my cheekbone down to my lower lip. Chills spread out from the invisible tracks his fingers made, down my neck. "So beautiful," he murmurs.

Then he kisses me.

Those chills change to heat waves that engulf me entirely. His hand moves to my belly and under my shirt, caressing me as it rises to my chest. I gasp. But I don't make him stop.

He pulls away and helps me out of my buckle.

"Come," he says, and climbs into the back seat. My heart is beating wildly. I follow.

"Lay back," he instructs.

I look up at him, as he shrugs off his jacket. His grey-blue eyes are almost black, full of desire, his face flushed.

"Oh my God," I say, unable to stop my words, "You are so hot."

"And you are too sexy," he whispers, kissing along my jawline. He slips his hand under my shirt and kisses me again. He groans. I melt into him and a moan escapes. He moves his hand to my waist, unbuttoning my jeans. He works the zipper down, sliding his hand into my panties.

My eyes flash open. My vision resumes spinning. I thrust myself up and bash my forehead into his chin.

"Crap!" he shouts, holding his face.

"I'm going to be sick!"

"What?" Jeremy backs away like I've got rabies. "Not in my mom's car!"

I cup my hand over my mouth and struggle with the door handle. Jeremy reaches over me, releases the lock, and pushes the door open wide.

I tumble out and land hard on the road. My hands scrape on the icy pavement. Crawling on my hands and knees I make it to the back of the car before I vomit. Over and over. My throat burns. It feels like I am spewing up chards of glass.

Jeremy lays his hand on my back and I jump, retching. Finally, it stops and I lean back against the car's tire. My head is clear. Jeremy's face is distorted, his desire gone. I yank up my pants zipper.

"I'm sorry, Jeremy," I say, trying not to cry. My stomach cramps. *Oh, God, no more.* I clench my teeth, willing myself not to throw up.

What is wrong with me? Maybe I do have sex issues. He has every right to be angry. I am a sex loser.

"Let's go," he says, pulling me up under my arms. He leads me around the front of the car and buckles me in. The clock on the dash reads 11:50. He passes me his tin of mints, but doesn't say a word. I pop in three. I am too numb to speak.

As we drive home the silence builds, forming a wall between us. In moments we're in my parking lot.

"I'm so sorry, Jeremy."

He doesn't respond.

"Jeremy—"

"I'm not going to wait forever Julia," he says.

"But, Jeremy, I just drank too much. I—"

"You better go in," he cuts me off.

"Okay," I say, waiting for a kiss goodnight. He doesn't make a move. And why would he want to kiss me? "I'll see you tomorrow."

Still no response. I open the door and climb out.

"I love you," I say, as a light flashes on behind me. The back door swings open as Jeremy speeds down the back lane.

"His Royal Nibs couldn't walk you to the door?" Grandma's voice rings out across the dark cold night.

"He had to get home too," I lie as I brush by her, stomping inside.

Grandma grabs my arm, forcing me to face her. My head spins. I concentrate hard on staying upright. It would totally blow my cover if I fell in a heap at her feet.

She stares hard at me, her grandma senses must be tingling.

"What?" I ask. I can't bear her scrutiny.

"Just looking," she replies, smoothing her pale green toque. Since she cut her hair, she loses all her heat through her head and she gets too chilly at night to sleep.

"For what?" I'm careful to speak clearly.

"I'll know when I see it."

"O-kay."

"There is something," she says, taking a step back and running her gaze over me from head to toe. Her eyes narrow, her brows don't flinch. "I'll be watching you, my dear. Closely."

I squeeze by her in the narrow hallway. "I'm really tired."

She follows me as I carefully walk a straight line down the hall. I don't feel nearly as wobbly as I did at the party, but I can't mess up.

"Nice jacket," Grandma says.

"Thanks. Jeremy gave it to me."

"Looks expensive." She doesn't sound impressed. "Better soak those pants. Vomit stains."

Crap. Busted.

CHAPTER 20

What happened?

My phone buzzes on the bookshelf that is doubling as my nightstand. Ugh, my head. A tiny hammer is pounding at my temple, sending spasms of pain across my skull. I blink to clear the sleep from my eyes. My clock shines 1:42 AM. I stare at my phone and the text that shines back at me.

> LEDZEP: Hey teach! Thx again.

Tyler?

I sit up and stare at his text. What is he talking about? I scroll back to the start of our conversation.

> JULES: Hey. I wl tutr u
>
> LEDZEP: Awesome! THX!!! What should I pay u?
>
> JULES: $15 hour ☺
>
> LEDZEP: Cool. Since we don't have school can we start tomorrow?
>
> JULES: Sree
>
> LEDZEP: Huh?

JULES: Sure. Come 3 my hsoe

LEDZEP: What?

JULES: Srryy. Fingrs wont tupe. Come 2 my housse after lunch

Holy Crap. When did I do this??? I place my hand on my chest; my heart feels like it's going to leap out of my body. My mind races back through last night. Annika storming out, Tyler texting me at Jeremy's, driving to The Creek, two drinks and then... *what?* I close my eyes, thinking hard. *Annika!* I totally snubbed her. I rub my hand across the back of my head, finding a large goose egg.

"Youch." Okay, that I remember, and then we left.

Oh my God! The car! I barfed. *What is wrong with me?* I look at my phone. When did I text Tyler?

I look at the time of my texts. 10:41 PM. I was still at The Creek. How come I can't remember sending them? Was I completely wasted? I cringe. Why did I take that first sip?

As I lie back down, a draft from the window makes me shiver. I pull my comforter up to my chin and curl into the fetal position. Closing my eyes, I hear only the oak tree outside my window. It taps its long gnarled branch against the pane in a subtle pattern. Whenever there's even the tiniest gust of wind the tree starts rapping. I've never told anyone, because I'm sure they'd think I was crazy, but I like to imagine that the tapping is Dad's way of telling me he's watching over me. I stare into the dark night, the moon hidden behind clouds.

Hot tears slide down my cheek. I let them.

Dad. I miss you.

CHAPTER 21

"No point living in the past, when the present is giving you the middle finger."

I ease my broken plastic door open. Mom must have rehung it when I was out last night.

"Morning," I mumble to Grandma. I step cautiously so I don't jar my head.

"Morning, sweetie. How's my girl?"

"Fine."

"You don't look fine. You look wiped."

"I had a hard time sleeping." Truthfully, I was up most of the night thinking about Jeremy. When I finally fell asleep I had this nightmare where Tyler and I were in the library studying and Jeremy walked in screaming that I never had any time for him. He then fled into the hallway and I ran after him. I chased him down the school halls and even though I was sprinting and he was walking, I could never catch up.

Must be an omen. I have to text Tyler and cancel the tutoring session.

I rub my eyes and focus on Grandma. She's got yet another scarf—this one is grey with tiny rhinestones. Right before her first treatment she decided to beat the chemo hair loss and got her hair "styled to beat cancer," which to the rest us means she has a cute pixie cut. She then ran around town picking up a couple dozen scarves. She said by the time she is completely bald, she'll be a pro head wrapper. She's flipping pancakes on the electric fry pan. One of the best things about having Grandma here this past week is her amazing cooking. She gave me her secret cookie recipes, which once I "Juliafy," I'm going to serve to our book clubs. What is surprising is that it's before 9 AM and she's out of her pyjamas, makeup-ed, and head-scarfed.

"Why are you already dressed?"

"Chemo day. I'm meeting with the oncologist again right before my treatment. I gotta' look my best so he remembers what he's working to save," she says, fanning herself with the metal flipper while batting her long black eyelashes.

How had I forgotten something so important? Her humour unsettles me. She's been acting like this is all no big deal.

"Oh, okay." The pounding in my head begins to beat in time with my heart. Just perfect.

Grandma pulls me in for a hug.

"You don't need to worry. I'm going to be right as rain, soon enough."

"I'm sure you will be." A lump forms in my throat. My eyes burn. She shouldn't be comforting me—she's the one with cancer. I should be taking care of her. I didn't even remember about today's appointment.

"Now that's what I want to hear. Have to be surrounded by good energy right now."

"Oh, not you too. Has Mom got you reading her new age hippie books?"

"Don't knock it, 'til you've tried it."

She slides a book across the dining room table to me.

"Healing Yourself—From the Inside Out," I say as I spin it right side up. "Yup, that sounds like something Mom would read."

"Actually, there's a chapter in there about 'healing the grieving soul' that you might find interesting."

"No thanks. I'm taking care of my grieving soul my own way."

Grandma places her hand on mine and gives it a squeeze. "I still want you to look through it. I've marked the chapter that I'd like you to read." She points to the bright orange sticky note that pokes out the top of the book.

Grandma returns to the griddle and flips three massive blueberry pancakes onto a plate and sets it down in front of me. Normally, I would dive right into the stack, but the sweet fruit smell churns my stomach.

"Uhhh, I'm not very hungry."

"Now why might that be?" She asks, in a tone that tells me she already knows the answer. She removes my plate, placing another one upside down on top to keep the pancakes warm.

I shrug. "I, uh—" What am I supposed say?

"No use lying, my dear. I know what a hangover looks like. And smells like. Thought you may need these," she says, shaking a bottle of Tylenol. She places it and a tall glass of water on the counter.

"I," I stall. She's onto me, and my head feels like it's going to shatter into a zillion pieces. I don't need the water for the pill, but my mouth tastes like I sucked on sawdust all night. I down half the glass in one swig.

"Hmmm, I hope you weren't drinking like that last night," she says.

I sputter. Water comes precariously close to spurting out my nose. "Grandma!"

"Sweetie, your Mom may be blind to what is going on right before her eyes, but I have 20/20 vision when it comes to you."

I pull over the tall wooden bar stool from the corner of the kitchen and sit down. What's the point of arguing? My Grandma is like the frickin' KGB.

"I feel like garbage. I am never, ever drinking again." I hold my throbbing head in my hands, willing the thumping to stop.

"I should hope not. I did some Googling last night. You are walking a very dangerous line."

"I dunno what you mean."

"I think you do. Alcohol and depression medication of any sort can be a disastrous combination. And that anxiety medication isn't any better with booze. I will not have my granddaughter ending up in the hospital because of some very stupid choices."

"Grandma, I won't—"

"Don't. Start. Remember, I know what drunk looks like and I know what a liar sounds like. I am watching."

"Morning ladies," Mom says, as her arms wrap around me from behind. She kisses me on the top of my head.

"Good Morning," Grandma says. "Coffee's just about ready."

"Pancakes, coffee, and a morning welcoming committee— I could get used to this."

As mom gives her a hug, Grandma stares at me over Mom's shoulder, not saying anything about my drinking admission. I mouth "thanks" to her and she purses her lips in response. Her eyebrows narrow. I know she won't tell Mom, but that look means she hasn't let me off the hook.

Grandma draws away, but Mom won't let go and holds tight. She begins to cry and her back rises and falls with her sobs. Grandma strokes her hair and makes the exact same shushing sound that Mom does to me when I can't stop crying. My throat tightens. Pressure builds and spreads up the back of my neck, across my skull, adding an unwelcome intensity to my already throbbing head. I push away from the counter and race to the den. I can't handle Mom crying. Sitting on the pullout bed, I stare out the window at my oak tree.

"Dad, are you there?" I whisper. The tree sways its mighty branches, seemingly in response, and they hit the windowpane. Tap pause tap pause tap slide. Too bad I don't speak tree Morse code. *Fantastic. Now I'm talking to trees.* Massaging my skull, I close my eyes and take a deep, calming breath.

I quickly change into my favourite hole-ridden jeans and pull on a bright yellow hoodie Grandma brought me from Arizona. It's huge but cozy. I send Jeremy a quick text before stuffing my phone into the front pocket. Forcing my curls into a loose French twist, I search my backpack and find my bottle of anti-depressants. I dump one tiny blue pill into my hand, tilt my head back and pop it in. No water needed—I'm a pro pill popper now.

My phone buzzes in my pocket. *Please be Jeremy. Or Annika.* I slide it out of my hoodie, willing for a text from either one of them. What would I say to Jeremy? Sorry I was too drunk to have sex? Sorry that my barfing ruined the mood?

And what would I say to Annika? Sorry I dumped you for Jeremy? I wasn't as blitzed as you thought I was.

Or was I? I can't even remember half the night. What else happened? Shivers run my spine. I wish I could get a do-over for last night. If only I didn't take that Xanax. I won't repeat that mistake.

I stare at my phone. Just a sales alert from Le Grotto. I have to apologize to Annika.

JULES: So sorry Annika. Will u forgive me?

Turning the ringer to loud, I slip it back into my pocket. *Please respond, Annika.*

I gently slide my wobbly door open. Mom and Grandma are chatting in the kitchen. Mom's stopped crying and is clutching her self-help book to her chest. I tiptoe across the apartment hoping to slip away before Mom can ask me about last night.

"Are you okay, Jules?" Mom says, giving me the third, fourth, and fifth degree stare. She says she learned how to sniff out a liar in her first year of teaching. I actually think it's genetic and she inherited it from Grandma—thankfully she's not as good at it.

"Yeah, I'm fine," I say, moving towards the staircase.

"I'd like to talk about last night."

"Uhm—okay, but not right now. I have to open the shop, so you can get Grandma to the oncologist."

"Later then—after we close."

"Good luck today, Grandma." I give her a quick hug and peck on the cheek, careful not to let Mom catch my eye.

I race down the stairs, faster than my legs are willing to move, slipping on the last few. Grabbing the handrail, I stop myself from crashing into the door at the bottom. My head resumes its rhythmic painful beat.

Unlocking the door to the bookstore, I take a deep breath of new book smell—dry, inky, warm. All inviting. The bookshop design is an eclectic fusion of everything Mom finds comforting and inspiring. Last spring, she painted each wall a different shade of orange, with quotes from Dickens to Margaret Laurence written across the walls. Pots of ivy and other climbing plants vine up the sides of bookshelves and cling to the two pillars that stand in each of the four corners of the store. The cash desk is my favourite feature. It sits right in the middle of the store. Dad built it using three old mahogany doors they found at a flea market. He stripped the robin's egg blue paint from the wood and then fashioned a stand out of old bookshelves, creating a u-shaped desk.

To be honest, I have a love/hate relationship with the shop. I love it, in theory. I adore books, the store itself, and Mom's passion is contagious. But I don't want to live here. I don't want this to be my entire life. Especially when Mom won't listen to any of my ideas about expansion and, though I would never say this to anyone, not even Annika, I feel trapped. I need to get a scholarship out of here or I'm scared the bookshop will become my future.

I trudge across the dark store. How different would my life be if Dad were still alive? Grandma would've arrived with her cancer news, but Mom wouldn't have fallen to pieces like she did just now, and we would've been comfortable and cozy in our old house, where we had an actual guest bedroom, not a cell-sized den. But most importantly, Dad would've taken charge. Through his university connections with the school of medicine, he would've made sure Grandma had the best doctors looking after her through every test and procedure. Not that any of that helped him. He was too far gone for any miraculous interventions when we got his diagnosis.

I kneel behind the counter and slide what looks like an ordinary row of old dusty leather books down the shelf that sits under the till. It's actually a faux book wall that hides our small safe. When Mom first opened the shop she crazy-glued seven old classics together. Dad teased her about how very Nancy Drew she was, but she was super proud of her secret hiding spot.

Dad. I wish Mom would talk about him.

I pull out the cash tray from the safe and sigh, muttering to the empty store, "No point living in the past, when the present is giving you the finger." I read that on a T-shirt I saw online. I totally wanted to buy it, but it would've crushed Mom.

Mom. I wish I could talk to her like I talk to Grandma.

CHAPTER 22

Flustered.

"We're back," Mom calls as she enters the store from our apartment entrance.

"Hey!" I call back from the top rung of our old wooden ladder. It sits on a track that's nailed to our bookshelves and slides along the longest side of our store. The ladder adds an old world feel and I love to sit on the very top with a good book and read my shift away. I often trace the initials that are carved into the top step and dream about who the ladder used to belong to. *Who was* J.M.R.*?*

Mom bought that ladder and track at an auction when she first opened the bookstore and it only took Dad a few hours to figure out how to install the rolling mechanism. I like to think the ladder was shipped to Canada, along with a vast library, from England over a hundred years ago. In my mind, J.M.R. was a wealthy young woman and it was part of her dowry. She must've been excited and nervous as she set sail to begin her married life in a strange land, intent on bringing some "culture" to the wilds of the new world.

I shove the last few books into their spots and scale down the steps. Mom passes me a cardboard cup.

"Thanks," I say, taking a sip. "Where's Grandma? How did it go?"

"Pretty good. She went straight upstairs to rest. She—" Mom pauses, as if considering if she should tell me more. I hold my breath, not wanting to hear bad news. "She's going to be just fine."

"That's good." I don't ask for more details, even though I know I should. "Do you want me to set up for tonight's book club?" I offer.

"Sure, honey. I put the cookies in the little fridge."

I can feel Mom watching me as I cross the store. At least she's not on me about last night. I hurry down the hallway, grateful for an excuse to avoid further scrutiny.

I love the book club room. It's tucked down a narrow hallway at the back of the store. You'd expect the corridor to open into a storage room, but instead it leads to a perfect size meeting room. It's big enough for at least twelve people but small enough to still feel homey. Mom and I argued over how to decorate it. She wanted it to be all clean lines, minimalist, IKEA-ware, but I really thought our customers would prefer a softer space, more of a "Cottage Chic with Comfortable Couches" than "Doctor's Office Waiting Room with Hard Plastic Chairs." When I sketched out my vision, Mom immediately fell in love with my plan.

I glide my fingers along the green wall, remembering when I told Annika the paint colour was called "mottled fern." She thought it looked more like an Irish Mist or Shamrock Swirl. Then she linked her arm with mine and we danced a jig while she hummed some Irish tune, purposely off key. We twirled each other around the room until we got too dizzy and crashed onto the sofa, breaking into laughter.

Annika. Will she ever forgive me after last night? I check my phone. No response. Can I blame her?

Sighing, I pull out the tin of cookies I baked yesterday from the mini fridge that's tucked into the far corner of the room. It was Annika's idea to drape it in a pink check tablecloth and place a lamp and a small old-fashioned brass clock on top to help disguise it. I arrange the treats on three plates and lay them in the middle of the table.

"Honey, someone's here for you," Mom calls down the hall. "I'm heading to the basement to sort books, so you'll have to listen for the door chime."

I peer towards the front of the store, but the hall light is burnt out so all I see is a dark figure ambling down the corridor. The figure waves at me. Then it speaks, which sends a chill down my spine. *How did I forget to text him?*

"Hey, Julia. Cool store."

"Tyler," I say as he steps into the light of the book club room. "You're here." I jump up from the couch.

He looks around and pretends to be surprised, staring at his hands and then patting his arms and legs.

"Oh my gosh, you're right," he says and laughs. "I am here." He gives me this huge crooked smile.

"Of course, sorry. I just—I'm setting up for one of our book clubs."

"Need some help?" he asks, picking up a plate. He spins it on his finger, faster and faster. "Did I ever tell you I used to bus tables at The Big T Steak Shack?" I suck in my breath. If he drops those cookies I'm screwed. I have zero time to bake another batch. He then stops the twirling plate just as quickly, without losing one. "Ta-da!"

"Bravo!" I cheer. "You totally deserve a cookie for that!"

He takes a bite and his eyes widen. "These are the best cookies I have ever tasted," he says.

"Thanks," I say, feeling flustered by his compliment. "About me tutoring you—" My head recommences pounding. *I need to get out of this.* "I'm not sure it's a good idea."

"Please Julia, I'm begging you. If I don't pull up my math grades, I'm toast." He looks as desperate as he sounds.

"I dunno." How am I going to tell Jeremy? Maybe he won't mind, because it's Tyler. Tyler clasps his hands in front of him. My resolve erodes.

"I'll be in your debt. Forever."

"I guess," I sigh. I am crazy. At least the extra money will be handy. I can't keep relying on Jeremy to pay for everything.

"You're the cat's pyjamas. The bee's knees. The rootinist, tootinist—"

"Very funny," I say interrupting his blast from the 1920's past. "Let's see how hilarious you find algebra."

And please let me figure out a way to tell Jeremy of my newest student.

CHAPTER 23

Julia Forever

"Jeremy," I call, darting down the middle of the staircase, pushing through a throng of tenth graders to the second floor. "Jeremy!"

He stops and turns. His face is blank for a moment, like he doesn't recognize me, then a smile takes over his face.

"Julia," he says, rushing to me.

"Why didn't you return my texts?"

"I was busy." He bends down and nuzzles my neck. "You smell great."

"I wanted to talk about the other night. I'm so sorry."

"Yeah, me too. I shouldn't have come down so hard on you," he says. He takes my hand and we weave our fingers together. "Come on. I want to show you something."

We walk past the science labs to the shops classes. No one is around.

"You want to show me how to build a birdhouse?" I ask.

"No, this," he says, rolling up his sleeve.

"Oh my God, Jeremy," I gasp. That's why he was too busy to text. "A tattoo. Did it hurt?"

"You are incredible, you know that? I get 'Julia Forever' tattooed on my arm and the only thing you're focused on is if it hurt."

"I'm sorry. I—"

"No, I love having someone that cares about me like that."

"Can I touch it?" I ask. I can't take my eyes off the black swirling writing.

"Sure. It doesn't hurt. It's just temporary. To see if I like it enough to go all the way with a permanent tattoo."

I trace the scrolling letters.

He strokes his fingers across my cheek, trailing down my neck. He cups the back of my head, pulling me to him. He kisses me along my jaw, slowly, finally reaching my lips. Desire builds in me, and my kissing becomes more urgent. His hand moves down my back to my butt, which he squeezes before lifting me off the floor. I wrap my legs around his waist as he presses me up against the wall, grinding his pelvis into mine. He moans deep in his throat.

"Jeremy," I gasp, my head spinning.

"I want you," he whispers. "So much."

"You two need to get a room!" Harley calls. "Whoot-whoot!" He thumps Jeremy on the back as he passes by and enters the woods shop.

Jeremy lowers me to the floor but keeps me pinned with one arm against the wall next to my head. His free hand runs down my side, resting on my hip.

"I have to go on an ice fishing trip this weekend with my dad. We leave tomorrow at 6 AM."

"Can we still do our study session tonight?

"I wouldn't miss it."

"And ice fishing is fun, right?"

Jeremy shrugs.

"At least you get to hang out with your dad." Even though I know he doesn't get along with his dad, I can't help but feel jealous of Jeremy. My dad and I used to go fishing all summer at the lake. Mom sold his old fishing boat when we moved. One more link to Dad severed.

"Hardly. Dad rents this lodge up north and invites his business partners and top clients. He only drags me with him so he can pretend he's the world's best father. We appear like the perfect father/son team for the weekend, but as soon as we get back to the city, we're back to our real normal; Dad will leave on a business trip, Mom will remain in l.a., and I'll be on my own. Except for Angelina. And I'm a little old for a nanny." His laugh is bitter.

"Jeremy, I'm so sorry."

"Don't be. I can handle it," he kisses me lightly on the lips. "I'll miss you."

"Me too, but we'll have tonight." Jeremy drapes his arm around my shoulder as we stroll down the hallway. The bell rings.

"We'd better hurry," Jeremy says.

"I don't care if I'm late for class."

Total first for me.

"But what about your grades?"

"You got a tattoo for me. Being late for class is nothing in comparison."

"Temporary tattoo." He clarifies.

"Whatever. It's still a big thing."

"Wanna' skip?"

"Skip? The entire class? Uhm—sure."

"I love you." Another kiss. Warmth flows from my lips, across my cheeks, and streams down my neck.

We race down the stairs, through the kids rushing to class-es, and out into the crisp February air. The sun reflects off the snow, blinding us as we run hand in hand down the sidewalk to the back of Prairie Trails to the parking lot and Jeremy's BMW.

"When do you get to drive the Hummer?" I ask.

"Whenever my dad's out of town, but right now it's in the shop getting the brakes fixed. He wanted it to be safe to drive on the highway this weekend. Not that he was at all concerned when we took it to Holiday Mountain."

We zip out of the parking lot.

"Where are we going," I ask.

"My house," he says. "No one's home." We'll have the house to ourselves.

"Great," I say. I feel better than great. I think—no, I know—I'm ready to do it. Finally.

Jeremy races down the streets, past Annika's house and my old street. I crane in my seat to try and spot our old house at the end of the block. All I see is a flash of red siding before it's completely out of sight.

"Hey Jeremy, about the other night—"

"Don't worry about it. You already apologized."

"That's not what I wanted to talk about. You know how Harley smokes a lot of pot…"

"Yeah?"

"Do you ever do that?"

"No, not much anymore."

"Oh, okay, it's just—"

"Don't worry about it, Julia. A little pot is no big deal."

"I guess."

Totally the opposite of Annika's zero pot viewpoint and another reason for her to hate Jeremy. Another secret I'll have to keep from her.

"Trust me."

The car slows as we approach Jeremy's winding, tree-lined driveway. He zooms towards the garage, braking at the last moment. The wheels squeal on the perfectly shoveled pavement.

"Yikes!" I say, gripping the dashboard.

Jeremy laughs and bounds from the car.

"After you, m'lady," Jeremy says in a ridiculous English accent, holding my door open.

"Thanks."

Like every other time I've entered Jeremy's house, I am blown away by the smell that greets us. To me, it's what rich would smell like if you could bottle it. Fresh flowers, lemon-scented wood polish, and expensive cologne blend to create a wealthy potpourri aroma. If Dad were still alive, he could figure it out in his basement home lab, recreate it, and sell it, making us a fortune.

"Wait here," Jeremy says, leaping up the stairs to the second floor.

I take a few tentative steps through their marble-floored foyer and peer into their massive living room. A glossy black grand piano sits in the far corner of the room, surrounded by white leather couches and chairs. The entire back wall is floor to ceiling windows that showcase the manicured back yard that ambles down to the now frozen river. Taking a few more cautious steps, I peer around the corner into the seldom-used main kitchen. All I can see is the large white island and its sparkling black granite countertop. Mom and I would die for that kitchen. With two ovens, we'd be able to make book club cookies en masse.

"Hey," Jeremy says, making me jump.

"You scared me," I say, feeling guilty for snooping.

His laugh echoes through the entryway, rebounding off the three-foot tall sleek white vase that stands across from me. The only flowers I recognize amongst the exotic spray are long-necked orange birds of paradise. The splash of blue in those flowers pops against the other yellow and red plumes that fill an entire corner of the foyer. That arrangement must have cost a fortune.

"I want to play you something," he says, his eyes shining as he pulls me into the living room.

"Okay." I laugh with him. He's bouncing on the balls of his feet like a kid on Christmas morning. "You sure are hyper."

His grin intensifies, if that is possible, and he sits on the piano bench, his fingers hover above the keys.

"I've never played for anyone other than my parents and my piano teacher."

"Really?"

"Nope, so feel honoured." His smile is smaller now but more sincere.

"Okay," I say.

Jeremy closes his eyes, his body rocking slowly forward as his fingers press the keys. Softly he plays a vaguely familiar classical song. Bach or Beethoven maybe? He sways with every bar, his movements growing more intense as the music quickens.

He is amazing.

"Jeremy!" A male voice blasts behind me. I scream and stumble into the piano.

"Dad!" Jeremy shouts. "I thought you were in Toronto."

Jeremy the Second stands in the middle of the living room, less than a foot from me. I was so entranced by the music that I didn't hear him walk across the hardwood floors.

"What are you doing home?" His tone is stern, his voice sounds like he gargles gravel for mouthwash. He gives me a head to toe inspection, hovering too long on my chest. Ew. He doesn't ask to Jeremy to introduce me. Nice.

"Why do you care?" Jeremy crashes the piano cover closed, knocking over the bench as he storms towards his father. "And what are you doing here in the middle of the day? Is *she* here?"

"What I do is none of your business. You and your"—he gestures to me—"girlfriend better get back to class. I won't bail you out of another school, Jeremy."

Jeremy's fists tighten into balls, his knuckles whiten.

"Let's go, Julia," Jeremy growls between gritted teeth.

"Don't be late coming home tonight," his dad bellows. "We leave at 6 AM sharp." Soft jazz music follows us out the front door.

"He is such a frickin' asshole," Jeremy says.

"I—" I don't know what to say.

He doesn't answer. Without speaking we climb in his car. He races down the driveway, barely slowing as we approach the street. We swing out of the driveway, accelerating down the road.

"Do not say anything about that," Jeremy says. His voice is quiet. Angry.

"I wouldn't."

"I am serious, Julia. Not a word."

"I won't."

He veers to the side of the road, ramming the car into park. He lunges at me, gripping my shoulders and slams me against my door. The handle digs deep into my back. White pain spiderwebs out across my shoulder blades.

"Ow! Jeremy! Stop!"

"No one can ever know about my dad. Ever. If I hear that you said anything about today, you'll be sorry."

His fingers embed themselves into my arms. He squeezes tighter. I gasp.

"Jeremy you're hurting me." He pushes me even harder against the door. The handle burns into my spine. "Please stop."

His face is inches from mine. I close my eyes and turn my face from his. Panic fills me, making breathing difficult. I take shallow breaths to control my mounting terror.

"Look at me!" he yells.

My eyes snap open as I face him.

"Jeremy, please stop," I whisper, my voice rasping in my throat.

"Crap." He releases me and sits back in his seat, slamming the gearshift into drive.

I grip Dad's button so hard my fingers begin to cramp as we drive the few blocks to school in silence. My back pulses where the handle implanted itself. I can feel waves of anger ripple from Jeremy.

He coasts past the parking lot, stopping by the side entrance off the street.

"Aren't you coming?" I ask.

He doesn't respond.

"Jeremy?" *Isn't he at least going to apologize?*

"I'll talk to you later," he says, without looking at me.

"Fine."

I slam the door behind me, and he races away. My hands start to shake.

I need to talk to Annika.

But I can't.

She's not talking to me.

CHAPTER 24

How many beats can your heart skip
without completely stopping?

Knocking echoes up the staircase and fills the apartment. I glance at the clock on the stove. 7:00 PM. *Jeremy? Is he still coming?*

I peer down the staircase. The knocking resumes.

Out of habit, I slide my hand along the rail as I race to the bottom. No need to slip down the final few and land in a heap.

I peer through the peek hole.

I unlock the door and swing it open. "Jeremy!"

"I am so, so sorry, Julia," he says, his arms full of brown paper wrapped flower bouquets. "These are for you," he says, his voice quiet. "I got so mad about my dad, but that wasn't your fault. I don't know why I snapped at you."

"It's okay, I understand." Sort of. I get he got hurt by his dad's comments, but why did he take that out on me? "Jeremy, you want me to trust you, but you need to trust me, too. I would never tell anyone about your private family business. Honest."

"I know I should believe you, but it's hard for me. My parents lie all the time. They're not exactly trustworthy, you know?"

"I guess. Yeah."

"Can I come in?"

I look down at my bunny-slippered feet. What am I supposed to say? Part of me wants to yank him inside and forgive him instantly. But the other part? That part is confused. And bruised. And a little pissed off.

"Uhm, I—I—Jeremy, you really hurt me in the car. You jammed my back into the door handle."

"What?! Oh my God, Julia! I am so sorry. I didn't even realize. Please forgive me. I will never do that again. I promise."

Tears fill his eyes, and my eyes tear in response. He looks like he's in physical pain.

"It's okay. It doesn't hurt anymore." Another almost truth. As long as I don't lean back against anything like a chair, couch, or mattress, it feels normal.

"Are you sure?"

"Yeah, just—just," the last residue of Jeremy-focused anger dissolves as his pleading stare stays on me. "Just come on up."

He follows my creaky climb up the stairs into the apartment, kicking his boots off on the mat at the top of the stairs. He remains quiet as I take his coat and drape it along the top of a dining room chair.

"Here," he says holding the packages out to me.

"You didn't need to do this," I say, as I lay them on the kitchen counter. "Can you get a vase from the cupboard above the fridge?"

I unwrap each one, revealing a total of forty-eight long stem white roses.

"Jeremy, this is too much! It's going to look like a florist shop in here."

"Nothing is too much for you Julia."

"Better grab three more vases, then." I point back to the cupboard.

We place the roses around the dining room and living room, their musky perfume wafts into every corner of the apartment.

"And I have a surprise planned for next weekend."

"Oh," I say. I hate surprises. I force cheer into my words. "Sounds great,"

"You're going to love it."

Jeremy glances at the dining room table.

"You're ready to study?"

"Yup, I can't fall behind," I pause before continuing. It's now or never. "I sort of took on another student."

"What?"

"I've been meaning to tell you, but the time never seemed right." I take a breath and continue. "It's Tyler. He needs help in math or he's going to fail."

"But, you're so busy already. This is going to cut into our time."

"A little bit, maybe, but I could use the money and he looked so desperate."

"I'm not so sure," he says. There's something extra in his voice...doubt? Jealousy?

"What do you mean?"

"Julia, do you realize how amazing you are? You're gorgeous, brilliant, and kind. There is no one at school like you. Are you sure he isn't interested in more than just being tutored?"

"Jeremy! That's sick. First, he's been your friend since forever, and second he's totally interested in Annika. You have no need to worry."

"I suppose—"

"And you need to trust me, remember?"

"I remember. I'll try."

"Good. Now let's get at it."

He pulls me close and kisses me along my neck. It feels so good.

"Jeremy," I say, putting my hands on his chest and pushing him away. "My grandmother is asleep in my bedroom and we have a ton of work ahead of us. Focus."

"Focusing is so boring."

"So is summer school."

We sit at the table and I pass him a piece of loose leaf.

"Okay, let's work on this equation," I say, pointing at a problem in the textbook. "Once you understand the basics, you'll have no problem."

"I sure hope so. It's like a different language."

"Well, math sort of is its own language, but a very logical rule-based language. Once you master those rules, you'll be set."

"It will take me forever to do that."

"Don't worry. We'll go over this as many times as you need."

"Careful what you promise. I suck at math. It's what got me kicked out of two prep schools."

"You need more confidence. You don't doubt yourself when you play basketball, do you?"

"That is totally different. I know I'm good at it."

"Yeah, but you weren't that good the first time you shot a basket, were you?"

"What?" Jeremy pretends to be horrified.

"Okay," I say, laughing. He can be so easy to be around. Sometimes it feels like we've known each other all our lives. "Maybe you were some sort of child basketball prodigy. I'm just saying that for us mere mortals it takes time to get really good at something. Most of us aren't immediate masters at anything."

"Yeah, but you're a math whiz."

"Math came easy to me, but I am a hopeless mess at anything sports related, which was apparent at Holiday Mountain. Even bouncing a ball is a definite skill I lack."

"Hey, I just got the best idea. I could teach you to shoot hoops as a thank you for sharing your killer math skills."

I shrug. "No need. You're already paying me."

"You are worth way more than $15 an hour."

Jeremy grabs an oatmeal chocolate chip cookie from the stack on the plate in front of us.

"I can't believe you made these for me," he says, grabbing another cookie.

"As if. They're for tonight's book club, The Mad Mavens."

"They have a name?"

"Yup and they're my favourite. They have a seriously predictable old-lady name, but the women are hilarious. They come dressed as their favourite character from whatever book they're discussing."

"Wow. That's crazy."

"They're a bunch of Grandma's old sorority friends, and they were our first book club last year. They even kept coming in when Grandma went down to Arizona for the—" a thump from Grandma's room stops me mid-sentence.

"What was that?" Jeremy asks.

"I dunno."

Shoving away from the table, I rush to her bedroom.

"Grandma, are you okay?" I push on the door, but it doesn't open far before banging into something.

"Grandma!" She's lying on her side on the carpet. Her body is blocking the door. "Jeremy, get my mom! She's downstairs."

I squeeze through the narrow opening, careful not to fall onto her as I step over top. Her scarf has fallen off, exposing her pixie hair cut. Wrapping my arms under Grandma's head and upper back, I ease her further into the room away from the door. With care, I rock her onto her back, stuffing a small throw pillow under her head. She weighs next to nothing and she feels too hot. She has a gash along the side of her head above her ear. She must have hit the nightstand when she fell because it's lying on its side next to her. The bedside ceramic lamp hangs precariously upside down by its cord over the side of the table. Blood's oozing into her hair. Her eyes flutter open and a look of confusion clouds over them.

"What, what happened?" Her voice is whisper soft.

"You fell, Grandma." She tries to push herself onto her elbows, but she's so weak she collapses. "Just stay where you are. Mom's coming."

Her eyes close. I try to control my breathing and stem my rising panic. *Focus Julia! Pull it together!* I take slow, deep and steady breaths as tears sting my eyes. They stream down my face, feeling as hot as Grandma's skin.

I glance towards the sound of Mom and Jeremy barrelling across the apartment towards us. Mom squeezes through the doorway.

"What happened?" She kneels next to Grandma.

"It's okay, sweetheart. Just a bit of a tumble," Grandma smiles and pats Mom's trembling hand. She glances towards Jeremy who is peering through the partially opened doorway. "Who's the hunk?" she asks.

I blush and when I look at Jeremy his face looks as red as mine feels. I'm too mortified to hold his gaze for longer than two seconds. Leave it to Grandma to try and deflect the attention away from her and embarrass me in the process.

"This is Jeremy. He's my boyfriend. You met him before."

She smiles tenderly and lets out a long sigh, as her eyes slowly close. I stroke her soft curls away from her forehead. A little shiver tingles up my arms. Grandma used to do this to me when I was little. It feels strange to be taking care of her, rather than the other way around. She glances back at Jeremy and smiles, "Your father's here so no need to worry."

"My father?" Mom looks confused and twists to look at Jeremy.

"Yes. He's back home from..." Grandma begins, a frown replacing her smile. "From...the cottage...I think...." Her eyelids flutter to a close and she drifts off.

Mom lays the back of her hand across Grandma's forehead.

"She's burning up," Mom pronounces, her voice quivers. She pulls back the blood-wet curls above Grandma's ear and her face blanches. "Julia, would you please run and grab a clean facecloth?"

Jeremy jumps out of my way as I run into the bathroom and race back.

"Place pressure here to stop the bleeding," Mom's eyes meet mine, and the fear I see there propels me back to when Dad was dying in the hospital. Suddenly, I can't seem to get enough air. "Stay here with Grandma, I'm going to call an ambulance."

"Okay, okay," I stammer, too scared to ask the question I really want to know. *Is Grandma going to be all right?*

Two small red circles sit high on Grandma's cheekbones and her eyes are still closed. Her breathing is slow and shallow.

She's mumbling something about Grandpa, but it makes little sense. I stroke Grandma's hand. She remains still. The muttering stops and she looks as if she's asleep. I lean over her, placing my ear over her mouth. Her breath is so slow and quiet that I'm scared she's going to stop breathing.

"I need to pack a bag for Grandma," I say to Jeremy, my voice low. I don't want to disturb her. "Can you hold onto the cloth?"

He nods. I grab my duffle bag from the bottom shelf in the closet. Grandma will want her own robe and slippers in the hospital. On my dresser, she's placed a picture of Grandpa and her sitting in beach chairs in Oahu. It was taken the winter before he died. Grandma's fearless grin meets the camera straight on, but Grandpa is staring at Grandma with this look of wonder. It's like he still can't believe he's lucky enough to be with her. They met in high school, married at nineteen, and never spent more than a few nights in a row apart from each other in their thirty-eight years of marriage. When Grandpa had a massive heart attack and died five years ago, Grandma was in shock for over a year. Now Grandma takes this photo with her whenever she travels. She even packs it when she spends a weekend at a friend's cottage in the summer. She's going to want Grandpa with her, so I carefully wrap the picture in her robe and place it in the bag. Funny she thought Jeremy looked like Grandpa. I can't see the resemblance, but it's been a long time since I've seen pictures of him as a teenager.

"You look like your Grandma," Jeremy says.

"That's what everyone says. Mom says she was quite the beauty when she was young."

"Just like you."

"Oh, no that's not what I meant," I stammer, totally embarrassed. He's going to think I was fishing for a compliment.

"I know, but it's what I meant."

He smiles and I swear my heart misses three beats. Possibly four.

And it feels amazing.

CHAPTER 25

Hospital Veteran.

"I need you to call Mrs. Henderson and let her know their book club is cancelled tonight," Mom says as she climbs into the back of the ambulance with Grandma. "And you'll have to lock up before you head to the hospital. And grab some money from the cash register so you can take a cab."

"I still have my $40," I say.

"No. I don't want you using that."

"I can drive her," Jeremy offers.

Mom looks at him and gives him a fast head to toe inspection.

"I'm not sure that is a good idea."

Jeremy looks embarrassed and I wince.

"Mom, please give him another chance."

Mom gives him a more thorough assessment.

"I'm not super happy about this, but he can drive you. But Jules, please don't forget to lock both doors when you close up and I suppose you can leave the cash in the safe for tonight." Wringing her hands, her brow knitted, she repeats herself. I know her look. She's scared.

"Mom, don't worry about it. We can handle this."

"We've got to go now," interrupts the paramedic.

"I love you Grandma! I'll be there soon," I call as the ambulance door slams shut. I wave to Mom even though I can no longer see her.

I take two steps through the back door into the shop and burst into tears. Jeremy pats me on the back, which makes me cry even harder. He wraps me into a hug, but I gently push away, wiping my face with my sleeves.

"I need to hurry," I say, as I run through the store. "I'll just be a few minutes."

I empty the money from the cash register into the safe and grab the store bible from the drawer to the left of the cash register. It's a coffee-stained blue scribbler that has several curled sticky notes poking out from its top. I flip to the page that lists our book clubs, searching for Mrs. Henderson's number. Fingers trembling I dial and it goes straight to voice mail.

"Mrs. Henderson, this is Julia Collins from The Littlest Bookshop," my voice quivers then breaks. "Grandma's been rushed to the hospital, so we have to cancel tonight's book club. Sorry."

I hang up and sling Grandma's bag over my shoulder. I dropped it in the middle of the store when the ambulance arrived.

"Let's go," I say to Jeremy. As we step into the night, the cold air brings everything into focus. *Time to pull it together, tears can wait. Mom's going to need me.*

Perfect Christmas snowflakes swirl around me as I head towards Jeremy who's standing beside a black car I've never seen before. What would it be like to have a whole fleet of Beamers at your disposal?

He's pulled the car around so the passenger door faces me. Dad always did that for Mom and me. Mom said it was his inner Prince Charming breaking free from his outer Mad Scientist shell. As Jeremy opens my door, I notice rust stains eating at the doorframe and a spiderweb crack expands across the windshield. His car isn't in much better condition than Aunt Mildred.

"Thanks," I say, as I sit down. The grey leather seats are cracked in places and a particularly nasty tear criss-crosses the entire driver's seat. He's used silver duct tape to keep the fabric together. The scent of pine emanates from a green cardboard tree that hangs from the rear view mirror. Not too surprising, the rear view mirror is cracked. What does surprise me is that I feel more comfortable in it than any of Jeremy's other cars.

It's hard for me to see Jeremy through the thickening snow-fall as he runs around to his side of the car. A gust of wind and snowflakes chase him inside. He sits down and bats his head and arms free of snow.

"I like your car."

He lifts an eyebrow.

"Seriously? Brutus is a complete junker, but he's all mine." He rubs the dashboard in small circles. A slow smile emerges. "Every time Dad gets mad he thinks he's punishing me by making me drive Brutus. If I told him I actually like this car, he'd have it recycled into pop cans in a second."

"I'm sure he wouldn't go that far."

"You have no idea." His voice is quiet as he stares out the front windshield. Silence descends and my nerves rise to the occasion.

"So, you named your car, too. I, for so many obvious reasons do not own a car, beater or otherwise, but I named

Annika's mini, Aunt Mildred." I chatter, chipmunk style. "We could double date! You and me in Brutus and Annika and Tyler in Aunt Mildred."

Jeremy's grin returns and my nerves dissolve in the after effects of his radiant smile.

"You always make me feel better. I knew there was a reason I loved you!" he says.

"And here I thought it was because of my math mind."

"Oh, right and that too." We both laugh as he reverses through the parking lot. Brutus coughs and spews in protest. "What's the best way to the hospital?"

My stomach flutters at the mention of hospital. "When we visited my Dad, we always took Pembina to Stafford, continued down Academy and then…" I begin, but can't finish.

"Right, it turns into Maryland and you keep heading north and then you can't miss it," Jeremy finishes for me. We turn towards Pembina Highway and yield into traffic.

"I wish I could miss it," I say.

Jeremy doesn't respond, but I can feel him stare at me, before he returns to watching the road. We drive in silence down the darkening street. Shame rolls over me as I try to block out the feelings of not always wanting to visit Dad. Especially at the end, when he looked so different, and not just sick different. In the days before he died, he looked like he no longer wanted to live; he was tired and he was done, but I think he was hanging on for Mom and me. And I'm ashamed to admit that I wanted him to hang on, even though he was so drugged up he wasn't even fully aware near the end. *I am so sorry, Dad.* My breath catches.

The snowfall picks up, and the perfect Christmassy flakes churn into a full winter storm as we zigzag through the city.

"We're almost there," he nods to the hospital looming ahead of us on the left.

We park at the first meter we find, and I have little room to squeeze out of the car. I struggle up the three-metre high snow-bank that skirts the road. Jeremy reaches for my hands and swings me down to the sidewalk. The wind barrels against us, forcing us to bend into it to keep from being blown backward as we trudge towards the hospital doors. We pull up our hoods and turn our faces to block the worst of it. By the time we go through the emergency doors, the inside walls of my nostrils have frozen together, my lips are burning and even my teeth hurt from the freezing wind. Jeremy's cheeks are a dark brick red and snow crystals coat his eyelashes and eyebrows. His eyes sparkle with wind tears. He looks like a frozen Greek god.

"You look cold," I say, pulling off my gloves. Without thinking, I reach out to smooth off the frost. The stubble on his cheek prickles my cold fingers. Jeremy gently clasps my hand in his and pulls it towards his mouth.

"You're like ice yourself," he says. His voice sounds deeper and huskier than normal. He blows on my fingers, sending bolts of electricity through my body. My knees wobble and I sway closer to him. The scent of his musty cologne makes my hands shake. I stare up into his eyes, and he stares back at me with an intensity that sends my brain swirling. *Oh my God.* I need to say something funny and witty to cool me down. We are here to see my Grandma, not to make out in the waiting room.

"You are so gorgeous," I say. So much for funny and witty. My blush is immediate. I'm pretty sure I am radiating enough heat to start a fire. Jeremy smiles down at me.

"Thanks. I think you're pretty gorgeous too."

I step back from him, to clear my brain of lusty thoughts. *What the heck am I doing?*

"We should go," I mumble, walking to the admittance desk. Grandma's comments about Jeremy play over in my head. Was this how Grandpa made Grandma feel?

The clerk buzzes us through the security door, and with the first step into the emergency room, I'm assaulted with the pungent smell of antiseptic. A barrage of painful memories of Dad's visits to this hospital smashes into me. Our first glimmer that something was seriously wrong with Dad was revealed to us behind door number three, on the left. I'm sure my hand must have left an imprint on the silver doorknob. I spent countless hours here and little has changed since we rushed Dad in that final time, less than a year ago. Nothing but the patients has changed. The same faded mint green walls, the same too-bright quietly buzzing fluorescent lights, and the same constant beeping monitors. All those machines chiming out information that hospital rookies don't understand. I feel like a veteran after being here so often with Dad, and I immediately recognize the long siren-wail that pierces the air. Heart failure. A nurse, with her hair tied back in a no-nonsense bun, jams her pen into the back of her hair, and rushes to the heart attack patient. I turn away, not wanting to eavesdrop and a new alarm, a rising high-pitched whine, grabs my attention. Someone's blood oxygen levels are falling low, but I don't feel any concern. Most likely their finger sensor has just slipped off. Its beep will cry out for a few minutes before a nurse investigates.

Jeremy follows me as I approach the nurses' desk, where doctors and nurses huddle in clumps discussing charts, poring over X-Rays or making calls to other departments. Even after being here so often, I still feel intimidated by their orderliness. I clear my throat, hoping someone will look up from their work.

"May I help you," asks a young nurse in plum-coloured scrubs. She slowly draws her eyes up from the file she's reading and gives me a weary smile. It's not the kind of smile that reaches her hazel eyes. Her smile's not even strong enough to lift both sides of her mouth. She looks like she's on the tail end of a long shift, and this weak half-grin is all she can muster. There's a half drunk Tim Hortons cup sitting next to her keyboard with a film of scum milk settled on the top. I glance at the clock hanging on the wall behind her. 7:20. Thank God shift change is at 7:30 and we'll have a batch of well-rested, fresh recruits to look after Grandma.

"Yes, I'm looking for my Grandma, Cora Roberts."

"Let me see what bed she's in," she replies, as she types Grandma's name into a computer. Her elbow grazes the coffee cup and it teeters for a moment before she grabs it and chucks it in the trashcan.

"Bed six, right at the end. The doctor is in with her now."

"Thanks," I say. A torrent of dread cascades over me. Part of me wants to rush to her, but the other part wants to run away and find some quiet corner to curl up in and wish this all away. Of course, the reality of being in a hospital where there are no quiet corners to be found is too glaring, and I have no choice but head towards bed six and just deal with it.

The florescent lights hum brightly as I scan down the hall and see Mom backing out of a room with a white-haired doctor, deep in conversation. He reaches out and gives Mom's arm a squeeze and a comforting smile, which I immediately recognize.

"Dr. Grandpa," I call and run to give him a big hug.

"Julia," he says, and holds me in front of him. "My granddaughter…from another grandmother!"

We all laugh. Dr. Donovan was Dad's oncologist and when he was taking care of Dad, it felt like he was a part of our family. He looks so much like the classic Grandfather picture with his white hair, glasses, slight paunch belly, and pockets full of candies. One day as a joke I called him Dr. Grandpa, Dr. G. for short, and the nickname stuck.

"How are you? What are you doing here?" I ask.

"I'm much better now that I've seen the two of you. I don't normally make ER rounds, but your mom called me and I was up on a ward, so I just popped down," he replies, and looks meaningfully at me over the top edge of his wire framed glasses, "I'm sorry about your Grandmother, Julia."

"How is she?" I blink away tears that prickle my eyes.

"I was just telling your mother that Cora is one tough cookie. She's actually doing remarkably well and her prognosis remains very positive. We're running a few tests, but I'm not expecting to find anything too surprising, beyond dehydration. But even so, you did the right thing bringing her in. Dehydration can cause a lot of problems when you have a compromised immune system."

"Really? That's all?" A surge of relief flows through me as I lean against Mom. She wraps her arm around my waist and gives me a kitten kiss on my temple.

"Really," Mom says. "Dr. Donovan is going to consult with Grandma's oncologist later today or tomorrow about tweaking her meds to help control the nausea."

"And how is my favourite little rebel?" Dr. G asks.

"Annika? Good, she's good. Her hair's pink now." Annika was often with me at the hospital and she and Dr. G. hit it off immediately. He has six kids of his own and fourteen grandkids and he just sort of understood Annika.

"Well that would be quite the change from the last time I saw her," he chuckles and rubs his chin, "what did she call her hair color?"

"Swamp Thing!" Mom and I say at the same time. We laugh, remembering Annika's green-tinged, long black hair.

Dr. G clears his throat, drawing our attention. "And is this your young man, Julia?"

I turn and blush fiercely hot. I've seriously got to put an end to this blushing. I'm not sure what I'm more embarrassed about—Dr. G calling Jeremy "mine," my crazy blushing, or that I didn't introduce Jeremy myself. To be honest, I sort of forgot about him when I saw Dr. G.

"I'm sorry, yes, this is my boyfriend, Jeremy. Jeremy this is Dr. Donovan."

Dr. G. shakes his hand and I can see Jeremy wince, slightly. Jeremy is a big guy, but at 6'3" Dr. G., makes Jeremy look like a sixth grader. He peers over his glasses at Jeremy, trapping Jeremy's hand in his own larger one.

"A pleasure to meet you, Jeremy."

"Nice to meet you too," Jeremy replies, his eyes dart down to their handshake and back up to meet Dr. G's intense stare.

Dr. G still hasn't released Jeremy's hand from his kung-fu tight grip. "Now this here is a very special young lady, which of course you already know," says Dr. G., smiling at me, "and she deserves to be treated like the remarkable woman she is."

"I agree."

"Good," he says, giving Jeremy a thump on the back and finally freeing Jeremy's hand.

"Why don't you pop your heads in and say hi and then give Grandma time to rest," says Mom. She pulls a $20 bill from her purse. "You can head down to the cafeteria and bring back some coffee and muffins and I'll go over Grandma's care with Dr. Donovan."

I stuff the money in my pocket and watch Dr. G wrap his arm around Mom's shoulder leading her to the nurse's desk.

"I think we've been dismissed," whispers Jeremy.

"Sort of looks that way," I agree.

We slip into the room and find Grandma propped up with three pillows. Her head is neatly wrapped with her scarf. Her eyes slowly blink open.

"Oh, sweetie," she murmurs, "I thought I heard your voice."

"How are you feeling Grandma?" I squeeze in between the monitors and Grandma's bed, careful not to bump any cords.

"Looks like I'm going to be fine, just like I told your mother in the ambulance." Her eyelids waver and then close. She purses her cracked lips, as she shakes her head slightly, "You two need to learn not to panic."

"Grandma, Dr. G was pretty glad we brought you in."

"Dr. G.," Grandma smiles and her eyelids flash open. "Now that's one hot sexagenarian!"

"Grandma, he's married!" We both laugh.

"Well, there's no harm in looking, my dear. Now off you go so I can get some beauty rest," she says and pulls me in for a hug. "How am I supposed to rock n' roll this headscarf looking like a dog's breakfast?"

"Grandma, you'd rock the headscarf, not rock n' roll it," I explain, amazed that she's still throwing out jokes. "And it's impossible for you to look bad."

"That's why you're my favourite granddaughter."

"I love you Grandma. We won't be gone long." I give her another gentle hug. She feels frail and I'm scared I'll crush a bone if I squeeze too tightly.

"Love you too, sweetie." Her eyes shut; she's already drifting off to sleep.

Jeremy and I tiptoe from the room, closing the door so it makes little sound. We weave through the fresh batch of doctors and nurses arriving for shift change and make our way toward the exit and the hallway that will take us to the cafeteria.

"Is, Dr. Donovan always that..." Jeremy asks, searching for the right word.

"Protective?" I finish for him.

"That was pretty intense."

"I've never seen Dr. G like that, but I never brought a boy to the hospital with me when Dad was his patient. If it's any consolation, I think you passed the test." I give Jeremy a sideways glance. He catches me and smiles.

"Are there any other tests I should know about?"

"Well, the head nurse may give you a lie detector test, but beyond that, nothing special."

"Piece of cake. I ace tests—except for math. And science. And anything academic."

"Yup, should be no problem. The needle of truth serum should be painless," I try to sound dark, sinister, and Russian KGB, "Ve have vays to make you talk!"

Jeremy laughs. It's deep and rolling. I'm not sure I've heard him laugh like this before. It sounds...real.

"Oh yeah? I have ways to make you talk, too." He reaches over and tickles my ribs. I squeal, totally sounding like a Pom-Pom-in-training, and wriggle away from him. He chases me down the hall.

I feel like I could run for miles.

CHAPTER 26

Reinforcements.

Thank goodness Jeremy is driving us home and not me. It's close to 1 AM and I'm having a hard time keeping my eyes open. My head keeps nodding forward and then I jerk awake. The snowstorm has subsided, leaving the streets slippery under the fresh layer of snow. Jeremy still looks wide-awake. He hasn't even yawned once, while my mouth spent half the evening springing open into an enormous yawn. I'm sure my face looked like a black hole. He pulls into our dark parking lot.

"Do you need me to walk you in?" He asks.

"No, I'm good. Thanks for coming with me tonight. It meant a lot having you there, even if you got the third degree from Dr. G."

Jeremy finally meets my gaze. A brief smile flickers across his face and he looks like he's about to tell me something important, but our motion detector light flips on and his smile vanishes, his eyes darken.

"I'll see you on Monday," Jeremy says and gives me a quick kiss on the cheek.

"Oh my God! I totally forgot. You're leaving early tomorrow for your fishing trip with your dad. You're going to be exhausted."

"Don't worry about it. He won't care if I sleep all the way to the lodge, I just have to be "on" in front of his precious guests." He sounds bitter.

"I'm sorry about your dad."

"Don't be. You have enough to worry about."

"Thanks for tonight."

Grabbing my purse, I climb out of the car and trudge through the snow to our back door. I wave to Jeremy, but even with the back door light, it's too dark to see if he's waving back. He waits for me to get into the shop before driving away.

I shuffle through the bookstore, up the staircase to our apartment. Mom is staying at the hospital tonight, so I'm going to sleep in her bed. I head straight for her bedroom and scurry under the covers. Normally sleeping in jeans would drive me nuts, but I'm too exhausted to change into my PJs. My teeth can rot, for all I care—all I want to do is sleep. My head drops to the pillow, which moulds around my head like a massive, mountain-spring scented marshmallow. I just have to set the alarm for the morning, which I'll do in a second...

I bolt upright and get tangled in the sheets as I climb out of bed. Sitting back down, I unwrap my legs. Someone's creaking up the stairs.

Crap. I was supposed to get back to the hospital by 8:00 AM to relieve Mom. As I emerge from her bedroom she reaches the top of the stairs. Her face sags from exhaustion, her hair juts out in odd angles. I can imagine her spending the entire night running her hands through her hair, her whole body full of worry. She lifts her arm and gives me a limp wave.

"Mom, I'm so sorry. I forgot to set the alarm."

"That's okay Jules," she replies, shuffling to the sofa. Her voice remains soft and low. "Reinforcements arrived about an hour ago, with arms full of fresh baking, magazines, and piles of books."

She plunks herself onto the couch and sinks into the over-stuffed cushions, putting her feet onto the coffee table. She must truly be wiped if she's breaking her own house rules. I sit down next to her.

"Reinforcements?" I'm puzzled. Mom and I are the only family Grandma has in the city.

"The Mad Mavens," she explains, "When you told them what happened last night, they spent the evening planning how to help Grandma and then they went into action. They brought supplies this morning—books, magazines, and piles of baking to bribe the nurses and orderlies, so they'll keep an extra-special eye out for her."

She wearily pushes herself up from the couch. "I'm heading to bed. The Mavens have us covered until 2:00. Can you handle the store until then?"

"Sure. When do you want me to wake you?"

"About 1:00, that'll give me a few hours sleep."

She stumbles to her bedroom.

"Mom," I call. "She's going to be alright, isn't she?"

She adjusts her glasses, and pats down a lock of kinked hair.

"Yes, of course. No need to worry," she says, her eyes narrowing. "Are you okay?"

"Oh, yeah. Everything's great." I lie, which I'm getting better at. Annika's not speaking to me, Jeremy's roller coaster emotions and anger is freaking me out, and Grandma ending up in the hospital is freaking me out even more. Yup, smooth sailing here.

"That's a huge relief. I'm not sure I could handle anything more right now."

"Just focus on Grandma, Mom," I say as I head to my room to get my morning pill. "I can take care of myself."

Which isn't a total lie.

CHAPTER 27

Tragic, star-crossed lovers.

Sitting in a sunbeam at a desk cubical, I swivel in my chair and glance out the library windows. Blowing snow drifts in waves across the frozen football field, swirling around the group of boys tossing a football. Jeremy's red toque weaves through the others as he races towards the end zone. They seem impervious to the -30 windchill. I shiver just thinking about being out there. I'd pick my cozy library nook over that open field any day.

"Hey," Tyler says, interrupting my thoughts. He taps on his textbook. "I still don't understand this equation."

"Sorry, brain drain. I need lunch. Can we continue tomorrow?"

"Sure." He watches me as I gather up my stuff, zipping and unzipping his bag about two inches. Open. Close. Open. Close. He clears his throat. "I, ah— I asked Annika to the dance."

"Really? That's awesome."

"Yeah, she said yes."

"Great." An awkward silence follows us as we leave the library.

"I didn't know you guys were fighting," he says.

"Uhm, we're not fighting. It's just—I—totally messed up," I glance at Tyler. He nods his head but doesn't say anything. "Is she still mad?"

"I don't know if she'd want me to say anything."

"Crap. She's pissed."

"Yeah, that's a good summary." Tyler pauses before continuing. "I don't know you very well, and The Third is my buddy, but just be careful."

"Don't worry, I don't ever plan on a repeat creek performance."

"That's not exactly what I meant. I don't think you know—"

"Hey, Julia," Jeremy throws his arm around me as he appears from behind us. He leans his head close to mine. "Should I be jealous?" he whispers loudly enough for Tyler to hear.

"No, of course not. We were just studying."

"Yup, she's teaching me everything she knows," Tyler says, stepping away from Jeremy and me.

"I think I'm failing as a tutor with Tyler. I totally blanked out in the middle of our session."

"Nah, you were just caving to hunger. Anyway, I gotta' go. See you later," Tyler says.

"Later," Jeremy says, watching Tyler sprint up the stairs to the second floor.

"Hey, how was the lodge?" I ask as he faces me. I run my fingers over the stubble that covers his face. His eyes are bloodshot. Really bloodshot "You look tired."

"Let's just say my dad owes me. Big time," he replies, as he squeezes my hand. "I'm really excited about next weekend."

"Next weekend?"

"Yeah, your surprise." Right.

"Can you give me a hint?"

"Hmmm. Let me think," he smiles. "Your surprise will happen after the dance."

"So, we're going to the dance?"

"Of course."

"It's just—you never actually asked me, so I wasn't sure." I blush again. "I've never gone with a date before."

"Sorry, I should've asked you." He runs his hand gently across my cheek then gets down on one knee and reaches for my hand. "Julia, will you do me the honour of going to the Valentine's Day dance with me?"

I start giggling, feeling self-conscious as passing students stare.

"Yes, of course."

"Woohoo!" he yells. "The most beautiful girl in the school is going to the dance with me!"

"Shhhh! Jeremy! People are staring."

Jeremy stands up and pulls me to his chest. His grey eyes are intense as his hand caresses my cheek.

"What do we care?"

"I guess we don't," I reply, breathless.

In the past, the sight of cherry red and Pepto-Bismol pink hearts snaking their way along the halls would've made my stomach roll with a toxic blend of jealousy and dread. Jealous of those girls with dates who counted the days until the school dance and dreading that wallflower-loser walk of shame each time I entered the dance sans date.

But for the past two days, it's all I have been thinking about. We just need to agree on costumes.

Letting the last few bites of my chocolate bar slowly melt on my tongue, I lean against the wall outside the chemistry lab and wait for Jeremy. The bell rings and I lick all chocolate traces from my fingers.

"Hey," Jeremy says, smiling. We walk hand in hand towards his locker. His shirtsleeve is rolled up and I can see his trial tattoo.

"My Grandma came home yesterday," I say.

"Oh, yeah? That's great," he replies, sounding distant. He pulls out his phone and texts.

"Yeah, it is. She—" I begin, but he interrupts me.

"Hey, so what do you want to go as for the dance?" he asks, stuffing his phone back in his pocket. He's never once asked about Grandma. Even though I text him updates of her recovery on a daily basis, he never engages. The most he says is, "that's good." I've tried not to let it bother me, but it really hurts that he doesn't seem to care about how she's doing. I know he has his own family drama to deal with, but his lack of interest stings.

"Well, since the theme is Romantic Couples, I thought we could go as the most tragic star-crossed lovers: Romeo and Juliet," I suggest.

"Romeo and Juliet? Ah, no way am I wearing tights."

"You don't have to wear tights."

"No kidding. I'll rent us costumes from Malabar's."

"Okay. When should we pick them out? We're running out of time."

"I'm going to do it myself and surprise you." Another surprise. *Fantastic.*

"Aw, I wanted to pick them out," I say. I've never dressed up before because I always thought the theme dances were lame. Until now.

"Nope. It'll be part of Saturday's surprise."

Jeremy gives me a quick kiss on the lips and then frowns, licking his lips.

"Have you been eating chocolate?"

"Ah, yeah. So what?"

"You better watch how much you eat. Don't want a whale for a girlfriend."

"What? I'm not fat." I say, but something about the way he lifts his eyes and tilts his head makes me doubtful. "Am I?"

"Not fat. Yet. But you better watch yourself. I don't want you to turn into a Rachel Aarons."

"Oh. I won't."

I blanch, feeling like I'm betraying her. Not that we were friends, but not defending her feels mean. Something happened to Rachel. She was super skinny up until tenth grade. She came back from summer vacation at least twenty pounds heavier and she kept gaining more and more weight. Rumour was that she went on a date with her cousin's best friend and he tried to rape her. No one knows if it's true or just gossip, but once that rumour surfaced it swept across Prairie Trails like cancer. Rachel ended up transferring to a private girls' school for eleventh grade. Who could blame her?

Jeremy opens his tin of mints.

"Stick to these. Fewer calories," he says as I pop one in my mouth. He smiles and pulls me close, kissing me. "So beautiful. Let's go."

We move hand in hand, through the crowd. Up ahead I see a familiar swath of pink hair poke out of the throng of students. Her head twists back and for a moment her gaze meets mine. She looks sad. *Has she been crying?* She then glares briefly at Jeremy before darting away.

My heart pounds.

We exit the school, his arm now draped over my shoulder, heavy, protective. His dad's Hummer is parked as usual, diagonally, in the far corner.

"OPAP," I whisper.

Annika, I miss you.

CHAPTER 28

"Sometimes what you imagine is going to bother you, isn't what is most upsetting when the time comes."

I watch Jeremy's tail lights disappear down the street. Light fluffy flakes float through the air and settle weightlessly on my hair. Skipping up the snow-covered stairs, I reach for the door handle and my feet fly out from under me. I land hard on the stoop. You'd think by now I'd be used to falling, yet I'm still surprised every time I crash to the ground.

It's remarkably comfy lying here in the fresh snow. I watch the sunset's pinks and oranges glow against the darkening sky. The snow white clouds float by so slowly that at first they look like they're stationary.

Watching the clouds reminds me of Dad. At the cottage we'd lie on the beach for what felt like hours and look for shapes in the clouds. *Dad?* I search the cloud formations for messages from him. What shape of message-cloud would Dad send me? A horseshoe for good luck? A heart to say he loves me? A Golden Boy so that I know for sure it's him? I search the sky, but all I see emerge is a dark grey boot-shaped cloud. I guess that means I need a swift kick in the tush to get to work.

Time to get shovelling.

"Be right with you," Mom calls, without looking to see that it's me. She's high on the ladder with a red feather duster stuffed in her hand. *Hmmm, must've been a slow day if Mom's had time to dust.*

"It's just me, Mom." I shrug out of my jacket and rip off my toque. I'm drenched from shovelling.

"Oh, hi Jules." She sounds relieved and eases her way down the steps. "How was your day?"

"Fine. Actually, better than fine." I continue in a jumbled rush, "I wanted to tell you on Monday, but with Grandma in the hospital it wasn't a good time. Jeremy and I are going to the Valentine's Day Dance this Saturday!" I'm on the verge of a solid happy dance, but Mom looks so tired that her limp smile sucks the "joy" out of my overjoyed.

"Why don't you go tell Grandma about it? She could use a granddaughter pick-me-up."

"Oh," I glance towards to the staircase. "Is she okay?"

"She's starting to lose her hair from the chemotherapy and she's not terribly happy about how she looks."

"But she already got that pixie hair cut in preparation. I thought she was fine with it, trying to 'out-do chemo' and all that."

"Well, there's a big difference between having very short hair, when that's your choice and no hair, when you can't do anything about it. Sometimes what you imagine is going to bother you, isn't what is most upsetting when the time comes." Mom sniffs, her eyes grow misty and cloud over with a faraway look. She strokes my bangs off my forehead and behind my ear like she always does. A wistful smile plays on her lips. "Can you even imagine what you'd look like bald, like a baby, all these gorgeous locks gone?"

I gulp. The thought of losing my hair makes me shudder. I don't want to appear shallow and brag, but my hair is my one defining feature. I may not be a style goddess and I have too many freckles to count, (not to mention my larger than average teeth), but my hair, although frizzy on occasion, has a wild look that I love. It's my security blanket.

"No, actually I can't imagine what that would feel like." It must be killing Grandma. She's so proud of her appearance. A wave of Grandma-love soars through me with such intensity that it brings a lump to my throat and tears to my eyes. "I'll head upstairs right away."

Mom nods, that same wistful smile appears for a moment as she climbs back up the ladder.

As I dash up the stairs, my stomach knots. *What if she looks really horrible? What am I going to say?* Mom says my emotions play across my face like a movie, so I won't be able to hide my immediate reaction. If I try to lie, which I never do well, I'll end up jabbering on and on, making Grandma feel worse and worse. Ugh.

I pause at the top of the staircase, taking a deep, supposedly calming breath.

"Grandma," I call, when I'm near the top of the staircase. "I'm home."

"I'm in my bedroom. Come on in." Her reply is faint.

I gulp. My legs feel heavy, wooden. Hesitation marks every step. Before I even enter my old bedroom, her lilac perfume greets me and soothes my worry. *This is Grandma*, I remind myself. *She's a tough cookie.*

"Hey Grandma."

She's standing in front of my full-length mirror, her back towards me. I'm relieved that she's in day clothes and out of the nightie and fluffy bathrobe that has been her uniform in the hospital. Even sick, Grandma looks chic. Her tiny frame makes her resemble an older actress, like a Grandmother from a TV series or movie. Aging Hollywood Royalty. She's paired her slim fitting dark jeans with a long body-hugging light grey knit sweater. She fusses with a grey and cream coloured tam, pulling it to off angles on her head. The tag on the hat juts out at the back and as I reach for it I notice small dark curls scattered across her shoulders. I stop mid-reach and my arm hovers, like a crooked tree branch.

Involuntarily, I draw in a quick breath, loud enough to pull Grandma's attention away from her primping. Our green eyes meet in the mirror.

"Yes, sweetie," she says. "I am shedding like a dog. Moulting like a moose. Sloughing my outer layer, like a snake." A small smile plays on her face, as she makes a pathetic attempt at humour.

I know she's trying to cover up her true feelings, so that I don't worry, which makes me feel guilty and selfish.

Of course she's not going to show her true emotions. Every time anyone exposes something deep or scary, you cry or have a panic attack.

So this is what people mean when they jokingly say, "It's not all about you." Grandma's cancer scares me, and the thought of losing her terrifies me, but she's the one with cancer, not me. A tingle runs up my spine. I feel weird, like I'm all "one with the universe" like Mom chants about.

Time to buckle up, Julia. It's not all about you.

CHAPTER 29

Bald is beautiful.

I take a deep breath and slide Grandma's tam off her head. Tufts of auburn hair stick to the inside of the small hat.

She grabs my hand and gives me a gentle squeeze that I return. Our eyes find each other again in the mirror and I'm struck by the intense green colour of her eyes, a perfect match to mine. Forever connected. Her eyes become glassy as she unlocks her gaze and looks back at her own reflection. Her scalp resembles a patchwork quilt, but rather than swatches of different fabrics, her head is covered in fuzzy, short hair patches and bald spots. She looks like…a cancer patient.

"What would your Grandpa say?" she asks. Her voice is quiet. She's close to weeping. "He loved my hair."

"He'd say that 'no one can keep my girl down'."

Grandma cocks her head. Her smile is laced with memory. "You're right. I can hear his voice in my head." She chuckles.

"Me too."

She sighs. "So Julia, what do I do with this mess?" She runs her hands over her short black hair. Her head looks so small without her wavy chin-length hair. It's perfectly round, no dips, or bumps or uneven spots.

"Hmmm," I say, a thread of an idea weaving its way through my brain. "I think you need to commit to one look or the other."

"What do you mean?" She looks perplexed as she smooths down a swath of longer locks that stick out from behind her ear.

"I have an idea. Come with me."

I take Grandma's hand and lead her to the bathroom and position her in front of the mirror. Across her narrow shoulders I drape a bath towel and search the tall, skinny cupboards for Dad's old shaving kit. For some reason, it was one of the things Mom couldn't throw out when he died. I find it at the back of the top shelf and when I bring it down I immediately know why she kept it. Dad's cologne fills my nose and wave after wave of Dad-memory hit me. Dad fishing off the dock at the cottage. Dad working in this basement lab at the old house in the middle of the night. Dad passing out Christmas presents in his fake white beard and Santa hat.

His memory calms me as I wrap my fingers around his electric shaver. I place it on the counter and search for the small scissors. The cool metal sends a chill through my hand. *Dad, give me strength.*

I can feel Grandma watching me. When I turn around I have the barber tools in my hands, and when she sees them she just nods her head, like she'd been expecting this.

"I've done this a few times for Annika, and I watched Mom shave Dad's head."

Her eyes grow glassy and she wipes a tear away. "I trust you sweetie. Just take it slow."

I pick up the scissors and carefully trim off the handful of longer strands so that her remaining downy brown fuzz is all the same length. Every hair is now less than an inch long.

"Ready?"

"It's now or never." Grandma closes her eyes. "Tell me when it's done."

Her trust in me pierces my heart, my eyes sting. I slowly exhale and steady my hand. The buzz of the razor zings me with déja vù. I've been in this moment before, with Mom and Dad, but in our old bathroom. Before I was merely a witness to this unwanted caner ritual. Now I've a part to play and it's cruddy. Cruddy ritual. Cruddy cancer.

I place one hand lightly on Grandma's shoulder, an inner strength surging through me. My throat burns as I swallow back my tears.

"I'm starting now," I tell her. She grips the edge of the sink and readies herself. "You are going to be stunning when I'm through with you."

"I'm going to 'rock the bald'?" Her voice trembles. I smile.

"Of course. Bald is beautiful."

Grandma closes her eyes as I place the razor to the nape of her neck. I run the blade up to her crown, in slow perfect lines. I then work on the front and shave from her hairline to the top of her head. Dark fuzz drops to rest on the white towel on her shoulders, reminding me of spots on a Dalmatian.

I find a fresh hand towel and brush off the few feathery cut hairs that lie scattered on her smooth, completely bald head. Bunching up the towel from her shoulders, I collect every last hair. I fold the hand towel into the larger one and stuff the entire bundle out of sight in the bottom of the cupboard. No need for Grandma to see what little was left of her hair.

Stepping back to inspect my work, I am amazed by how truly elegant Grandma looks. Even bald and white knuckling our pale blue sink, she has a regal air.

"Can I look?" Her voice is small, her eyes still closed.

"Yes, and as promised Grandma, you look stunning."

Grandma's eyes blink open and she searches mine for reassurance. "Really?"

"No lies Grandma. Look at yourself."

I step to the side as she squares her shoulders, tosses her head, and looks intently into the medicine cabinet mirror. Gingerly, she traces her fingers from her vanished hairline to her ear, as if tucking wayward hair behind her ear. The thought, "phantom hair," burns on my lips, but I bite my tongue so that it doesn't tumble from my mouth.

"Sweetie, you have done a marvellous job," she says, turning her head from side to side, examining every inch of my hairdressing skills.

I hold up a large oval hand mirror and angle it so she can see the back of her head. She runs her hands across her head and sings the first few bars of Grandpa's favourite song.

"Five foot two, eyes of green," she begins. She changes the first line of "eyes of blue" like Grandpa always did when he sang it to her. I sidle up next to her and we hold hands, our eyes locked on each other.

Together we sing the next line of Grandpa's rendition, "Oh what those five feet could mean."

Our singing grows louder with each note. Mom stumbles into the bathroom, she looks confused, her eyes wide. Her chest rises fast as she sucks in air. She still has the feather duster in her hand.

"Mom," I say, as she clutches the doorframe.

"What's wrong?" Grandma asks and pulls Mom into the washroom with us. She searches Mom's face for the cause of distress.

"I heard this horrible noise and I thought something terrible happened," she says, taking in all of Grandma.

"Hey, not fair," I say, laughing. "Our singing's not that bad."

Mom ignores me and gestures at Grandma with the duster, causing dust bunnies and red feathers to float to the bathroom floor. "What happened to your hair?"

Grandma's eyes grow round and she clamps her lips shut, stifling a chuckle deep in her throat. Mom takes a deep gulp of air, her shoulders sagging and confesses, "I thought you were both crying."

Grandma starts to giggle, which makes me start too. Mom can't fight it. She starts laughing with us and we gather close for a squishy group hug. The edge of the sink digs into my butt.

"What do you think of Julia's handiwork?" Grandma asks. She pulls away and does a 180-degree turn for Mom, bumping into the tub as she slowly spins.

"All the ladies at your book club are going to line up for their turn in Julia's barber chair," Mom says.

"Can you imagine twelve beautifully bald Mad Mavens," Grandma says. "What book would we have to read to make that look work?"

I laugh. "Harry Potter? You could all be the evil Lord Vodemort."

"That might be a nice break from the complete collections of Jane Austen that we're currently slogging through," says Grandma.

"But He Who Must Not Be Named is more gruesomely bald than beautiful," I say.

"Don't argue the details, sweetie. The devil is in there," says Grandma, giving my chin a firm shake.

We shuffle out of the bathroom and Mom strolls into the kitchen.

"I have a slow-cooker ready. I'm going to grab some food and head back downstairs. You two can eat when you get hungry," says Mom.

"I'll come down when I'm done," I offer.

"No rush."

"So," I say to Grandma, once I can no longer hear Mom's footsteps on the stairs. "Jeremy asked me to the Valentine's Day dance."

"Jeremy. The one who abandoned you at the ski hill and to make amends, brought you home drunk as a skunk?"

"Well yes, but he's totally made up for all that and you were the one who said he looked like Grandpa."

"What? I never said that."

"Yes, you did—when you fell in the bedroom."

"Well," she says, smoothing down her sweater and lifting her chin. "Clearly I was delusional."

She drags a stool to the kitchen counter as I ladle out the beef stew. Her stare bores into me, as if she's attempting to read my mind. Even with their 50-year difference, Grandma and Annika have a lot in common. Finally she relents. Sighing, she stirs her bowl of stew.

"Alright, share the details," she says.

If you had asked me two months ago if I would share girl talk with my Grandma, I would've booked you a room on a Psych Ward. But now, it seems natural and normal. I don't know how we got along without Grandma before she moved in. All I know is that I don't want to get along without her ever again.

I want Grandma with us forever.

CHAPTER 30

"Is this what love is supposed to be?"

"When is he supposed to arrive?" Grandma asks, as she passes me a dish to dry.

"He said 7:00, and then everyone's heading to Madison's house for pizza and to get ready," I reply.

"Will Annika be there, too? We haven't seen much of her lately."

"Uhm, I, I don't think so."

"That surprises me." She stops washing dishes and stares at me, giving me what Grandpa called her "Green-Eye Gaze." It's like a visual truth serum. No one is immune to her intense scrutiny. She can get anyone to spill their beans.

"We sort of had a disagreement."

"That's a shame. Annika's such a thoughtful girl and you've been friends for so long. More like sisters, your mom and I used to say."

It's impossible for me to reply. I have a lump in my throat the size of Texas and it's crushing my voice box. All week I've tried to talk to her. I've texted. I've called her house. I've written notes and slid them into the crack of her locker door—

and no response. I'm scared I've lost her. Forever. Closing my eyes, I force my tears to stay in my sockets and take a deep breath. Slowly I exhale, willing my lip quiver to cease. Calmer, I reach for a pot to dry. As I grasp it, Grandma squeezes my hand. Her rubber-gloved fingers leave soap bubbles on mine. In silence we finish up the day's dishes.

"And you really have no idea what your costumes are?" Grandma asks, as she pulls the stopper from the drain.

"None. He didn't let one clue fly, and you know I don't like to be surprised."

"No, sweetie, you never did. Keeping you out from under the Christmas tree was nearly impossible when you were younger."

"Remember how Dad had to hide them at work? He said his office looked like a department store leading up to Christmas."

Grandma grabs my hand again and squeezes.

"Your dad would've done anything for you. He'd be so proud of the young lady you're growing into."

But would he? What would he think of my fight with Annika? And getting drunk? The biggest question by far is what would Dad think of Jeremy? The memory of my spine slamming into Jeremy's car door handle leaps to mind. No way would he be okay with that.

"I have to get ready, Grandma," I say, and head to my room.

I close the door with care and sit on the edge of the sofa bed. The cold metal frame digs into the back of my thighs. My oak tree taps against my window, as if Dad's saying, "I'm here."

As I stare into the black night, the tears I kept in place in the kitchen spill down my cheeks. I love Jeremy. I do. But there is something so angry in him. I've seen a glimpse and it terrified me.

But then he went and tattooed his arm for me. And he keeps talking about making it permanent, which is a huge thing to do for someone. And all those roses. That was a florist shop full of sorry. But then he totally ignores the fact that my grandma has cancer. He's never once asked about her. Not once. Jeremy confuses me and excites me at the same time.

Is this what love is supposed to be?

I wipe my wet face on my sleeve and lay back, my legs over the side of the bed and stare at my flaking stipple ceiling. I wish I could talk to Annika. Maybe I can talk to her at the dance tonight. Sitting up, I sigh deeply.

My alarm clock reads 6:45. I check my purse for my essentials: Dad's grey button, my Xanax, and Mom's $40 emergency cash. Better hurry.

Can't be late for Jeremy.

CHAPTER 31

Signs, and boobs, and thigh-high boots. Oh my.

"Curfew is 1:00 tonight. No later," Mom reminds me as we walk across the apartment to the staircase.

"Okay," I say.

She hugs me and as I draw away she tightens her grip.

"Uhm, Mom I sort of can't breathe." Her hug lessens, but she doesn't detach.

"I just," she pauses. "I just want you to know how much I love you—we love you—your Grandma and I. Even if it hasn't seemed like it lately, I'm here for you—we're here for you. So if anything—" She draws away to look at me. I think she's trying out her Grandma-like spidey senses again. They still aren't working.

"No. Mom. I'm fine. Really."

"Okay, but we're here. I'm here."

But is she really? What I really want to talk about is Dad. What would she do if I said that to her? Demanded she tell me what Dad would think of my going to a dance with a boy for the first time. Mom's face is drawn, grey circles her eyes. If I uttered the word Dad, she'd crumple. Worry lines crisscross her forehead and crevasse deep between her eyes. She gently squeezes my hand.

"Julia? Did you hear me? We're here—"

"Yes I know. I gotta go."

"I love you, Jules."

"I love you too, Mom."

I can feel her watching me as I walk down the stairs.

"Have fun!" she calls to me.

"Thanks, see you later." I enter the bookstore, hoping to dart across the shop without running into Grandma.

"Grandma!" I screech, as she pops out from behind the mystery novel stack. My fight or flight instincts take control of my brain and I leap to the side, knocking over Laura Ingalls Wilder.

"Ready for the big dance?" she asks.

"Yes." Grandma helps me stand up Laura, which is difficult as I squashed her legs when I sent her sailing into the cash desk. "Poor prairie girl. She just keeps getting demolished. We had a mom with a toddler in yesterday and that little girl dragged Ms. Wilder around half the store." She rubs a black dust smudge from the cutout's forehead.

Grandma's mood quickly lifted since her moment of despair when I shaved her head. I expected her to be more depressed and scared, but her reaction has been just the opposite. If you look beyond the headscarf and her thinness, she actually looks healthy. And happy.

"Grandma, I have a strange question."

"Then I may have a strange answer," she replies with a chuckle.

"It's just...I'm not sure what I really want to ask, or how to ask it—" I trip over my words and have to stop and start over. "It's just that you seem so happy and you act like you're not sick at all."

"That sounds about right."

"Oh." I'm surprised by her easy agreement, but I'm still concerned. "But Grandma, you *are* sick."

"Well, I wouldn't recommend getting cancer to anyone." She smiles and tweaks my chin.

"Grandma I need you to be serious for a second."

"Okay."

"Are you hiding your true feelings because of me? Because you don't need to, I can handle it."

Grandma guides me behind the counter. We sit on the tall stools and face each other. She holds my hand in hers.

"Sweetie, I've always known that you are far stronger than you realize. You always have been. You get that inner strength from your father. Nothing could fluster him."

"Really?" His unflappable attitude was legendary, so I know this is true, but I love hearing stories about him. I want Grandma to keep talking.

"Oh my, yes. Your Grandpa used to say that your dad had shoulders as wide as Niagara Falls. And it was true. Your mom found a man as wonderful as your grandfather and we were proud to have him as our son-in-law." She smiles and then continues. "Do you remember the fire in his lab at the house when all his brand new equipment melted?"

Grandma laughs, although her face remains smooth, only tiny crowfeet appear around her eyes and teensy faint lines are barely visible on her forehead. Grandma's decided to stop further Botox treatments even though her face has aged more in the past two weeks than in the past five years. Those new wrinkles haven't bothered her at all. She says they're a badge of honour and a sign she's making small victories over the cancer.

"How could I forget? The smell of melted plastic oozed into every inch of the house."

"He was a picture of calm as he sprayed down his microscope and that other odd device. What was that called?"

"It was a microplate sealer. He used it to make slides of his specimens." After he put the fire out, both tools were just lumps of fused metal and glass. "He was more upset that we were all in the house when it happened than his destroyed lab."

Grandma nods her head in agreement and squeezes my hand.

"Julia, I know you have the same grit that your father had and you can deal with the toughest of what life throws your way. It's not always going to be easy and you will occasionally stumble and even fall, but you've got the pluck to stand back up."

"Thanks Grandma." She hugs me close. Have I really got that "pluck?" Am I really as strong as my dad? I'm not 100% sure, but I think I'm getting there. I ask one final question. "So you're really feeling okay?"

She pulls away from me, holding my face in her hands and looks directly into my eyes.

"Sweetie, at the end of every day I feel like I've run a marathon. I'm tired, a little nauseous, but thankful that I'm still here to run another marathon the next day. Losing my hair was a shock, but I'm not a moper by nature. I've had my little cry and now I have to make the best of it and carry on. So yes, I'm feeling okay."

"Good."

"Any other questions? Grandma's chat line is still open."

"I do have one other, but it's not really a question…"

"Well, give it a go. What is your concern?"

"It's Mom. I really want to talk to her about Dad, just like you and I did right now. I want us to talk about all the good times and the funny stories."

"I know you do."

"I'm scared if we stop talking about him, we'll forget him. I'll forget him."

"My dear, you will never forget your father. He was far too special to be erased from your memory."

"But how do I get Mom to start talking about him? Do I just keep bringing him up in conversation and force her to talk? Isn't that mean?"

"Is it mean to want to talk about someone who meant the world to both you and your mom? What do you think?"

"Not when you put it that way, but Grandma you make it sound so easy."

"Oh, sweetie it will be far from easy. It will be damn hard. Most things worth their weight are hard to accomplish. It may feel like we're chipping through a marble slab to get your mom to open up about Richard, but don't you think it will be worth it? To see your mom's face brighten again? To be able to share all the wonderful stories about your father over dinner or a game of cards?"

"Of course."

"And not to worry. I'm working on her, too. I even promised to go to her yoga class."

I laugh, picturing Grandma in mountain pose on the community club floor.

"Now that is huge."

I give her a tight hug and only pull away because my phone vibrates in my pocket. I check the display as I slip off my stool.

"That's Jeremy," I say.

"Have fun tonight," she says, following me to the back door. "And Julia, don't do anything that doesn't feel right. Stay true to yourself."

Am I hearing things or is by Grandma alluding to sex? Or drinking? Or my judgement in guys? Or something else?

"Stay true to myself," I repeat her words and laugh. "You sound like a bible thumper."

"What I mean is to listen to your gut and follow your instincts. If you're not sure about something or someone, simply ask yourself is this what Julia Collins really wants? Is this who Julia Collins really is?"

"I think you and yoga are going to be a natural fit."

"Julia, did you—" I interrupt Grandma, worried she may launch into an exceedingly long lecture and Jeremy is waiting.

"I'll be fine," I say.

"Are you sure?"

"Trust me. Anyways, I've always got Dad with me." I pull out my button from my purse and she smiles.

"And you always have us. Just a phone call away," she gives me a quick hug.

"Bye Grandma."

I step into the cold evening and pull my scarf tighter to block the biting wind. At least it isn't snowing.

"Hey," I say to Jeremy, tossing my purse in the back seat.

"Just a sec," he says, texting.

I strum my fingers on my leg and look back at the bookstore. Mom has joined Grandma at the back door window. I give them a little wave. They both wave back. Neither smiles. They look displeased.

"We should go," I say. Who knows what those two will do if we sit here much longer.

"Crap."

"Pardon?"

"Sorry, not you, I'm trying to get something for tonight. Something to make your surprise perfect."

"I'm sure whatever you planned will be great, Jeremy. It doesn't have to be perfect."

"Yes it does. When you see what I—" he stops and grins. He glances into the back seat to where two plastic Malabar's bags hang, hiding our costumes. "Hey, you almost got me there. You just have to be patient."

We race out of the parking lot, towards Madison's house. It's another poorly laid out McMansion, similar in design to Jeremy's. They have a turret too—must have been a sale on Castle architecture plans. It's been five years since I've been in her house, so I'm curious to see what atrocious artwork her mom has on display now. Her mom thinks she is an art connoisseur, and I remember she hung this papier-mâché monstrosity in the dining room. Apparently the artist used real eggplant and pumpkin to add to the overall appeal. If the sun shone on it too long, a slight rotten stench would waft through the room. Talk about an appetite suppressant. But that was a long time ago. Maybe she's moved onto watermelon and banana collages.

If I'm completely honest I'm also nervous about going to her house. For sure Hannah will have her be-atchness shined to a glistening perfection. She'll be sure to point out all the ways I fail—at everything. Hopefully Chloe will be there. She offsets Hannah's evil mojo.

Madison's long circular driveway is packed with cars. Harley's SUV is right outside the front door. "What's he doing here?" Jeremy asks, staring at a sliver BMW parked behind Harley. It looks like Tyler's car. My breath quickens. Is Annika here?

"Tyler? Why is that a problem?"

"He's been asking Harley a bunch of really weird questions about us."

"Why?"

"I don't know, but I'm going to find out."

"I'm sure it's nothing. Please don't get angry."

He glares at me and then throws his car into reverse. My hands immediately go clammy as I search my purse for Dad's button. No room for his typical OPAP, he parallel parks behind Harley and jumps from the car. He hurries to the beamer, muttering under his breath. Cupping his hands around his eyes he peers into the driver's side window. I stay beside Jeremy's car and focus on breathing and not freaking out. Hyperventilating right now is not an option, and I really, really would like to avoid another Xanax emergency. How does he get so furious, so quickly?

"Nope. Not his."

"How do you know?"

"There's a Minnie Mouse bobblehead figurine on the dashboard. It's Chloe's car."

"I guess everyone has a silver beamer but me." I gulp, trying to make a joke, trying to calm him down. It sounds lame. I hope he didn't hear my voice tremble.

"Let's go." He walks past me to his car and grabs our costumes, leading us to Madison's front door, which he opens without knocking. Music thumps at us as we stack our boots near the twelve or so pairs that are piled on a large Persian rug near the mirrored doors of the closet.

Madison's foyer is not quite as grand as Jeremy's. It's still impressive, but the vaulted ceiling is only fifteen feet high, rather than twenty and there isn't a square of marble tile in sight. I scan the pristine white walls, unable to draw my eyes from the eight-foot tall by four-foot wide painting that faces us. Madison's mom has moved on from fruit and vegetable based art, which I guess is a good thing. This artist applied black and grey oils in long jagged lines, some hair-strand thin and others as wide as a ruler. Crimson red splatters cover the middle section of the painting. Something, maybe a hunting knife, was used to slash three great arcs across the entire canvas: two running the length of the painting on the outside of the red centre and one that dissects the middle. Not exactly the warm welcome you expect when you enter a home.

I check my hair in the mirror, slowly releasing my breath. I can do this.

"You look gorgeous," Jeremy says, all traces of his rage in the driveway have vanished. "Come on."

He takes my hand and we walk across the dark mahogany hardwoods to the living room. Kids in costumes are everywhere. Tarzan and Jane are standing in front of the white granite fireplace, Cleopatra and Mark Antony are sitting at the dining room table, and a "his and her" bacon and eggs are making out on the leather sofa.

"Hey look," I say to Jeremy, pointing to the kissing couple, "Who knew breakfast foods could be romantic?"

"Pathetic. Wait 'til you see our costumes," he says.

Beyond Tarzan and Jane, Hannah is pinning a long white veil to the back of Madison's hair. Her shining blonde hair falls in long loose curls around her shoulders and she's wearing a strapless rhinestone encrusted bridal dress that hugs every curve. Her entire body sparkles. She looks stunning. Her mother, in addition to having atrocious taste in art, owns the largest bridal salon in the city. She takes Madison to New York on numerous buying trips every year.

I hope Jeremy has picked out something equally elegant for me.

"Hey!" Harley appears from the kitchen, in a tuxedo, with a beer in his hand. He hands it to Jeremy. "I'll grab another. Julia, can I get one for you?"

"No thanks," I say, very aware that Madison and Hannah have stopped their fussing and are staring at us. "Not yet," I add.

"Madison, looking gorgeous," Jeremy says as he gives her a full body appraisal. "Where can Julia and I get changed?"

"You can have my brother's room and Julia can take my bedroom. You remember where my bedroom is, don't you Jeremy?" Madison's voice suggests that would be impossible to forget.

"Hey, I'm still in the room," I say, trying to sound like their exchange doesn't bother me. I fail.

"How cute," Hannah says, wriggling closer in a too-tight iridescent turquoise mermaid costume. Her face shimmers with silver glitter. "She's jealous."

"No, I—" I say, my face scorching.

"Really no need to be concerned, Julia. I'm long past Jerem—The Third," Madison says.

"And I picked you, so don't worry," Jeremy says, grabbing my hand and guiding me down the hallway. "Let's get changed."

We stop outside Madison's bedroom and he passes me my costume bag.

"When you're ready, wait for me here," he says, pecking me quickly on the cheek.

"Okay."

I close Madison's door, setting the lock. My toes sink deep into the white plush wall to wall carpet. Her room has changed since seventh grade. Gone is the loft bed and in its place is a king-size bed with a beaded white leather headboard. The pale pink comforter has been replaced with a luxurious bright white duvet with silver piping. Solid-coloured throw pillows of silver and lilac are strewn artfully against the headboard. Madison has none of her mother's poor taste. The entire look is exquisite. And probably represents a whole month of our bookstore profits.

I lay the costume bag across the sleek black wooden chair that sits in front of her desk and unzip it, revealing a black pin-striped suit with a white tie. The shoulder strap of a Gatling gun loops around the hanger. We're dressing as 1920's style gangsters. I try to push down my disappointment and not think of how incredible Madison looked in that wedding dress.

Someone pounds on the door.

"Hey, Julia," Jeremy calls. His voice is muffled. "We got the wrong bags. You have my costume."

"Oh, oh," I call, my words jumble as I open Madison's door as hope leaps deep in my chest. Maybe my costume is better than I thought.

Jeremy is standing in a white tank undershirt. The tattoo on his arm seems to glow.

"You must've thought that was a pretty crazy costume."

"Yeah, I uh—yeah, I did. Wild West. Blam-Blam." I pretend to shoot a gun. I sound like an eight-year-old.

"Is everything okay?" he asks as we exchange our costumes.

"Yes. Yes, of course. Everything's fine. Just fine."

"Alright," he says, and hesitates, like he doesn't quite believe me. "Don't take too long. I can't wait to see you, Beautiful."

He takes a step and turns back.

"Julia, I—I wanted to tell you how much it means to me that you're here with me tonight. Especially after…what I did. After my dad…" His voice trails off.

"Oh, I—"

"You just need to know, it means everything to me. No one's ever been there for me like you. No one's ever meant so much to me."

He pulls me to him, gently and slowly he lowers his mouth to mine. His kiss is feather light. Tender.

"I love you, Julia. I need you," he says, his voice is deeper and hoarse. *Is he about to cry?* He turns away too fast for me to search his eyes for tears. "Don't be too long."

Jeremy saunters down the hall and disappears into a bedroom. I close Madison's door, locking it again.

Hands shaking, I tear off the thin plastic Malabar's bag. Staring back at me is a black satin and very small-skirted costume. The bodice is actually an old-fashioned corset rimmed with white satin along the bustline. A shiny white necktie and black fedora hat complete the outfit. I lift the tag that is fastened to the hanger. It reads, "Sexy Bonnie." Of course. We're going as Bonnie and Clyde.

It's bad enough that we're going as such a predictable couple, but a sexy costume? How am I going to pull this off? What would Jeremy say if I refused to wear it? He'd be crushed for sure. He is so excited about this. I plop onto Madison's bed as a wave of disappointment surges over me. Madison looks stunning and elegant and incredible and I am going to look like…what?

I take a deep breath, trying one of Mom's yoga breaths. I can do this for him. Maybe it won't be so bad.

Slipping out of my clothes, I step into the gangster costume. Which is the misnomer of the century—I mean how could anyone shoot up the Wild West dressed in a slippery miniskirt? A nervous giggle bubbles out of me as I spin to face myself in Madison's mirror.

"Wow." I look—hot, although slightly trashy. My breasts look like they are attempting to flee out the top of the corset. Thank goodness I got dressed here. Mom and Grandma would never let me leave the house looking like this. I pull the tie over my head and perch the hat on my head. My curls cascade down my shoulders.

"Julia," Jeremy calls, through the door. "Are you almost done in there?"

"No," I say, my voice a whisper. Louder I reply, "I just need a few more minutes." I fuss with my hair, first pulling it over one shoulder and then the other. I try stuffing it all under the hat, but large sections keep sliding free.

Jeremy hammers on the door.

"What is taking so long?" he asks.

"Jeremy, I'm not sure about this outfit. It's very," I search for the right word. I don't want to insult him, but I feel half naked. "Revealing."

"I'm sure you look gorgeous. Let me see. Please."

I let my hair fall naturally and stick the hat back on. Taking a deep breath, I open the door.

"Oh my God. You look better than I imagined."

He scoops me into his arms and his mouth crashes down on mine. Unprepared for his wild kiss, I am breathless. I push back, gasping for air.

"Sorry, Beautiful. You're irresistible."

"It's okay. Good thing I don't dress like this every day."

"I think I could get used to it." He pulls his white fedora low on his forehead, his grey eyes dark with desire. "Let's go downstairs. I want everyone to see me with the hottest girl in the room."

"Oh, I don't know."

"Trust me. Your body looks fantastic."

"Thanks, but this skirt—it's so short. I don't even think I can sit down." I flatten it against my legs, willing it to somehow become longer.

"Then stand."

"I—I think I look cheap," I say in a rush, blurting out my worst fear. I know he's all about appearances and no way would he want me looking trashy.

He pulls me to the mirror. "Look at yourself. You are gorgeous."

I examine his face. He doesn't look like he's lying. In fact his eyes can't stop travelling across the reflection of my body.

"Jeremy," I say, his compliments embarrass me, yet make me feel wanted, sexy. "I didn't think you'd like me looking like this."

"Hey, this is between us," he pulls me away from the mirror and holds me close, his gaze intense. "I got this for you, because I knew you could pull it off. When you're with me, you'll never look anything but classy. You don't have to worry about anything. Together we are a killer couple. Trust me."

Jeremy's confidence is hard to deny. I close my eyes and let out a long sigh.

"Okay. Let's go."

He steps into the hallway and picks up a pair of tall black leather boots.

"I forgot these in the car. They complete the outfit."

Thigh high boots. You've got to be kidding. I struggle into them and take one wobbly step.

"I am going to kill myself in these."

"Then just stay next to me," Jeremy says, linking his arm through mine. He leads me down the hallway. I tug up my bodice. *Boobs, please stay put.*

"Ho-ly," says Harley as we enter the living room. His eyes are huge as he stares at me. His obvious appraisal causes my temperature to shoot through the roof. Hannah rolls her eyes. I can't hear her words, but I can read her lips. I'm pretty sure she didn't say "chuck sir."

"Wow, Julia," says Madison.

"I picked out the costumes," Jeremy says, "We're Bonnie and Clyde." He sounds as proud as if he sewed them himself.

"Oh, that explains it," Madison says. I can tell she's fighting hard not to laugh.

"Are you even going to be able to sit in that?" Hannah asks. She then stage whispers in Madison's ear. "Total WT." White Trash. *Ouch.*

I blush hard, almost painfully. This is a disaster.

Chloe is also staring at me. When our eyes meet, she looks away. *She looks embarrassed for me.*

Jeremy looks at his phone and frowns.

"Everything okay?" I ask.

"It will be," he replies, and pats me on the butt.

"Jeremy," I say, swatting at his hand. I absolutely hate it when he does that. He smirks in response.

"Want a drink?" Jeremy asks.

"No thank you." I smooth the satin skirt again and take a step behind the sofa in a feeble attempt to hide myself.

"Are you sure? You look a little...jittery," asks Harley. *A little jittery?* It feels like my legs are going to completely collapse.

"Okay. Maybe just a small one," I say, folding my hands in front of me to stop them from shaking. After the debacle at the creek, I never thought I would have another drink, but maybe it will calm my nerves. It is a sedative and booze must be called liquid courage for a reason, right?

And I'm going to need vats of courage if I'm going to make it to the dance like this.

Jeremy and Harley disappear in the kitchen. Madison and Hannah return to their last minute makeup touches and Chloe heads for the front door. I slip behind a tall leafy plant in the corner of the living room to hide from view. Instinctively I pat my hip, looking for my pocket and Dad's button. Of course it's in my purse.

"Why would Sexy Bonnie need pockets anyway? She's only supposed to rob her way across the Midwest, running from the law," I mutter. "Totally lame gangster chick outfit."

I guess I'm on my own. For now.

CHAPTER 32

Seek, but you might not find

We pull up to the school. Jeremy parks as usual—OPAP. My vision spins.

"Jeremy, I shouldn't have had that drink." No way do I want another creek-like drunk fest.

"Don't worry about it. You'll be fine. I'll take care of you," he says, grasping my hand.

"Okay." I move to open the door, but he holds tight to my hand. I turn and face him. He looks intense.

"You know, Julia, my mom would never let my dad pick out anything for her. Not a sweater, not one Christmas present, not even her engagement ring. She had to control everything. Nothing he did was good enough. Now my dad…" his voice grows quiet. "Well you know."

"This costume really means that much to you?"

"Yeah, I guess it does." I squeeze his hand and he smiles. "Let's go."

We walk slowly through the snow towards the school doors. I'm not sure what's making me wobble more, the four-inch heels or the alcohol. Harley, Madison, Hannah and her newest boyfriend, Sam, are waiting for us between the doors.

"The party is now on!" Harley says. Jeremy hoots in response. I pull my jacket tighter as we follow the surging music down the hallway.

"Wait up!" Hannah calls, her nasal whine as irritating as usual. She's fallen behind since she can hardly walk in her fish tail. Sam is dressed as a pirate and he lifts Hannah with little effort, slinging her over his shoulder. She flounders upside down, her fin flapping close to his face.

"Stop it! You're messing up my hair!" Hannah's carefully coifed hair sways wildly as she pounds her fists on his butt. What would Kimmie, her housekeeper, say? I stifle a giggle. No point redirecting Hannah's wrath my way.

"Hey! Quit it, or I'll drop you on your Mer-head," Sam says. Hannah stops beating him but continues to complain.

Music reverberates through my chest as we turn the last corner to the gym. Pink and purple heart-shaped balloons are tied together to form an archway over the main entrance to the gymnasium. Faux red rose petals cover the ticket table, where Chloe is sitting. She gives me a tentative wave and smile. I smile back as we pass her our tickets.

"Do you want to use our coat check? All proceeds go toward Winnipeg Harvest," Chloe asks as she hands me a ballot for the Most Romantic Couple Contest.

"Sure," I say, reluctantly handing her my coat. Without it I feel semi-nude. And cold. Goosebumps cover my arms. As Jeremy stuffs the coat check tags into his pocket, his phone pings.

"I'll be right back," Jeremy says, texting as he walks back down the hallway.

"Why aren't you in costume?" I ask. Chloe's short black hair is slicked back and the only makeup she has on is heavy black mascara.

"I've got it on under this," she tugs at the collar of her grey hoodie and I see a swath of green fabric underneath. "I left Madison's early to help run the table. A few more minutes and I'll be in there for the rest of the night." She points to the gym with a big grin.

"Ready?" Jeremy asks, linking his arm in mine. I can feel the phone in his pocket vibrate.

"Is everything alright?"

"Of course, why?"

"Your phone, it keeps buzzing. I wondered—never mind."

We follow Han Solo and Princess Leia under the balloon archway into the music thumping, strobe light pounding Valentine's dance. Every few feet or so balloon hearts hang from the ceiling. A huge balloon chandelier hangs in the middle of the gymnasium.

I yell over the live band to Jeremy, "The decorating committee sure went all out."

"Yeah, it's pretty cool. Do you want a soft drink or something?" he asks.

"Sure. Whatever they have is fine."

We find one of the few remaining empty tables along the edge of the dance floor, close to the door.

"Wait here," he says.

I watch Jeremy skirt the array of costumed kids jumping, gyrating, and thrashing to the music on the packed dance floor. He stops to talk to a guy I don't recognize at the beverage table at the far side of the gym. Dancers block most of my view, but

I can see they are both laughing hysterically. I scan the room looking for Annika. *Is she even coming tonight?*

Three green-faced aliens with painted green rubber bald caps are doing a slow motion robot dance. It's incredible. When one stops, he taps the other one, and that alien continues. A girl alien races by me, her short skirt flaps as she squeezes through the other dancers and joins them. Everyone moves away from the group, making a large circle around them, blocking my view. I stand up to see what they're doing and crash into Madison. The pink plastic cup she's carrying goes flying, her white sheer veil slips forward, covering her face as she stumbles and nearly falls.

"Oh my God! Are you blind on top of being a total spaz?" She screams at me, pushing her veil back.

"Sorry I didn't see you." I'm flustered by her yelling and my hands begin to shake. "Did your drink splash on you?"

She looks down the front of her white bridal gown and I look at the back of her dress, scouring it for stains. The back cuts down low, adding another element of glamour.

"You are so lucky. Do you know how much this retails for?" Madison says, sounding almost disappointed not to have found a mark. I assume this is a rhetorical question so I don't answer.

"So, where's the groom?" I ask, trying to redirect her attention from her haute couture gown. I scan the gym, looking for Harley.

"He's getting us more mix."

"You're drinking at the dance? What if the teachers find out?"

"Oh my God. How did you ever snag Jeremy?" Her voice matches the sneer on her face. I didn't wreck her gown. Why is she so angry with me?

"I didn't snag anyone."

Madison stares at me. Here eyebrows narrow. Her grimace slinks into a cat-like grin—a cat that has just trapped its prey. Something tells me I'm her prey.

"You really have no idea, do you?" she asks.

"What are you talking about?"

"The Third—" she begins.

"Did you miss me?" Harley says, stumbling into Madison. Liquid splashes over the side of his cup.

Madison jumps back, scowling. "Careful!"

"Whoa. Chill babe," Harley says. A mellow smile plasters his face. Madison searches her dress.

"Idiot," she mutters.

"What?" Harley asks, just as the electric guitar player wails into a riff that echoes through the gymnasium.

"Just come," she says, pulling Harley after her. They exit out the side door, presumably to mix their drinks.

I perch on the edge of the chair and tug at my skirt. Every time I sit down it slinks too far up my thighs. I pull my phone out of my purse and text Annika.

JULES: Hey. Are u coming to the dance? I'm here.

I stare at the display, willing her to respond.

JULES: I'm really sorry. Please don't hate me forever.

Nothing.

"Here you go," Jeremy says returning with two red plastic cups.

"Thanks." I place mine on the table.

"Aren't you going to take a sip?"

"In a while. Do you want to dance?"

"I—" he doesn't finish. He pulls out his phone.

"I'll be right back." He marches away before I can answer.

"No worries. I'll just wait here." I mumble, staring out at the dancers. More and more kids have packed the gym. In the middle of the crowd, I see Annika dancing.

I whisper her name and wave, but she doesn't see me.

She's with Tyler and they look like they've time warped here from somewhere in the future. They could be dead ringers for Pris and Roy from *Blade Runner*—one of Annika's favourite movies. Annika tilts her now bleach-blonde head to the side and does a little curtsey to him, her hands pulling at her all-in-one leather top and short-short outfit as if she wore a skirt. She's attached this black gauze-like material along her neckline and down the arms. Over it all she's thrown a tattered leopard print, thigh-length coat. I especially like the leg warmers and garter belt. The frayed black stockings are such a good replica, they could be from the movie. Tyler dyed his hair to match Annika's and it's shorter and spiked. He's wearing black leather pants and a silver-studded leather jacket. Just like Pris, Annika's painted black racoon eyes across her own. It adds an element of otherworldliness. I find it a bit disturbing but then she smiles at Tyler and she resembles more of her Annika self.

My heart beats hard in my chest.

Oh my God.

I miss her.

That's it. This is crazy. I am going to talk to her. I take two hurried steps in my ridiculously high-heeled boots and wobble precariously.

"Whoa, where are you going?" Jeremy asks, steadying me by the elbow.

I can't tell him I want Annika back. I know he'd get angry. "I want to dance."

"Okay. Let's go."

Jeremy takes my hand and leads me to the edge of the dance floor. We're still too far from her to make eye contact. Somehow I have to get her attention without Jeremy noticing and then talk to her—again while keeping Jeremy clueless.

The song ends before we start dancing and the DJ takes over to give the band a break. A slow beat begins. The dance floor empties and we're able to weave between the remaining dancers to the middle of the gym. Jeremy stops directly beneath the balloon chandelier. I can't see Annika anywhere.

He places his hands on my hips and I reach up to his shoulders, lacing my fingers together behind his neck. We find the rhythm of the music and with each slow turn we're drawn closer to each other until our bodies are moulded together. In these heels, I'm only a few inches shorter than him and each time my eyes meet his he gives me a grin that makes my whole body tremble. I'm locked in his stare, his gaze holding fast. My breathing quickens. My legs slow. We dance like this for bar after bar until Jeremy bends into me, one hand high up my back. He presses me into him and…kisses me. For a moment, I'm embarrassed. The whole school is here, and they can see us. But it feels so good. *Who cares what anyone thinks.* I kiss him back. Hard. My heartbeat pounds in my ears and I can feel it thumping through me, faster and faster. Growing dizzy, I have to pull away, panting to catch my breath.

The song ends and I remain in his arms, staring into his eyes.

"Now that was steamy," says Harley.

Harley and Madison must've joined us on the dance floor during the song, but I was too focused on Jeremy to notice. Okay I was too focused on kissing Jeremy to notice— huge difference.

"Mr. Jacobs was on his way over to break you two up," says Harley, his eyes sparkling.

I blush fast and hot. So much for not caring what everybody else thinks. I'm still searching my groggy brain for a witty comeback when a hard beat rap song echoes out of the speakers. Tyler sprints past us to the centre of the dance floor. I search the crowd for Annika.

"You totally gotta' see this," Harley says pointing after Tyler. "You know his mom runs a dance studio, right?"

Annika appears directly across from me to watch him dance. Tyler joins the aliens and a Mr. and Mrs. Claus and they take turns showing off their B-Boy moves. He tosses his leather jacket to Annika, throws himself to the floor, spins on his head and rolls down to his shoulders. He flips back to his stomach then somehow pushes off the floor, landing effortlessly on his feet. Annika's clapping to the music, a smile of complete joy on her futuristic-looking face. I wave at her again. This time I catch her attention. Her mouth slides into a complete "o." Her clapping ceases. She gives me a tiny wave, mutters something, and then she's blocked from view as more kids join Tyler on the dance floor.

The DJ seamlessly blends the end of the song into Michael Jackson's "Thriller". The Thriller video is projected on the wall above the bleachers. Kids flood the floor and Jeremy and I attempt the Thriller line dance. A couple dressed as John Lennon and Yoko Ono seem to have memorized it, but I'm hopeless.

I bash into Jeremy after the first direction change. "I have to get these boots off before I break my neck."

We step out of the throng of kids and I shuffle to our table, tossing my boots underneath. I take a sip of my soda, frowning at the bitter aftertaste. *Did Jeremy put booze in it?* I push it across the table. In bare feet, I race back to Jeremy and we squeeze back to where Annika and Tyler do a respectable Michael Jackson imitation. I step on Jeremy's feet four times, turn into him twice, and punch him once in the ribs. For me this is success. The music ends, and we fall into each other, panting for air.

"I wasn't sure I was going to get out of that alive," says Jeremy.

"Was I really that horrible?"

"Don't worry about it. It isn't your dancing I'm interested in. You have other talents."

"Jeremy," I begin, wanting to ask him if he's okay, but he kisses me and my words evaporate as I melt into his chest. He pulls me close. Our hips mould into each other. He moans.

Someone taps on my shoulder. Reluctantly, I pull away from Jeremy. He sways into me and I stumble back under his weight.

"Break it up lovebirds," Harley says. "You're gonna' get kicked out for sure."

I look around the gym and notice Mr. Jacobs and Mr. Benoit staring at us.

"Let's go vote, they're going to count the ballots soon," I say. Maybe I can find Annika and force her to talk to me—accept my apology.

"Okay, but we won't be here that long."

"Why?" I ask, as I grab my boots from under the table. Jeremy holds me steady as I slip them on.

"Your next surprise. It's on its way."

Crap. The other surprise.

CHAPTER 33

Asshats do not a good friend make

I drop my ballot into the box, hoping Annika and Tyler win the contest. In tiny steps I walk to the end of the hall to the trophy case. Jeremy's taking forever in the washroom, and I couldn't stay back there waiting for him. It felt like everyone was staring at me.

I rest one hand on the glass case to steady myself.

"Hey, Julia."

I spin too fast for my high heels and stumble into Annika, twisting my ankle in the process. She grabs me before I hit the ground.

"Are you okay?" she asks.

"Yes, I'm fine. Sorry about that. These boots are insane." I flex my foot and wince. Pain zings through my foot as I put a bit of pressure on it. "Youch."

"You need to put some ice on it."

"I'll be fine. I just need to rid myself of these stupid boots."

"They sure are…tall." Annika's eyes widen as she looks at me—at all of me. I feel more naked than ever. "Who are you supposed to be?" she asks.

Feeling defensive, my whole body tenses. I try to keep the snark out of my voice. "I am 'supposed to be' Clyde's Bonnie."

"Oh."

"And who are you supposed to be?" Why is my snark on overdrive?

"Pris, from—" she begins, but I interrupt her.

"I know. *Blade Runner.* I knew who you were, I was just—"

"Trying to make me feel bad? Taking lessons from your new pals?"

"No, that's not what I was going to say! It's only—I felt— this costume—" I stutter to a stop, my arms run up and down my sides, like a gimp game show host, trying to show the best features of the lamest prize in TV history. I stumble backwards into the display case. My ankle rolls. These boots have to go. I unzip the boot on my good foot first and yank it off. Much slower I unzip the other, wincing as I ease my ankle free.

I can feel Annika watching me with her Pris racoon eyes. *Is she looking for the inner secret of me?*

"That costume is ridiculous. What were you thinking?"

I hang my head.

"It was Jeremy's idea—part of his 'night of surprises.'"

"But you hate—"

"Yes, I know. It seems everyone is keenly aware of my aversion to surprises, except him."

We stare at each other.

"Annika, I miss you and I'm really, really sorry about the night at The Creek. And for ditching you for Jeremy and for being the world's worst best friend."

Annika doesn't respond. She strokes the black feather earrings that dangle down to her shoulders.

Oh no.

She might not forgive me.

My hands shake as I fiddle with my teensy white satin tie, smoothing it across my chest.

"Julia, it isn't that simple. You act like an asshat. I forgive you. You then act like a bigger asshat. Again I forgive you and you respond by becoming a colossal asshat. Why should I believe you this time?"

"Because you're my best friend and I miss you. I miss everything about you. Your laugh. Your sense of humour. I miss hanging out together..."

"I miss you too, but missing each other is not the basis of a good friendship. At least it isn't for me."

"What do I need to do to convince you?"

"I'm not sure. I have to think about it."

"You have to think about it?" She sounds like she's considering what pair of shoes to buy. I'm supposed to be her best friend!

"Yeah, cuz' I don't think you really understand how it felt to be pushed to the side time after time. How humiliated you made me feel."

"I made you feel humiliated? Oh my God, Annika. I am so sorry."

What have I done?

"Yeah, well," she says, glancing down the hall. "We can talk later. Looks like your next big surprise is waiting."

Jeremy stands outside the washroom. He's peering through the crowd gathered around the ballot box. His gaze is fixed on me—on us.

"I have to go," I say, my voice a croaking whisper.

"Fraidy," she says, grabbing my arm. "Be careful."

I frown. *Be careful?* Of what? Was she behind the questions Tyler's been asking?

I hobble past her, picking up my boots. My throat burns. I fast limp down the hall. My vision blurs, but this time alcohol has nothing to do with it.

Sorry. I am so sorry.

CHAPTER 34

Far too many surprises.

I stumble towards Jeremy. Swiping at my tears, I attempt to squeeze through the kids that jam the hallway.

"Julia," Jeremy calls. I can just see him over the heads of the students. He's standing by the doors with his jacket on. My coat is in his hands.

I push my way through, my ankle throbs with every step.

"Finally," he says. "What were you talking to Annika about?"

"I—nothing."

"Are you sure? You look upset. What did she do?"

"I'm fine. She didn't do anything," I say, which is the most honest thing I've said in a long time. "I did twist my ankle in these boots though." I wave them at him. He glances at my foot.

"But you're okay now, right?" He wraps my coat around my shoulder and picks me up. He doesn't wait for my answer. I guess my pain doesn't fit into his plans. "Your surprise has arrived. Come on." Jeremy pushes through the doors and we head into the cool night air. It's refreshing after the heat in the gymnasium—for a moment. A gust of arctic chill blasts us, pelting snow in our faces like dozens of tiny frozen needles.

"But we're going to miss them announce the winners."

"Who cares?"

I do. I need to talk to Annika. Find a way to make amends. Find out what she meant by "be careful." If she was behind Tyler's questions, then she still cares, she still wants to be friends, right? At least I pray she does. But I don't say any of that to Jeremy, because waiting at the curb is a black stretch limousine.

"Is that for us?" I ask.

A large man in a dark suit opens the door for us and Jeremy sits me inside on a glistening black leather seat. I yank at my skirt, trying to pull down what little fabric is there to cover more of my thighs. Jeremy climbs in and the driver shuts the door. It hardly makes a sound. Quiet R&B music wafts through the car as we pull away from the school.

"I've never been in a limo before," I say. I hear the awe in my voice. I sort of hate that—the awe, not that I haven't been in a limo before. Dark cherry wood and mirrors cover the walls. The black ceiling looks like the night sky with teensy clear lights dotting the entire surface and on a low wooden table in the centre of the car is an ice bucket, complete with a bottle of champagne.

"It's just the beginning of our night." Jeremy says. He lifts the bottle out of the ice water and pops the cork, which flies to the far side of the limo. He snatches a fluted glass off the table as champagne bubbles down the side of the bottle. Not more booze.

"Can we drink in here?" I'm nervous we're going to be pulled over and spend the night in jail. I twist the leather strap of my purse around my fingers. Jeremy gently pulls it from my hands and lays it on the couch next to him, placing a glass of champagne in my hands.

"They follow a different set of rules, and the owner of the limo company is one of my dad's clients."

I nod. Limos, champagne, out on a surprise filled night— I should feel excited that it's all happening to me, but in reality I just feel completely out of my element.

"Cheers," he says. We clink our crystal glasses. The bubbles tickle against my nose as I take a small sip.

"Mmm, nice," I say. I actually find it too dry and bitter, but I don't want to hurt his feelings. He's gone to a lot of work for me.

"And look at this." He grabs a remote and presses a few buttons. A wooden panel at the back of the limo slides to the right and a TV screen appears. "Everything in here is high end."

"Wow, this must have cost a fortune."

"You're worth it."

Jeremy flicks through the channels, stopping at music videos. Some rap song replaces the R&B. He looks out the window, his face reflects in the glass, removing all the hard edges. He looks like he stepped off a 1920's movie set.

"We're almost there," he says, leaning back in his seat. Jeremy brushes my curls over my shoulder and runs his fingers under my hair to the nape of my neck. Gently he pulls me in for a kiss. I close my eyes and attempt to melt into the moment. He rests his other hand on my knee. Shivers tingle up my leg. He slides his hand up to the edge of my skirt—my dangerously short skirt. My eyes flash open. I place my hand over his.

"What's wrong?" he asks. He doesn't remove his hand.

"The driver."

"He can't see us."

"What about cameras?"

"What are you talking about?"

"Don't they have cameras back here to keep an eye on their customers? I saw it in a movie."

"Not this limo company. They are very discreet."

I gulp. I'm not sure I like discreet. I feel caged. Trapped.

"I've taken care of everything tonight," he continues, and smiling he removes my hand from the top of his. "Just relax, Julia." He entwines his fingers in mine and begins kissing me again. He moves my tie so it hangs over one shoulder and traces the top edge of my bodice with his index finger.

I close my eyes. *Be careful.* What did Annika mean by that? *Be true to myself.*

What is wrong with me that my Grandmother's sage wisdom is floating through my head while my boyfriend tries to make out with me?

I tense. Jeremy pulls back.

"Julia. Seriously. You've got to chill." His words sound more demanding than comforting.

"I'm sorry. I'm just overwhelmed, I guess. The champagne, the limo—it's all so much."

"Have another sip." He watches me as I hold my glass to my lips. I don't let a drop enter my mouth and pretend to swallow. "You're going to love the room I booked. It even has its own hot tub."

"Oh—I didn't bring my swimming suit." A room?

"Neither did I."

"What—"

"We're here," Jeremy says, as the limo slows to a stop. "Put your boots back on. I need to talk to the driver."

I can only nod as Jeremy leaves me to struggle with my boots. My brain is still digesting the news that we will be hot-tubbing nude. In a hotel room. Alone. I yank my top up as far as it can go, already feeling far too exposed.

Holy crap. Holy crap. Holy crap.

I gently slip the boot over my now swollen ankle, gasping when I slide the zipper over it. The door opens. The driver extends his black-gloved hand to me.

"Miss," he says, as he passes me to Jeremy. "Have a nice night."

A nice night.

What have I gotten myself into?

CHAPTER 35

No.

Jeremy opens the hotel room door, holding it wide for me to enter. The light in the room flickers. I hesitate, afraid. Yes, go figure, a girl nicknamed Fraidy is scared. Out of her wits.

"My arm is breaking here," Jeremy says.

"Sorry." I step over the threshold onto thick grey carpet. The room smells of flowers and something woodsy.

"Come in. The room is huge. It's only one step down from the penthouse."

"Wow, it's gorgeous," I say, which it is in an ostentatious, "look at us we're super rich" sort of way. All the furniture is dark brown wood with silver fixtures. The king-size bed is layered with white bedding and overflows with plush pillows. Crimson rose petals are scattered across the bed and a towel swan couple sits entwined, right in the centre of the flowers. Incense burns in an ornate holder on the coffee table next to another ice bucket. More champagne. My stomach tightens at the thought.

"I talked the hotel into giving us their honeymoon package. My dad books all his out of town clients here, so they wouldn't dare say no." His smirk looks beyond proud. He looks arrogant. His gaze slowly runs up my body, his head nods in approval. "No one says no to a Thurston."

"No, I guess no one does," I say as my eyes dart to the heart-shaped Jacuzzi that sits in the far corner of the room. A half dozen pink and sliver candles twinkle along the edge of the tub. It would be so romantic, if only—if only *what?*

"I need to use the bathroom," I practically shout.

"Is everything alright?"

"Yes, of course. I just have to—freshen up."

"Okay, that'll give me time to get your final surprise ready." He kisses me, one hand cupping my butt cheek as the other slides across my stomach. "But be quick. I've waited long enough," he whispers in my ear.

I plaster on a smile. My lips quiver with the effort.

"Be right back." I limp to the bathroom. My hands shake so hard that locking the bathroom door is a challenge. Leaning against the counter, I take a deep breath and stare at myself in the mirror. My face is devoid of colour, my lips blood red in comparison to my pale cheeks. I step back, tugging my bodice up. My boobs are fighting hard to explode out of my costume. I look like a hooker. Is this how Annika saw me at the dance? Is this how everyone saw me? Red blotches creep up my neck and scatter across my cheeks, returning some life to my face.

I don't want to be this girl staring back at me.

This is not who Julia Collins is.

It's that simple. This is not who I am. And Jeremy is expecting sex. Now. Which is only sort of completely obvious, since he all but demanded it.

Why didn't I see this coming?

This wouldn't have been a shocker to Annika. Maybe I should text her and ask her to come get me. Forget it. In her mind I remain an asshat. She isn't coming to my rescue this time.

And how can I blame her.

What am I going to do?

I just have to be honest with him. I am not having sex tonight. Not like this. He isn't going to like it, but I'll just have to make Jeremy understand.

No one says no to a Thurston.

Sweat beads along my hairline above my forehead. Opening my purse, I push Mom's $40 aside and find Dad's worn button. I close my eyes and wrap my fingers around its cool smoothness.

I can do this.

"Hey, Jeremy," I say as I enter the living room. My entire speech flees my brain when I see him sitting on the couch in a bright white bathrobe, his bare chest exposed. I squeeze Dad's button so hard it feels like it's going to shoot right through my hand.

"No." *Did I say that out loud?*

Jeremy blinks a few times. A slow smile crinkles around his eyes.

"No, what?" he asks, his voice honey thick.

I back towards the door. My sore ankle turns. I gasp as cold white pain shoots across my foot and up my calf. Losing my balance I bang into the wall. I grab for the door handle. It's locked.

"Julia, you aren't going anywhere. This is our night," Jeremy says. He saunters to me as I fumble with the lock. He whispers in my ear, his breath hot on my neck. "This is *our* night." He repeats. His voice is dead calm.

Shivers race down from my neck directly to my heart.

No one says no to a Thurston.

No way is he going to accept my "I'm not ready for sex" sermon. I fight the tunnel vision that is creeping over my periphery.

He grabs my hand and pulls me from the door. Dad's button tumbles to the floor. My skin crawls under his fingers as they wrap around my wrist. I flex my hand. His grip tightens. His fingers dig deep into my arm. I twist my wrist, his hand tightens. Pain radiates up my arm.

"Ow, Jeremy."

My breath catches. I can't get away.

No one says no to a Thurston.

"Come on, Julia. It's time to party." His grip loosens, but he doesn't let go. My arm pulses where his fingers bore into my flesh.

"But Jeremy, I—I," I run out of words. What words do I use to describe the revulsion my body now feels at his touch?

"Julia, you promised you would trust me."

"I know, it's just," I struggle to find the words, the right words, to stop this night from progressing. To get myself out of here. I point to the champagne. "I really shouldn't drink anything with my medication."

"Julia, why can't you understand? You don't need those pills. You just need me. I'll take care of you. Together forever." He finally releases his grip and passes me a glass of champagne. The candlelight casts dark shadows across my name inked on his arm. Jeremy glances at me and smiles. "Here's to us."

I stare at my hands. The angry red stripes left from his grip glare back at me.

No. This is not me.

I need to get out of here.

But first I have to get out of these stupid boots.

CHAPTER 36

I can take it from here.

I look around the room. A second bathrobe is slung over the back of the couch. I set the champagne glass on the coffee table.

"I'll just go and slip into this," I say, throwing the soft robe over my arm. It lands on the wrist he hurt and I wince. I pause. Jeremy hurt me. Again.

"You can change here," Jeremy says.

"No," I say too fast. I replace what I am sure is a panicked grimace with what I hope is a sexy smile. "I need a little privacy. You gave me your surprise tonight. Let me surprise you."

"Alright, I'll be in the Jacuzzi, but don't keep me waiting, Julia."

I look into his eyes, and instead of seeing the boy I thought I loved all I see is someone who I don't really know. And he doesn't know me, either. And how could he? I was trying to be the girlfriend I thought he wanted—that I thought I needed to be for him. And honestly, I thought I wanted to be, but just like those ripped designer jeans, the role of Jeremy's girlfriend just doesn't suit me.

"I won't be long." Which is partly true.

I hobble down the hall, out of Jeremy's sight. The hot tub jets rumble on. I duck into the hall closet and yank the zipper down the length of the boot on my good leg. More carefully I remove the boot from my injured foot. From my hiding place, I can see the front door. Dad's button is somewhere in that thick carpet. I examine the door and immediately realize why I had such trouble opening it. It has a bizarre double lock and the chain is on too. I place my hand over my heart, trying to muffle its thumping beat.

Can Jeremy hear it?

Pull it together.

I count to five. He must be in the hot tub by now. I take a deep breath and pick up one boot.

I tiptoe-limp to the door and slowly pull the chain off, placing it flat against the door jamb, silencing any possible jingle sound. I use both hands to slide the double lock open, hoping to keep it quiet too. The click is loud. I jump and look over my shoulder. No sign of Jeremy.

I prop the door open with my boot and scan the carpet. Still no sign of my button and no time to keep searching. I'm on my own. With fists clenched, I walk as steadily as possible into the suite. My long held breath comes out in a slow steady exhalation. He'll just have to accept that somebody is saying no to a Thurston.

Bubbles mound in the hot tub, tucked like a blanket under Jeremy's chin. He's holding up his phone.

It flashes.

"Hey, why are you still dressed? I told you to get changed," he says. His voice booms over the sound Jacuzzi jets.

Was he trying to take a picture of me naked?

"I'm leaving Jeremy. This isn't me—none of it. I'm sorry. I just didn't realize it before."

"What? How can you say that?" His mouth hangs open, disbelief clear in his eyes.

"I don't want to hurt you, and I appreciate you being honest about all of this, but I don't want it. I don't want you to take care of me. I don't want to feel pressured into doing stuff that doesn't feel right. I want to feel free to do whatever I want, when I want, not when someone commands me to do something."

"You can't leave! Do you know how much this cost?"

"I'm sure it was a lot—"

"I did this for you." He extends his fading tattooed arm at me. "Julia Forever. I meant that. All of this is for you."

"I know, I know," I say. My throat aches as tears slip down my cheeks. *I'm crushing him.* "But Jeremy, I didn't ask for any of it. None of it."

"If you leave, we are done. No more chances." His voice is loud, angry.

Chances?

Something inside me snaps. Anger flares through me.

"No. Jeremy *you* have no more chances. You hurt me. Just now," I hold up my wrist. "And in your car, when you slammed me against the door. I won't let you do that again."

"Julia, you are overreacting," he says and scoffs, as if my feelings are worthless. He stands up. Bubbles cling to his body, covering most of him. I look away. "Don't be an idiot. That was nothing."

His words slice deeper than his iron grip on my wrist and the door handle that he embedded in my spine.

"Idiot?!" I repeat, my voice straining in my throat. Dad's voice, clear as day, echoes through my mind. I know it in my bones; I am Einstein smart and I am too smart to be here. "I am not an idiot, but I have been stupid to stay with you. I deserve better. A lot better. I'm leaving."

Jeremy moves to the edge of the tub.

Flee, Julia, flee!

"Wait, Julia," he calls, but I don't turn back. I hobble as fast as possible through the doorway and down the long hall, trying to match my gait with the rhythm of my galloping heartbeat. My purse bumps against my hip.

I press the elevator button over and over.

"Come on, come on!" I plead.

"Julia, wait!" Jeremy calls. He's running down the centre of the hall, a towel wrapped around his waist. His face is twisted. *Oh my God. He's crying.*

The door isn't completely open as I stumble inside.

"Julia!" his voice races down the hall, squeezing into the elevator with me. I pound the elevator pad. The doors close. My finger hovers over the emergency button. I gasp for air, sobbing, my whole body shakes. Jeremy thumps on the door, but it doesn't open. "Julia!"

The elevator descends.

I stand right in front of the doors, praying it won't stop on any other floors.

Breathe, Julia breathe. It finally reaches the lobby and I push through the doors as they open. Hop-running, I bound through the hotel's front doors and into the winter air. With frozen toes I waddle over the well-shovelled sidewalk to the lone taxi that stands at the curb. Jeremy's limousine is gone.

"Where to?" the driver asks as I climb inside.

"Drive to Fort Garry—down Pembina," I say, pulling Mom's emergency money from my purse.

"Miss, I need an actual location," the driver says.

"Prairie Trails High on Doncaster. I don't know the street address," I say.

"That's close enough. You look like you've had quite a night."

"You have no idea," I say as he passes me a box of tissues. "Thanks." I wipe the tears from my cheeks, my head pounds from crying.

The driver pulls away from the hotel. I don't look back.

"Please hurry," I say.

If I'm lucky Annika will still be at school. If not, I'll track her down. I wrap my hands around my frozen bare feet. Not even frostbitten toes will stop me. I'll make Annika listen to me. I have a lot of apologizing to do.

I lean back against the cool leather seats, but the smell of bleach and b.o. makes me jerk back upright. I open the window a crack, close my eyes, and breathe in the cold crisp winter air. My thoughts clear as we drive through the dark night away from downtown, over the bridge towards the south end of the city.

I pull out my phone. Will she even read it if I send her a text?

What do I have to lose?

JULES: It's me. I broke up with Jeremy. I'm coming home

I stare at the display willing her to reply. *Please, Annika. Please.*

TKD4EVR: Huh

JULES: Yeah. It was a nightmare

TKD4EVR: So has being your friend lately

Oh God. She isn't going to make this easy, and why should she?

JULES: Yeah I know. I am a loser friend. Imma sorry. Really really really really sorry

TKD4EVR: Overkill. Have some self-respect. Don't be a desperate loser

A small smile creeps across my face, tears sting my eyes. If she is joking with me maybe that means…

JULES: Do u forgive me?

TKD4EVR: Maybe

JULES: I'll take maybe! I'll make it up to you. I'll be the bff u always deserved & never had!

TKD4EVR: Stop! Again too much. Just take it slow Fraidy. Did u learn nothing from your time with The Turd?

JULES: Sorry. Still learning

"We're here Miss," the taxi driver says. "That's $17.50."

"Keep the change," I say as I pass him one of Mom's $20 bills.

I open the door and stare at the brightly lit school. The dance is still in full swing. Some of the feeling in my toes should still remain by the time I make the twenty-metre dash to the entrance.

The school door opens.

"Fraidy, you are ridiculous," Annika calls to me.

I wince as I take my first bare-toed step onto the ice-covered sidewalk. I gasp as I wobble two more steps, trying not to slip.

"I know," I reply as I gingerly hop and limp from one foot to the other.

"Do you need help?"

"Nope. I got this."

Instinctively I search for Dad's button as I wobble and slip towards the open doorway. My heart sinks as it hits me. It's gone. But I know he'd be proud of me. I close my eyes and breathe easier than I have in months. I am amazed by how calm I feel. I smile and take another step forward.

I'm okay now, Dad. I can take it from here.

Love, Julia.

Forever.

ACKNOWLEDGEMENTS

They say it takes a village to raise a child and I say it takes a writing community to raise an author. *Forever Julia* would still be a plot-challenged mess if it weren't for my writing group, The Anita Factor; my mentor Carolyn Gray; The Manitoba Writers' Guild Sheldon Oberman Mentorship Program; my writing guide Anita Daher; and my family who have read many versions, made me coffee, and provided words of encouragement and pounds of chocolate while I wrote and rewrote this book.

The Anitas are my writing sisters, a collection of children's and young adult writers who offer support, critique, and hours of laughter. Every writer has their dark, "all hope is lost" periods and the Anitas pulled me through my darkest moments, reminding me that writers write because we can't stop!

I owe an enormous thank you to the Manitoba Writers' Guild and their Sheldon Oberman Mentorship Program for pairing me with mentor Carolyn Gray. She was integral to the publication of *Forever Julia*. She helped me locate the heart of this story and subsequently the plot buried deep in Julia's backstory, and in the process, Carolyn taught me how to be a better writer. We toiled for hours over pots of coffee, Belgian waffles, and Eggs Benedict at The Prairie Ink restaurant while reviewing her editing suggestions. We laughed, solved not only Julia's problems, but all of the publishing industries' greatest faults and emerged from the Sheldon Oberman Mentorship program as life-long friends.

Anita Daher is a treasure to Manitoba writers and lends support, enthusiasm, and provides tips along the way. When I grow up, I want to be just like Anita, but less organized. (Achievable goals are key.)

To my editor, Catharina de Bakker of Great Plains Publications. Catharina's editorial suggestions have taken *Forever Julia* to a place I couldn't even imagine. I can hardly wait for my earlier readers to see the difference your guidance has made to this novel. Thank you.

My parents have been to every book signing, book launch, speaking engagement, and writing presentation I have ever given. All I can say is, I am who I am because of you—all of you! I love you to bits.

My girls, Emma and Sarah. What a pair you are and I couldn't be a prouder mom. You're polar opposites in every way, yet equally awesome. You are patient with me when I am lost in one of my stories and offer 100% honest feedback when I read you my work. I love you two girls to the moon and back. (And yes that is even more love than to the cottage and back.)

And of course, The Drew. My best friend, my personal comedian, and most supportive, patient and loving husband. What a life we're having and what an incredible man you are, to live with a writer whose grand dreams and plans are often ridiculously unattainable, but yet after 26 years together you still say, "Why not?" I'll love you forever.

To readers of *Forever Julia*—thank you for reading! And if you or someone you know is being abused, know you are not alone. Sadly, violence against women is prevalent around the world. Please reach out to a trusted adult or care organization.

Kids Help Phone is 1-800-668-6868 and they offer web counselling and phone counselling. It is free and they are non-judg-
mental, confidential, provide services for individuals ages 20
and under, and are available 24 hours a day, 7 days a week.

"The World Health Organization recognizes sexual violence,
intimate-partner violence, and other abuse of women and
children as public health problems of epidemic proportions.
The United Nations has repeatedly called for the 'elimina-
tion of all forms of violence against women.' In the United
States and many other countries, law enforcement agencies
increasingly provide specialized training for officers deal-
ing with abuse situations. Yet violence against women is so
woven into the fabric of acceptable behavior that many wom-
en who experience violence feel that they are at fault or have
no right to complain about violent treatment."—*Our Bodies
Ourselves* (OBOS)